W9-CDL-771

Divalicious

Divalicious

Darrious D. Hilmon

NEW AMERICAN LIBRARY

New American Library
Published by New American Library, a division of
Penguin Group (USA) Inc., 375 Hudson Street,
New York, New York 10014, U.S.A.
Penguin Books Ltd, 80 Strand,
London WC2R 0RL, England
Penguin Books Australia Ltd, 250 Camberwell Road,
Camberwell, Victoria 3124, Australia
Penguin Books Canada Ltd, 10 Alcorn Avenue,
Toronto, Ontario, Canada M4V 3B2
Penguin Books (NZ), cnr Airborne and Rosedale Roads,
Albany, Auckland 1310, New Zealand

Penguin Books Ltd, Registered Offices:
80 Strand, London WC2R 0RL, England

First published by New American Library,
a division of Penguin Group (USA) Inc.

First Printing, August 2004
10 9 8 7 6 5 4 3 2

Copyright © Darrious D. Hilmon, 2004
All rights reserved

 REGISTERED TRADEMARK—MARCA REGISTRADA

LIBRARY OF CONGRESS CATALOGING-IN-PUBLICATION DATA:
Hilmon, Darrious D.
Divalicious / Darrious D. Hilmon.
p. cm.
ISBN 0-451-21207-x (trade pbk.)
1. Motion picture actors and actresses—Fiction. 2. Hollywood (Los Angeles,
Calif.)—Fiction. 3. African American women—Fiction. 4. Female
friendship—Fiction. 5. Actresses—Fiction. I. Title.
PS3608.I46D585 2004
813'.6—dc22   2004005814

Set in Janson
Designed by Ginger Legato

Printed in the United States of America

Without limiting the rights under copyright reserved above, no part of this publica-
tion may be reproduced, stored in or introduced into a retrieval system, or transmit-
ted, in any form, or by any means (electronic, mechanical, photocopying, recording,
or otherwise), without the prior written permission of both the copyright owner and
the above publisher of this book.

PUBLISHER'S NOTE
This is a work of fiction. Names, characters, places, and incidents either are the
product of the author's imagination or are used fictitiously, and any resemblance to
actual persons, living or dead, business establishments, events, or locales is entirely
coincidental.

BOOKS ARE AVAILABLE AT QUANTITY DISCOUNTS WHEN USED TO
PROMOTE PRODUCTS OR SERVICES. FOR INFORMATION PLEASE
WRITE TO PREMIUM MARKETING DIVISION, PENGUIN GROUP (USA)
INC., 375 HUDSON STREET, NEW YORK, NEW YORK 10014.

The scanning, uploading and distribution of this book via the Internet or via any
other means without the permission of the publisher is illegal and punishable by law.
Please purchase only authorized electronic editions, and do not participate in or encourage electronic piracy of copyrighted materials. Your support of the author's
rights is appreciated.

For Mr. Luther Vandross

You have the voice of an angel, the courage of a king.
God bless . . . and merci beaucoup.

Be humble, for the worst thing in the world is of the same stuff as you; be confident, for the stars are of the same stuff as you.

—Nikolai Velimirovic

Acknowledgments

My God is an awesome God. I bow before Him humbled by His love, mercy and grace. He is real, and He reigns supreme.

Never in my wildest dreams could I have imagined the outpouring of support and encouragement I've received from readers of my debut novel, *Five Dimes*. The e-mails, cards, and phone calls from friends and strangers alike have been an incredible boost to both my confidence and my spirit. Thank you very much!

This past year has been such an amazing one for me. Through it all I have had the astonishingly good fortune of being supported by some of the most loving, spiritually rich people you'd ever hope to know.

Gloria Hilmon (Mom), all that I am or ever hope to be is because of you. Your love is the foundation from which my dreams take flight. You are my queen and I love you. Javaki Hilmon, your humor, intelligence, and self-confidence never cease to amaze me. I'm so proud of you. Love you, baby sis! Toni (A.M.) Hilmon, you have been an inspiration since childhood. If I had a singing voice like yours . . . ooh wee! Love you madly. Leonard (Islord) Hilmon, you are some kind of brother. No one can make me laugh . . . or cry like you do. I love you. To my adopted brothers, Tiny (toy poodle) and Pee-Wee (Yorkie), I'm not at all bitter that Mom says you two are her favorite kids. Really (eye twitching), I'm not bitter!

JoAnne Gurley, what can I say besides I love you and thank God that you are my friend/sister/confidante/confessor/etc. I wake up every morning secure in the knowledge that ours is a lifelong association. Love you. To my goddaughter India Gurley, I meant what I said about that car. Take good care of your new little brother, Ian. Love you both.

Loren Brown, I consider your friendship to be one of my greatest treasures. Thank you for taking this crazy, joyous, chill-inducing ride with me and for always encouraging me to dare mighty things. I am *sooo* looking forward to the book we cowrote being published. People are going to be absolutely floored by your talent. Trust. Darice (pronounced "Dar-cee") Brown, you know I love you something awful. I will never be able to repay you for the marvelous job you did overseeing the Midwest PR campaign for *Five Dimes*. Carla Jones, thank you for masterful PR efforts on the West Coast. Michele Edwards, thank you . . . for everything.

To my editor at NAL, Janete Scobie, thank you for getting things back on track. John Paine, thank you for saving the day . . . and my sanity. Judy Burger, Randi Myles (baby, you rock!), Vicki Preston, Lady BG and the entire Radio One-Detroit family, mucho thanks for being so good to me. Let's do it again and again . . . and again. Nkenge Abi and everyone at Shrine of the Black Madonna in Detroit, thank you for wrapping your arms around me. Darnell Glover, congratulations on the twenty-year anniversary of *Salon on the Park*. I can't thank you enough for strong-arming, er, I mean *encouraging* every single one of your five hundred million clients to buy a copy of *Five Dimes*. You're the best, my brotha!

Michelle Wilson, what a force of power and light you are! Whenever I feel a creative lull coming on, all I have to do is go watch you perform on stage and my juices are once again flowing. You were wonderful on *ER* (yes, people, *that ER*!). This is your season, my darlin'. Much love (you too, Miss Stormi!). Sylvia Curtis and Monté Rice, thanks for taking such good care of me and Loren during our stay in Atlanta. More vodka gimlets, please! Monica Woodson, you remain my "down for whatever," and number-one enabler (LOL!). Love you. To Ava Mullen (regality personified), Ingrid Travis James (the best cohost ever!), Cheryl Day (my flower), Renee Hodge (my sister), Cyrus Gass (my brother), Andrea Ivory (the marketing guru),

Pete Knoop (the lil' big man), Camille Travis (thanks for the rides to the airport, Mommie ☺), Cheryl and Forest Hudson (ye merry makers of most delicious chocolatinis), Jeff Quinn ("No wire hangers!"), Joseph James, Christopher Russ and Wendy Wilson, thanks for having my back. My fellow authors, Asha Tyson, Camika Spencer, and Cheryl Robinson, thank you for your counsel, encouragement and for so graciously welcoming me into the fold.

To those friends and family I didn't mention by name, thanks for loving me without question or fail. And to you the reader, there are no words to appropriately capture how very grateful I am to you. Please know that I don't take your support lightly or for granted. It is my sincere hope that you will enjoy getting to know Angel, Erika and Faith as much as I did. These three divas are something else! After you've finished reading *Divalicious*, do visit me online at www.darriousdhilmon.com. I'd love to hear from you!

Be blessed,

D2

1

* * * * * * *

Gotta Have Faith

Soundstage 12 was permeated with an uneasy, finger-snapping energy. As they returned from their summer hiatus, the cast and crew of *Brave New World* served up plastic smiles and double-cheeked air kisses to one another, all the while doing their best to appear unfazed by the goings-on around them. Today, the latest chapter in the already eventful saga of the hit sitcom would play out.

"I didn't get much sleep last night," Angel said, studying her tired reflection in the light-encircled mirror. "You might want to give me a touch more concealer than usual just to be on the safe side."

"Chica, you look gorgeous like always," Ernesto said, working the foundation onto Angel's café au lait skin. "*Sooo*, what you think about the new girl?"

"Not sure yet," Angel said. Everyone had been shocked by the producers' decision to hire blond-haired, blue-eyed Faith Molaney to replace a black actress on a television show that—for its first two years on the air, anyway—revolved around the lives of three up-and-coming black women. That Faith was breathtakingly beautiful, and a clear favorite of Wellington Broadcasting Network's lecherous vice president of programming, Randall Hunter, only made the choice more suspect.

"She pretty, I guess," Ernesto said, trying not to appear too impressed with the newcomer. "I mean, if you actually *like* the blond-bombshell, creamy-skinned, hourglass-figure type."

Angel gave him a cool grin. "What is it about blond hair, blue eyes . . . and big titties that make you men lose your ever-loving minds?"

"I can't answer that one," Ernesto said smugly. "I'm immune to feminine charms."

Angel ran her hands through her shoulder-length, dark auburn curls, plumping them different ways to test out how they looked. "Well, that would make you the exception around here," she said, smirking. "It's almost comical watching the stagehands tripping over their boners to get within sniffing distance of her." She leaned back in the chair, studying her image in the mirror. "For all they know, that woman could be the biggest airhead this side of Betty Boop."

"Like it would matter to them if she were," Ernesto said.

"True that," Angel said, then smiled. "Wanna hear a blonde joke?"
Ernesto perked up. "Yes."

"How do you make a blonde's eyes twinkle?"
"How?"

"Shine a flashlight in her ear," Angel deadpanned.
Ernesto snickered. "That's funny."

"What do you get when you turn three blondes upside down?"
"What you get?" Ernesto asked.

"Two brunettes," Angel said, bursting into laughter.

Ernesto chuckled as he brushed the color onto Angel's cheeks. "Ooh, you wrong for that."

"Thank you very much," Angel said, waving at her nonexistent audience. "I'm here all week."

Ernesto shook his head as he continued applying the powder to Angel's face.

"What do you think of her?"

"She seem like a sweet girl . . ." Ernesto said, hesitating when he felt Angel's incredulous eyes on him. "But you my Gucci girlfriend," he said, raising his hand quickly. "So if you want me to hate her, I will."

"Oh no," Angel said, shaking her head. "We don't hate . . ."

"We appreciate," Ernesto said, finishing her statement.

"Exactly," Angel said. "If she doesn't step on my Manolos, I won't step on hers."

Ernesto nodded as he blew the excess powder off his brush.

"Hell, if I looked like Faith Molaney, I'd ride the gravy train till the wheels fell off."

"Lord knows, Randall's going to be trying to ride her," Ernesto said.

Angel rolled her eyes. "You can put money on that."

The second star of the show, Erika Bishop, strutted into the makeup suite. "Hey, colored people."

"Do you ever get anywhere on time?" Ernesto said cattily.

Erika cut her eyes at him, but decided against starting a fight with the makeup guru on such an important day. They were shooting the publicity photos that would be used to promote the new season, so she needed to look her best. Instead, Erika turned her attention to Angel. "Hey, girl."

"Hey now," Angel said with an easy smile.

Erika settled herself into the empty chair. "What do you think of the white girl?"

"I only had a chance to talk to her for a second," Angel answered, glancing at Ernesto. They traded smiles, thinking about the blonde jokes.

"Well, I don't like her," Erika said flatly. "Already sucking up to Randall's punk ass." She turned to Angel. "You know he wants to fuck her, don't you?"

"Erika," Angel said carefully. "We don't know that." What she did know was that Erika and Randall were having an affair. That was what Erika was concerned about—the new girl stealing her man.

"Come on now," Erika said with a raised brow. "Are you really gonna sit there and tell me that you don't have a problem with that girl infiltrating *our* show?"

"I'm not drunk with joy over her being here," Angel said. "But I suggest that you *not* go climbing up on your soapbox over this one."

Erika had a well-earned reputation around the set for being

outspoken. When she deemed something unfair, unflattering, or otherwise unacceptable, she made noise about it. Just as her stage mother had taught her.

"This is our show, Angel," Erika said emphatically, "and we have an obligation to our community to make sure that it doesn't become some watered-down, rainbow-colored piece of crap."

Angel sighed. Unlike Erika, *Brave* wasn't the alpha and omega of her world. The show was simply a stop on the road to her true goal: starring in motion pictures. And though she understood Erika's concern, the last thing Angel was interested in doing was making a potentially career-threatening stink over a hiring decision she was powerless to change anyway.

"Mother and I plan on having a talk with Jasper Wellington. We'll straighten him out."

"Erika, I really think you should leave this one alone," Angel said, then caught herself. Although she didn't consider her a close sista-friend, she did sincerely like Erika, and respected her outspokenness.

"Photo day, Ernesto," Erika said, ignoring Angel's warning. "Are you ready for me?"

Angel didn't push it. She suspected Erika—guided by her mother from hell, Victoria Steinberg—had probably already hatched a scheme to get rid of Faith.

"Make me look good," Erika said, tugging at the weave that fell to the center of her back. "And bring some life back into this damned hair."

Ernesto began applying a foundation two shades too light to Erika's dark skin. "I'm a genius, not a miracle worker," he said dryly.

"Ooh, no you didn't!"

"I just play with you." Ernesto grinned.

Erika gave him the finger.

Angel inspected her made-up face as she stood from her chair. "Boy, you *know* you good," she said, giving Ernesto a peck on the cheek.

"Chica, don't mess your lipstick," he cautioned her. "Marie, spray Angel's hair," he instructed his assistant. "Don't want her to go flat under all the hot lights."

"Excuse me," said a male voice, coming from the door.

Angel's head turned as the newest member of *Brave New World*'s writing team poked his head inside the suite. "Good morning, ladies."

"Good morning," Erika, Angel and Ernesto answered sweetly in unison.

Lucien gave Ernesto a confused grin. "I just wanted to bring you ladies . . ." he began, then hesitated. "I mean, Angel and Erika, the scripts for the season premiere."

Erika got up from the chair, tossed her hair back and sashayed over to Lucien. "Well, aren't you nice," she cooed as she took one of the scripts from his hand. "And handsome too."

Lucien ignored the come-on. He walked over to Angel, handing her the other script. "Here you go," he said formally.

"Thank you," Angel said, sizing him up. The dark-skinned cutie looked to be just under six feet tall, though she wouldn't be able to confirm that until *after* she got him out of the Timberlands he was wearing. His dreads complemented his smooth, angular face that featured dimples you could swim in. Angel didn't usually go for the roughneck type, but this sagging, FUBU jeans–wearing brotha intrigued her. Maybe it was his brooding-artist persona, or simply the lovely bulge between those tree-trunk legs. Whatever the case, Lucien had just moved up to the top of Angel's list of must-haves.

"Welcome aboard," she said, attempting to establish eye contact with him. "I'm Angel Hart."

"Lucien Alexander," he said, averting his eyes.

Angel's lips twisted into a grin. The tough guy was going out of his way to show her no love. That was fine. She figured he was being careful not to give the appearance of favoring one actress over another. The other writers had most likely warned him about the incident involving Erika's mother, a pink stiletto heel, and the head of the former head writer who cut one of her daughter's monologues.

"You work out, don't you, *Papi?*" Ernesto asked, gripping Lucien's muscular bicep.

"Uh . . . yeah," Lucien said, discreetly extracting his arm from Ernesto's grip.

"I can tell," Ernesto cooed.

Lucien chuckled uneasily. "Well, I better get back. Nice meeting you . . . ?"

"It's *Ernesssto*," the blushing makeup artist purred. "Ernesto Zolero."

Lucien extended his hand. "Nice to know ya, EZ," he said, then turned back to Angel and Erika. "Ladies."

Ernesto stroked his meticulously manicured goatee as he watched Lucien make his way out of the room. "He's *dickalicious*."

"Mm-hmm," Angel said, licking her lips. "Momma gonna have to get her a taste of that."

Erika looked up at Ernesto. "Well? Could you finish my face, please?"

Ernesto resumed the task of transforming Erika into a star. "You coming tonight, right, Mommie?" he asked Angel.

"I still don't understand how you're still celebrating your birthday two weeks after the fact."

Ernesto offered her a grin. "Because I'm special."

Erika smirked. "Is that what they're calling you people now?"

Ernesto ran the brush across her cheek a little rougher than necessary.

"Ouch!" Erika squealed. "Boy, be careful!"

"Oh be still, you, and let me finish rebuilding your face." Ernesto gave Angel a secretive smile. "Tonight is like the big finale," he explained. "Plus, I want you to meet my new *papi*, Jackson."

Angel chuckled. Ernesto fell in love about as often as she changed purses.

Ernesto glanced down at Erika. "You invited too," he said, eyeing her sternly. "So long as you promise to behave."

"No can do," she replied. "Got plans."

Ernesto turned back to Angel. "But you coming, though, yes?"

Angel smiled. "Of course I'm coming, *Papi*. Is it okay if I bring Jill and Benjamin?" she asked, referring to her two best friends from way back.

"Oh yes," he said. "The more the merrier."

While Ernesto powdered her face, Erika made one final attempt to garner support for her unofficial "oust the white girl" campaign.

"Am I the only one concerned about how this little cast change is going to affect *our* show?" Erika asked, cutting her eyes at Angel. "And no one is going to buy her as your half-sister either."

Angel didn't take the bait. She instead checked her outfit in the mirror, making sure everything was fabulous.

"What kind of message are we sending to the black community?" Erika asked.

"Since I don't have any control over this show, I'm not sending any message," Angel said.

Erika rolled her eyes. "You know what I mean."

Angel took the seat beside her. "Look, you know I appreciate your concerns," she said. "But if you make a public stink about this, it's you who's gonna come out looking bad, not the producers, and certainly not the white girl."

"Then what do you suggest we do?" Erika asked, less sure of herself. Angel was smarter than she was and Erika knew it.

"For the time being . . . nothing."

Erika's head snapped back. "Nothing!"

"Did I stutter?" Angel asked. "All we can do is hope that the viewing public will be so outraged, they'll demand Faith be put out on her ass by the second show."

"And if they don't?" Erika asked skeptically.

Angel shrugged. "Learn to peacefully coexist with our new costar."

Before Erika could respond, one of the production assistants entered the room, directing her and Angel onto the set.

"Hurry up!" Erika barked at Ernesto.

"If you woke up prettier, I'd be finished by now," Ernesto said.

"Bite me," Erika retorted.

"Maybe later," Ernesto said as he applied the last touches to her face. "There, finish."

Erika smacked him playfully across the rear. "Thank you," she said, then followed Angel out of the makeup suite.

* * *

As they approached the set, Angel gave Erika a look out of the corner of her eye. "Be good," she said through a painted-on smile.

"Always."

Angel tried not to stare as she approached the newcomer, Faith. No matter where you fell on the race issue, there was no denying that the new girl was incredibly beautiful. A less secure woman might want to shoot the Marilyn Monroe look-alike on sight. Angel glanced over at Erika, and sure enough, her jaw was set hard as rock.

"Hi, Angel," Faith said warmly. "I am so psyched to be working with you." She turned to Erika. "Oh, my goodness, I'm actually meeting Erika Bishop!" she said, brimming with genuine excitement. "I used to watch *Momma Knows* every week."

Angel eased her elbow into Erika's side, attempting to jar her out of her hate-induced fog.

"I am *so* looking forward to getting to know you," Faith said.

Erika gave her a cool smile. "We'll see about that."

"Ladies," Herb, the photographer, instructed, "let's start with some shots of the three of you together."

The three women took their places on a bench situated in front of a backdrop of the New York City skyline: legs crossed, hair teased and smiles seductive.

"Wonderful," Herb gushed as he began snapping shots. "That's it. Yes!"

As the shoot progressed, Victoria Steinberg positioned herself behind the row of cables running along the perimeter of the main set so she could watch the photo shoot. Her chosen location kept her close enough to the action that her daughter could see her, but far enough away that the producers wouldn't get angry with her. Victoria smiled as she spied the evil looks Erika was tossing at Faith. No white girl was going to upstage her daughter.

"If you could tilt your head a little bit more to the right, Erika," Herb instructed. "You're blocking Faith's face."

"Oh, I'm so sorry," Erika said, smacking Faith in the eye with her $2,500 hair before adjusting her position. "I didn't mean to block you."

Angel exhaled a bored sigh as she continued smiling for the camera. She knew Erika for her works. The insecure diva had given her an equally icy welcome when she joined the cast five shows into season number one. A minute before Angel was about to film her first scene, Erika "accidentally" spilled coffee onto her lap.

"*Ouuch!*" Faith yelped as her butt made contact with the floor.

Erika glanced down at her fallen costar. "Guess the bench is smaller than I thought," she said, flashing her mother a grin.

Angel remained silent as the producers rushed over to help the red-faced blonde to her feet. She was determined not to intervene. If Faith was to have any shot at surviving on this show, she was going to have to stand up to Erika—sooner rather than later.

"Let me straighten you out, Mommie," Ernesto said as he and one of his assistants worked on Faith's disheveled hair and smudged lipstick. He swatted the dirt from her backside. "Don't get nervous," Ernesto said with a sly smile. "I like boys." He took one more swipe at her rear. Even he was impressed. "There . . . good as new."

"Thank you," Faith said appreciatively.

"Herb, why don't we get a few shots with Faith sitting between Erika and Angel?" Randall Hunter suggested.

The too-perfect smile on Erika's face tightened as she switched positions with Faith. She looked over at Randall, annoyed by his stealth missile–like focus on the new girl.

Angel watched the dagger looks, grateful not to be a part of the ugly lust-triangle in the making. Randall Hunter was a damned good-looking man, albeit a little too smooth—and married—for her taste. He was a mesmerizing cross between Pierce Brosnan and Mel Gibson. His black hair fell to just above his shoulders, carefully gelled during office hours to ensure maximum manageability for him, and maximum acceptability for his colleagues. On the surface, he appeared to be the total package: smoky voice, befitting a quiet-storm radio DJ, intensely seductive gray eyes and a body to die for. Strutting around in his designer suits and black wire-rimmed Kenneth Cole glasses, Randall looked every bit the happily married, upstanding, hardworking wunderkind his publicity bio purported him to be. After hours, however, he preferred hair that moved, jeans that promoted his gym-enhanced butt, and the company of any woman other than his wife. Erika was the current other woman.

Faith let out a bloodcurdling scream as the heel of Erika's red Jimmy Choos made contact with her big toe. From the onlookers offstage, Victoria gave a delighted snort.

"Sorry." Erika smiled innocently. "Did I get you?"

Faith grimaced. "Yes."

"Oopsie."

The frustrated photographer threw up his hands. "All right, ladies, let's take five."

Angel decided to take the high road, going over to assist Faith. "Why don't you have a seat and wait for the pain to subside?" she suggested, helping Faith over to the blue canvas chair bearing her name across the back.

"Thanks," Faith said. "I guess I'm two left feet today."

"Just first-day jitters," Angel replied.

In the meantime, Randall marched over to Erika, wrapping his fingers around her arm. "Okay, you've had your fun," he whispered. "Now cut the crap."

Erika pressed her chest against his side. "Was I being a bad girl?" she asked playfully. "Maybe you can discipline me tonight."

But Randall's eyes had already strayed over to Faith.

"Hello?"

Randall's head snapped back toward Erika. "What?" he asked distractedly.

"I said, maybe you can discipline me tonight," she said, trying to sound seductive, but falling flat.

"Ah, listen . . . about tonight—"

Erika stopped him in midsentence. "Randall, no!" she said, almost shouting.

"Will you lower your voice, please?" He glanced around to make sure no one was listening. "You know how crazy things are at the start of a new season."

"But we haven't had any playtime in over a week."

"Maybe we can do something tomorrow, or Thursday," Randall said, his eyes returning to Faith. "I'll call you," he said, then dashed away.

"You have to watch out for her," Victoria said as she approached Erika. "She'll stop at nothing to steal your show."

"Oh, I'm watching," Erika snarled, eyeing Randall and Faith. "Look at her flipping her hair like she all that."

The mother-daughter team turned to each other and nodded.

Victoria hissed, "That bitch has got to go."

2

* * * * * * *

She's No Angel

ngel acknowledged the bouncer as he lifted the red velvet rope, motioning for her to come through. "She's with me," she said before he could lower the rope to stop her best friend, Jill Prescott, from entering as well.

"Sorry, Ms. Hart," the severely tanned brute said, giving Jill a polite grin as she passed.

"Okay, now I really do feel like the ugly fat girl," Jill said, tugging self-consciously on her cream-colored cold-shoulder sweater.

"Girl, please, you are one of the most beautiful people up in this piece," Angel said lightly.

"I appreciate the love, my dear," Jill said with a weak smile. "But something tells me that I'll be the only size ten in sight tonight."

"And one of the few who still has all of her original parts," Angel said, and they both laughed. "These heffas would pay up the wazoo to have your full lips and Indy 500 curves."

Amid the backstabbing world of show business, Angel treasured her lifelong friendship with Jill. She had been only eight years old when she went to live with her grandmother in the small middle-class town of Pomona, just east of Los Angeles. At the time, Angel was certain she was destined never to know happiness in her life again—not after her mother died. Then one day as she sat on the porch feeling miserable, she noticed a chubby girl watching her from the porch of the house next door. Twenty minutes later, Angel and

Jill were playing hopscotch in the middle of the street. They'd been best friends ever since. Each was an only child who found in the other the sister she never had. Through the years they'd kept each other's secrets and validated each other's pains. Jill was the yin to Angel's yang. Where Angel went off on creative flights of fancy, Jill was firmly rooted in reality.

As the homemaker wife of Compton-born surgeon Glen Prescott, everything about Jill was approachable and real. From her hair, which she wore in a short, gently relaxed afro, to her pleasingly plump, brown sugar–toned face, Jill preferred classic style and understatement over glitz and glamour. At five-foot-five and just over one hundred thirty pounds she wasn't Hollywood perfection. What she was was an honest-to-goodness normal person content living the life of a suburban soccer mom. Angel had spent many evenings sitting around the family room of Jill's four thousand-square-foot home in Ladera Heights—an area near LAX populated by formerly poor black folk who'd made good on the American Dream—watching movies with Glen and their two children, eight-year-old Glen Jr. and eleven-year-old Jasmine.

"This place just reeks of decadence," Jill said, her eyes glued to the backside of the Adonis-proportioned blonde passing them.

Angel gave her a devilish grin. "Just how Momma like it."

Jill smirked. "And you can, cause you're single."

"Blah, blah, blah," Angel said, prodding Jill through the draped entryway. "Tonight we're both letting our hair down and having some single-girl fun."

Jill sighed as they entered the lounge. "God help me."

The Sunset Room was one of L.A.'s most popular night spots. If you were beautiful, or famous—preferably both—the über-selective, thoroughly snobbish club was the place to see and be seen. If, however, you were of merely average looks and didn't have a two-movie deal, you were doomed to spend the night watching the parade of A-list celebrities and other industry types from the wrong side of the velvet rope.

"Ms. Hart, how nice of you to join us this evening," the club manager said, almost breaking his neck to get over to Angel.

"Good to be here," Angel said pleasantly. "This very important lady standing beside me is Mrs. Jill Prescott," she said, making certain that he realized she expected her best friend to receive the star treatment as well.

The manager extended his hand to Jill. "Mrs. Prescott, it's a pleasure to welcome someone as lovely as yourself to the Sunset Room."

Ignoring the stares from people nearby, Angel continued talking to the manager. "There's one more in our party," she said. "I want to make sure he's been added to the VIP list."

The manager lifted the silver pad he'd been holding.

"Benjamin Riley."

He scanned the list. "Yes, I have Mr. Riley on the list," he said, nodding. "Will Mr. Riley be bringing a guest?"

Angel turned to Jill. "Do you know if Phallon's coming?" she asked, referring to Ben's wife.

Jill stopped people-watching long enough to answer. "When I talked to her this afternoon, she said she had to work late at the hospital."

"Why don't I just list it as Benjamin Riley plus one, just to be on the safe side?"

"Wonderful," Angel said. "Has Mr. Zolero arrived?"

"Ah, yes, Mr. Zolero is holding court out on the patio," the manager said with a hint of fun in his voice. "If you'll come with me, I'll take you to him."

Angel and Jill followed him through one of the lounges toward the patio.

"I don't know how you don't completely lose your identity with this kind of constant adulation," Jill said, spying the men ogling Angel as she strutted by them in her red Diane von Furstenberg wrap dress and matching red fuck-me Manolos.

Angel chuckled as she elbowed her. "Like you'd let me get brand-new."

"Good point," Jill said, elbowing her back, hard enough to show she meant it.

"Besides, this life is about as real as those store-bought breasts fighting for freedom from that *fugly* red blouse," Angel said, referring to the woman giving them shade from the bar.

"Ooh, Angel!" Jill said, laughing.

"But am I lying?"

Jill gave the girl another look, then shook her head no.

Sitting with his piece du jour at one of the outdoor booths, Ernesto waved when he saw the women approaching.

"Damn," Angel said, noticing the muscular, midnight-black mountain of manhood sitting beside him. "I swear to God, that boy finds some of the hottest men."

Jill frowned. "The both of you need to settle your hot asses down with one man."

"Girl, please, I am too much woman for just one man."

"Mm-hmm," Jill said, choosing not to pursue the issue. Not tonight anyway.

"Angel!" Ernesto said as he stood to hug her. "You made it, Mommie." He turned to Jill. "And hello to you, pretty lady."

"Hey, sweetness," Jill said as she gave him a peck on the cheek.

Both Angel and Jill craned their heads skyward when Ernesto's date stood to his feet.

"Jackson, I'd like you to meet two of my favoritest people in the whole wide world," Ernesto said, smiling.

The towering testament to good genes and mucho gym time extended his large hand toward Angel. "Jackson Bennett," he said in an ocean-deep baritone.

She couldn't help licking her lips. "I'm Angel Hart."

"Of course you are," Jackson said, flashing teeth whiter than Denver snow. "You're even more beautiful in person."

Angel's lips twisted into a coy grin. "Well, aren't you just a tall drink of water on a hot night."

Ernesto tapped her meaningfully on the shoulder. "He's taken."

Angel raised her hand to her throat in mock embarrassment. "Oops, my bad."

The foursome laughed easily.

Ernesto turned to Jill. "And this fabulous creature is Mrs. Jill Prescott."

"Pleasure to make your acquaintance," Jackson said.

"Oh, the pleasure's all mine," Jill said, blushing like a schoolgirl.

Ernesto tapped Jill. "And you're married."

Jill smiled. "Oh . . . right."

They all laughed again.

"Come, everyone sit," Ernesto said, directing them to the booth.

"What would you ladies like to drink?" Jackson asked as Angel and Jill settled in their seats.

"Apple martini," Angel said.

"Just a Diet Coke for me."

Angel wrinkled her face in disbelief. "She'll have a cosmo." Turning to Jill she said, "Tonight you're going to forget you're a butt-old married woman and have some fun."

Jill popped her on the arm playfully. "Ain't nobody said nothin' about old."

Jackson laughed. "One apple martini and one cosmo coming up." He turned to Ernesto. "Baby, you want another sex on the beach?"

Ernesto blushed. "That would be fine."

Once Jackson went to get the drinks, Jill asked incredulously, "Are you sure he's gay?"

Ernesto grinned. "Ah, yes, he very much like the boys."

"Wow." Jill shook her head in amazement. "Where'd you meet him?"

"He pulled me over on South Hauser Boulevard last week."

Jill did a double take. "And you stopped?"

Ernesto gave her a playful grin. "Did I not mention that Jackson is a cop?"

"No, you didn't."

"He has handcuffs and everything."

Jill fanned herself. "My Lord."

Angel gave Ernesto the eye. "Were you speeding *again*?" She had lost count of the number of times she'd warned him that he would crash his Beemer.

"Aye, Mommie," Ernesto said, placing his forefinger over his thumb. "But just a little."

Jill smiled when she noticed the manager directing a man toward their booth. "Ben's here."

Ernesto's head spun around. "Where?"

"Down, girl," Angel said.

"Hey, good peoples," Ben said as he reached the booth.

Angel rose to greet him. "What up, playa?"

Ben kissed her on the cheek. "Nothin', just chillin'." He turned to Jill. "You losing weight?"

She smirked as she stood to hug him. "Boy, don't even be trying none of that agent BS on me."

"I'm serious," Ben said. "You lookin' damned good, girl."

Jill blushed. "Whatever."

Ernesto coughed loudly.

Ben turned to him. "So, do I get a hug from the birthday boy, or what?"

Ernesto leapt into his arms. "Yes, you get hug!"

"You know, if I weren't a boring old hetero, you and I could do some things."

"Oooh, *Benjameeen*," Ernesto purred. "Stop teasing me."

Jill spied Jackson returning from the bar. "Trouble at nine o'clock," she said in a whisper.

Jackson's muscular body tensed when he saw his date in the arms of the curly-haired, caramel-skinned stranger. If Ben were actually gay, Jackson would have good reason for concern. Ben was six feet tall, with the body of a track star and enough personality to charm the pants off a corpse.

Noting the look—a combination of jealousy and appreciation—on the law enforcer's lockjawed face, Angel moved in quickly to clear up any confusion. "I was disappointed when Jill told me that your beautiful wife couldn't join us tonight."

"Yeah, my baby is up to her ears in babies at the hospital," Ben said, disappointed.

Phallon was an OB/GYN at California Hospital Medical Center, the same downtown L.A. hospital where Jill's husband, Glen, was a surgeon. Jill—always the matchmaker—had introduced Ben and Phallon five years ago.

"I promised I'd be there to rub her feet when she got home," Ben said, giving Ernesto an apologetic smile. "So unfortunately, I can't stay too long."

"You need to go ahead and get that girl pregnant," Jill said. "If only so she'll finally take a day off from work."

Ben gave her a mischievous grin. "Trust me, I'm working on it."

"All right, Mr. Riley," Jill said, pleased.

"Speaking of good men," Ben turned to Jackson. "You're the one who has our Ernesto so happy, huh?"

Jackson flashed those beautiful teeth again. "I'm doing my best," he said. "Hey, can I get you something to drink?"

"I appreciate that, my brotha," Ben said, easing into the space between Angel and Jill. "Gin and tonic would hit the spot." He reached into his back pocket and pulled out his wallet.

Jackson waved him off. "Your money's no good here."

Angel and Jill gave each other the eye. Even back in high school Ben had a knack for doing or saying just the right thing to defuse a potentially explosive situation. That, along with an uncanny ability to make anyone feel as if she was the most important person in a crowded room, served him well in his chosen profession. As owner of Riley Artist Management, Ben was responsible for guiding the careers of a growing, and increasingly higher-profile, list of African-American and Hispanic entertainers. In an industry not known for hands-on service, or concern for a performer's artistic integrity or growth, Ben had built a reputation for being the exception. He wouldn't sign you if he didn't genuinely believe in your talent.

Angel kissed Ben on the cheek. "You are truly in the right business."

"So why can't I get you to sign with me?"

Angel sighed. She had been down this road with him before. "You know I'm with Brawner."

"So you enjoy being the ignored black fish . . ." Ben said, then smiled. "Oops, I meant little fish in the big sea."

Angel sucked on her teeth. "Could you just accept a compliment without turning it into an opportunity to tell me I'm making a mistake?"

"You are an amazing talent, Angel," Ben said, speaking in his best salesman voice. "If you'd let me, I can take you to the next—"

"Benjamin," Angel said, cutting him off. "You know I respect your skills as an agent, but Brawner is—"

Ben interrupted. "Brawner is what? White?" he asked, his voice tinged with disdain. "Come on, Angel, you know that kind of thinking—"

"Children, give it a rest tonight," Jill said, quieting them both.

"He started it," Angel said under her breath.

Ben bumped her with his shoulder. "I'll leave it alone . . . for now."

"Thank you."

"But when you're ready to be treated like the enormous talent that you are—"

"I got it, Benjamin."

Angel turned to Jill, changing the subject to one in which she was actually interested. "So how are my godchildren?"

"Growing like weeds," Jill said. "Junior is walking around like the HNIC since getting picked for peewee football."

"Little man is playing football?" Ben asked, surprised.

"He is until he breaks something . . . or I have a heart attack," Jill said sardonically. "And Ms. Jasmine has been on cloud nine since you offered to come over and help her with her tap dancing," she said to Angel. "Thank you for doing that, by the way."

Angel's face softened. "Thank you for letting me be a part of Jasmine and Junior's lives."

"Please, girl," Jill said, taking her hand. "You're family."

Ben looked over at Ernesto. "Women are so mushy."

Angel and Jill gave him the same synchronized eye roll they'd given him since their days together in grade school. "What*ever,*" the two said in unison.

Jackson returned to the sound of laughter coming from the booth. "What'd I miss?" he asked as he handed Ben the drink.

"Thanks, Action Jackson," Ben said. "Angel and Jill were just having a 'Lifetime television for women' moment while you were at the bar."

Angel threw her napkin at him laughing. "You make me so sick."

"Oooh, that's my song!" Ernesto cried when he heard the thumping beat of the Martha Wash dance anthem fill the air. He jumped up from the booth and turned to Jackson. "Come dance with me."

"Uh . . . baby, this is a straight club," Jackson said with a nervous chuckle.

Ernesto turned to Jill. "Come be our fag-hag," he said, pulling her to her feet.

"Be your what?" she asked, confused.

"If we all dance together, nobody know who with who," Ernesto explained.

Angel and Ben nudged each other, seeing Jill so out of her element.

"I swear you artsy people are strange," Jill said as she followed Ernesto and Jackson toward the dance floor.

"We gonna turn you out yet," Angel called after her.

Ben watched the three of them disappear into the crowd. "Gotta love it." He turned to Angel with an appraising look. "So what's the dealio on the reverse affirmative action happening on your show?"

She waved a hand. "I just found out about it myself when I returned to the set today."

"What she like?"

"Blond," Angel deadpanned. "I mean, she seems nice enough, but . . ." she hesitated.

"She still white."

Angel nodded. "Exactly."

Ben shook his head. "You know it's hard times when black folk can't even count on the few roles actually written for black folk."

"Tell me about it," Angel said.

"Maybe it's time for you to flip the script on them."

"Meaning?"

"Make a move no one would expect you to make."

"And what move is that?" Angel asked with a raised brow.

"Sign with Riley and let me—"

Angel stopped Ben before he could ramp up to full sales mode. "Benjamin, I love you like a play brother, but sometimes you are a freakin' dog with a bone."

"Okay, I'll let it go," Ben said. "I really am looking out for your welfare, you know?"

Angel patted his hand. "I know you are."

Ernesto, Jackson and Jill reappeared at the booth a few minutes later. Angel handed Jill a napkin, nodding toward her moist brow.

"Thank you," Jill said, wiping her face. She plopped down into the seat next to Angel exhausted.

"Whew!" Ernesto said as he sat down. "That was fun!"

"I'm gonna hit the restroom," Jackson said.

Ernesto was back on his feet in an instant. "I gotta go too," he said, heading off with him.

Angel winked at Jill. "So how was your first experience as a fag-hag?"

Jill continued fanning herself. "It's like sex on the dance floor," she said, still out of breath. "Those two mofos need to charge admission!"

Ben started laughing.

Suddenly, Ben cocked his head. "Why does that kid look familiar?" he asked, nodding toward the man making his way toward them.

Angel perked up, her hand floating to her hair. "Speaking of good sex."

"Almond Joy, I thought that was you," the man said, smiling at Angel.

"Tristan," she said, standing to greet him. "How you doin', baby boy?"

"Better now."

Angel introduced him to Jill and Ben. "Guys, this is Tristan. Tristan . . ." she said, struggling to call up a last name.

"Thomas," he said.

"Right. Tristan Thomas."

Jill fought the urge to laugh. She always said that Angel was worse than a man when it came to her treatment of the opposite sex.

"Tristan guest-starred on a few episodes of *Brave* last season." Angel motioned for the man, too beautiful *not* to be a model, to sit with them.

"Oh, right," Jill said, making the connection. "You were very good."

Tristan smiled brightly. "Thank you. Are you an actress as well?"

Ben almost choked on his drink.

Jill hit him in the arm as she answered Tristan. "No, I'm a mother and a homemaker."

"Oh," Tristan said, not certain how to respond. She might as well have said she'd landed from Mars. He turned back to Angel. "So how you been?"

"How do I look like I've been?" she asked flirtatiously.

As the two started getting friendly, Jill leaned over to Ben. "How much longer are you staying?" she asked in a whisper.

He looked at his watch. "I need to be heading out now."

"Would you mind dropping me off?"

"Sure, but didn't you and Angel come tog—"

The sound of Angel's wicked laugh stopped Ben cold.

"Tristan, if I didn't know better, I'd think you were putting the moves on me . . . again."

Ben smiled at Jill. "Question answered. My car's right out front."

Jill eased over to Angel. "Sweetie, we're gonna get going."

Angel popped out of mack mode. "But we just got—"

"I'm not asking you to leave," Jill said before she could finish. "Ben's gonna take me home."

"I can take you home."

"There's no reason for you to drive out of your way when Ben lives four blocks from me."

"You sure?"

"Yes, I'm sure," Jill said. "You stay and have fun."

Angel stood to kiss her good-bye. "Call me in the morning?"

"Don't I always?" Jill took a final look-see at Tristan, then turned back to Angel. "I'm gonna lay it on Glenn something good tonight."

"You lay it on him, Mrs. Prescott," Angel said.

Jill moved in closer to her. "Dance, have fun, but *do not* show that boy your panties."

"No worries," Angel said breezily. She ran a finger down her hip. "I'm not wearing any."

*   *   *

Lucien took another sip of his rum and coke, trying to appear interested as his date droned on about her planned career trajectory. Fortunately for him, she was easy on the eyes. When he'd met Toya a few weeks ago at the gym, his gut told him that she was just another wannabe. Boredom and horniness, however, made him accept her invitation to go out together for drinks—an invitation she extended only after learning that he was a writer on *Brave*.

So here they were at the Sunset Room, the embodiment of everything Lucien disliked about L.A. The place was overflowing with self-important, self-obsessed people strutting around swearing that their shit didn't stink. None of them had any real depth. They were simply players in the Hollywood shuffle. Lucien knew it didn't matter one bit to Toya that he had real opinions or passions. All she cared about was who he knew and how he could help advance her career.

"I'm as good an actress as any of these black girls," Toya said, giving a half-wave to up-and-coming actress Michelle Wilson as she passed by with her movie-director boyfriend, Trent Majors. "But they fear me too much to let me into the game," she added, her gaze continuing to roam around the crowded lounge. "Don't get me wrong, it's not like I don't get work," she said quickly. "I just did a Jay-Z video, and had two lines in a Tampax commercial . . . even though they made me shorten my hair."

Lucien eyed the lion's mane of curls cascading down around Toya's overly made-up face. Just as he figured: her hair was as real as her 36Ds. Why sistas insisted on buying into the Eurocentric definition of beauty—long hair, rail-thin bodies—was beyond him. Lucien liked to keep it real, demanding that the industry accept him on his terms.

Toya strained her neck to get a good look at the man entering from the patio. "Is that Benjamin Riley?" she asked rhetorically, her hand moving to smooth out her tight black cat suit. "I've been trying to get a meeting with that man for months." She looked at Lucien, but not really. "He's the agent who just signed Cassandra Douglass," she said, assuming the actress's name would register with him since she had starred on *Brave* its first season. "I auditioned for the role of Deana when she quit to do that Denzel movie . . . I could have done that movie," she said darkly. "Anyway . . ."

Lucien took a long gulp of his drink, then motioned for the bartender to bring him another.

"I know that high-yellow bitch Angel Hart fucked Randall Hunter to get the job," she sneered. "I, on the other hand, have too much self-respect. . . ." Toya hesitated when she saw the frown on Lucien's face. "I'm sorry if that's your girl," she said caustically. "I just don't like her uppity-acting self."

Lucien was about to tell Toya that he sincerely doubted that an actress with the talent Angel had would fuck anybody to get a job, but he let it go.

"Angel thinks she all that just 'cause she look mixed, but—"

"I don't know Angel that well," Lucien said, cutting her off. "But she doesn't strike me—"

"He's gonna talk to me tonight," Toya said, watching Ben and his female companion make their way through the crowd.

Lucien sighed.

"I'll be back in a minute," Toya said, then dashed away.

Lucien sipped his drink, hoping that she'd forget about him, thereby relieving him of having to listen to her the entire drive back to her Riverside apartment. As he stood at the bar thinking about all the things he could be doing besides wasting his time in this meat market with a gold digger like Toya, Lucien spied a woman making her way onto the dance floor, followed closely by some too-pretty-to-be-straight brotha. He leaned forward trying to get a better look. The guy was that model Tristan Thomas. Lucien couldn't quite make out the woman because her back was to him, but he could tell she had a kick-ass body. And from the way the crowd parted for her like the Red Sea, she was most likely a celebrity as well.

"Damn, I wish I could get me some of that," he heard someone say.

Lucien turned to the man standing next to him. "Excuse me?"

The guy nodded toward the dance floor. "Angel Hart," he said, rolling his tongue across his lips like he was looking at a big juicy steak. "I would give my right arm for just one tap of that ass."

Lucien almost choked on his drink. His head snapped back toward the dance floor.

"I heard she a freak too."

"Yo, bruh." Lucien glared at the man, the vein in the center of his forehead beginning to throb. "Show some respect for the sista."

The guy shrugged, surprised by the show of anger. "I'm just talking shit, man."

Lucien couldn't stand it when men disrespected women. And the fact that the woman in question was Angel only heightened his annoyance.

"You know her, man?"

"We work together," Lucien said, not taking his eyes off Angel.

"Really?" The tongue was hanging out again. "Can you introduce us?"

Lucien's head turned slowly. "Bruh-man, you need to bounce before you piss me off."

The man's eyes bugged as Lucien leaned toward him. "Aiight, man . . . I'm out," he said, hightailing it from the bar.

"Punk-ass nigga," Lucien growled under his breath.

For the next twenty minutes, he watched Angel dance. Her every move made him pulsate with energy and excitement, especially below the waist. Steadying himself against the bar, he looked on with envy as she moved teasingly toward Tristan, working her backside against him in perfect time to the throbbing music. The sight of her gyrating hips jump-started Lucien's breathing. He licked his dry lips as Angel extended her arms toward the heavens, her hands beckoning the lucky fool dancing with her to come closer.

"Damn," he said distractedly.

"You want another, buddy?" the bartender asked.

"No thanks, man," Lucien croaked. "I'm about to head out."

Flushed and hornier than any man sleeping alone should be, Lucien made his way toward the door, wishing he was the lucky stiff Angel had just worked into a rock-hard frenzy, the one who actually had a shot of taking her home tonight.

Toya appeared suddenly, blocking Lucien's path. "You weren't about to leave me, were you?"

"I was coming to look for you now," he lied. "You ready to get out of here?"

"Yeah, this place isn't happening tonight," Toya said. "We can go back to my place for a nightcap," she said, giving Lucien a look that made her intentions crystal clear. "That is, if you're interested."

Lucien looked over at the dance floor, then back to the date he'd almost forgotten. "Yeah, I'm interested."

3

* * * * * * *

Second to None

"Why are you avoiding me?"

"I've been really busy."

Erika took a deliberate breath as she tightened her grip on the phone. "Randall, it's been almost two weeks since we've been together," she said, trying not to lose her temper. "You aren't that busy."

There was silence on the other end of the line.

"*Hello!*" Erika yelled into the phone. "Don't try to play me, Randall!"

"Why are you making such a big deal about this?" he asked, his own level of agitation rising. "It's not like we're—"

Erika cut him off. "Are you fuckin' her?"

"Erika."

"Don't 'Erika' me!" she snapped. "Are you fuckin' the blonde?"

"Who, Faith?"

"No, the Queen of fuckin' Sheba," Erika said acerbically. "Yes, Faith. We both know you can't go more than forty-eight hours without getting laid," she said, edging forward on the bed. "And since your wife can't—"

Randall cut her off. "Don't go there."

Erika rolled her eyes at the phone.

"You know how crazy things get at the start of a new season," he explained smoothly. "We'll get together soon."

"Soon" wasn't the word she wanted to hear.

"Promise?"

"I promise," Randall said. "Look, I gotta go, I'll stop by the set to see you later . . . bye."

"Mm-hmm. Bye," Erika said, then hung up the phone. She rose from the bed, still not believing his lying ass. She glanced around her master bedroom—one of the twenty-two-room spectacle of opulence that was her Beverly Hills mansion. It was indeed a dream house—her mother's dream. Erika had wanted to purchase a smaller, less ostentatious place in Malibu, but Victoria wouldn't hear of it, insisting, "If you want them to think of you as a star, you have to live like one."

Just about every item in the showplace—the crystal chandelier hanging in the foyer, the marble floors in the great room, the gaudy oversized princess bed Erika needed a small ladder to climb into—had been hand-selected by Victoria. As with everything else in her life her mother's influence was unmistakable and, for Erika anyway, inescapable.

Making her way out of the bedroom and down the hall, Erika stopped when she reached Senghor Reid's *I'm Gonna Make You Love Me* hanging on the wall. The instant she saw the painting at the Fire & Ice Ball last year, Erika knew she had to have it. And though Victoria had implored her to spend her money on a more "important" piece, Erika for once went against her mother's wishes. At least one thing in her life was of her own choosing.

Erika admired the painting, hoping the beauty of it would help soothe her troubled spirit. Today, no such luck. She sighed. The start of a new season usually had her feeling on top of the world. Everything about it was special. The energy on the set was electric, the applause of the audience wrapping around her like a bear hug. But this season was making her uneasy. From the moment she'd laid eyes on Faith, things in Erika's well-calculated world had begun shifting off-kilter. That Randall appeared to be cooling to her—and warming to the unreasonably beautiful newcomer—only unsettled her more.

Erika took a final glance at the painting, sighed again, then continued down the staircase. She headed toward the kitchen, stopping short when she heard the shrill voice tearing somebody a new one.

"You promised me the cover!" Victoria yelled into her cell phone. "We turned down an exclusive with *Essence* because you said—!"

Victoria regarded the phone with an evil eye. "I don't care about Vivica A. Fox's fucking beauty secrets!" she barked. "Erika Bishop is the *star* of one of the hottest shows on television and—"

Erika pulled back to ensure she couldn't be seen.

"Bitch, if you interrupt me again, I will come down there and ram my foot up your bony ass," Victoria bellowed into the phone. "No! You listen to me, Kiara!" She rose from the chair. "You promised my daugh—*client* a cover story, not some piece of dribble hidden on page fifty-two."

Erika watched from the doorway as her mother adjusted her tight pale pink silk miniskirt. Victoria was a pretty woman, in better physical shape than women half her age. She took great pride in remaining a size six despite childbirth and five-plus decades of living. Her rock-hard butt and honey blond hair—cut straight and falling just past her shoulders—were attributes in which Victoria took special pride. Her high cheekbones, creamy beige skin, and legs that went on for an eternity still garnered lusty stares.

"I couldn't give a flying fuck if Halle Berry won two Oscars and a giant panda bear!" Victoria shouted. "Erika should still get the cover! Need I remind you who gave you the scoop about Khandi Long's drug problem, or the four-one-one on Janet?" she asked smugly. "And let's not forget the dirt on . . ."

Erika sighed as she listened. No matter what she thought of her mother, there was no denying that Victoria was doggedly committed to her life's purpose—the advancement of Erika's career. The editor up whose butt her mother was sticking her red Pradas could hem and haw until she was blue in the face; in the end she *was* going to give Victoria what she wanted. Sooner or later, everyone did.

"Yes, you *do* owe me," Victoria said, easing back down into the chair. "And if you want the juicy gossip hotline to remain connected, get Erika on that damned cover."

Victoria's lips twisted into a satisfied smirk as she checked off the entry on her Palm handheld. "I knew we could work this out," she said pleasantly. "Send the advance copy to my home office for my review and approval." Victoria nodded tightly. "No hard feelings at all. Bye now." She closed the phone, then shook her head. "A mother's work is never done."

Erika took a deep breath, then stepped into the kitchen.

"Well, it's about time you rolled out of bed."

"And good morning to you too, Mother," Erika said, taking a seat at the table. She cut her eyes at her housekeeper as she placed breakfast in front of her. Had Erika not already dismissed two servants in the past year, she would have fired Maria for letting her mother into the house without a heads-up.

Erika cringed as she looked down at the meal—half a grapefruit, one slice of unbuttered toast and coffee—her mother/manager/oppressor had taken the liberty of having prepared for her.

"You need to keep an eye on your weight," Victoria said, staring disapprovingly at her daughter's unmade face. "And stay out of that damned sun. Makeup can only lighten that dark skin so much."

Erika's jaws tightened. "Mother, why are you here?"

"To discuss strategy."

"What strategy?"

"Our strategy for getting that white girl off *your* show," Victoria said. "That bitch is dangerous."

Erika rolled her eyes as she raised the coffee mug to her lips.

"Don't you roll your eyes at me," Victoria said. "This is serious. Sam Rubin spent a good three minutes talking about that blond heffa yesterday."

Erika was about to roll her eyes again but caught herself. She stood up from the table and walked over to the cabinet. "He's an entertainment reporter, that's his—"

Victoria cut her off. "He also mentioned that Angel was up for an Emmy," she said, clearly pained at having to force the words from her pencil-thin, fire-engine red lips.

Erika gritted her teeth. She motioned for her maid, Maria, to hand her a bowl from the dishwasher. When Victoria was in her "don't let them get ahead of you" mode, it was best to just hear her out.

As a twenty-year veteran of the *business* of show, Erika was well aware of how the industry worked. Five feet seven and one hundred twenty pounds—according to her official bio anyway—she was, by most normal standards of beauty, an attractive woman. In the land of unattainable perfection called Hollywood, however, her dark complexion, full lips and flaring nose were—according to Victoria, anyway—imperfections that placed her at an unfair disadvantage. Erika might have been da bomb in Chicago, but in L.A. she was just another black girl.

Victoria used these perceived flaws as justification for her often ruthless interventions on Erika's behalf. Before the shoe-throwing incident that resulted in her being barred from the studio during tapings, Victoria used to saunter around the *Brave* set like she ran the show. She would demand—with modest success—that storylines revolve around her daughter, and the punch line of every joke be Erika's exclusively.

"Do you know what he said about you?"

Erika poured cereal into the bowl, not bothering to respond.

"Nothing," Victoria said, filling in the answer. "Not a damned thing. It's like you're not even on the show anymore." She slammed a fist on the table for emphasis. "We need to remind people that there wouldn't have *been* a show without you."

Her notion that her daughter was at the top of the *Brave* food chain was, to some degree, rooted in reality. The show had originally been developed as a starring vehicle for Erika—until it became quickly apparent to everyone involved that she, though a decent actress, couldn't carry a show on her own. Since they had already signed her to an ironclad five-year contract before realizing her acting limitations— Erika had Victoria to thank for that—the producers were forced to bring on two additional female leads to take up the comedic slack.

"*Brave New World* wouldn't even be on the damned air were it not for your star power. . . ."

Erika made her way over to the stainless steel oversized refrigerator. She removed a bottle of milk, trying to block out the sound of her mother's voice. If she let Victoria vent a little—while standing with her back to her—she might be allowed to have one bowl of Cocoa Puffs without being reminded that eating something that contained more than a gram of fat in it posed irreparable harm to her size-four figure.

"Am I the only one who remembers that this show was originally intended to be a starring vehicle for *you*?" Victoria said, pulling her

Palm back out of her red clutch purse. "Every time I look up, one of your supporting players is finding some annoying new way to upstage you," she said. "I'm making a note right now to get you booked on *The Tom Joyner Morning Show*."

Erika spun around. "No, Mom!" she cried out, almost choking on a Puff. "You know I don't like doing live interviews." She had a knack for putting her foot in her mouth, and she preferred doing taped interviews. They offered the option of editing her words before it was too late to take them back.

"Get over it," Victoria said flatly. Her eyes lowered toward the bowl. "Do you really think that's a smart choice?"

Erika shrank under the hot glare of her mother's spotlight. "A moment on the hips—"

"Yes, I know," Erika said with a defeated sigh. She walked over to the sink and emptied the contents of the bowl into the garbage disposal. "I'm on my way to the gym now to do penance," she said, heading toward the kitchen door. "Good-bye, Mother."

"We still need to decide how to tackle the Joyner interview," Victoria called out after her.

Erika yelled back, "I'm sure you'll tell me what *we* decide."

4

* * * * * * * *

A Familiar Refrain

Tentatively, Faith lifted the receiver to her ear. From the moment she had awakened that morning she'd been debating whether or not to make the call. It had been almost seven years since she had spoken to her grandmother directly, and she wasn't at all sure what to expect. Their relationship had been a tenuous one from the start. When she learned that her only child was pregnant, Ethel implored Faith's mother to abort, and she never forgave her when she refused. Well aware that her grandmother's feelings for her ranged from bare tolerance—on a good day—to downright contempt, Faith spent most of her childhood seeking the woman's approval and acceptance. She never got either. As far as Ethel was concerned, Faith's life was doomed before it ever began.

Her attempt to reconnect with her grandmother four years earlier hadn't resulted in the warm reunion Faith had hoped for. When the letter she'd sent was returned unopened, Faith, wanting to forge some semblance of a relationship with the woman who had raised her, left a message on Ethel's answering machine announcing that she was resending the letter, this time with a check enclosed. The delivery was accepted. Faith couldn't be sure if Ethel had ever actually read that letter or the four she'd sent since. But she knew the woman had cashed the checks.

Exhaling a weary sigh, Faith lowered the receiver back to the cradle. Maybe the past was best left behind.

The sound of the doorbell sent Jade—the cat Faith had rescued from an animal shelter last month—racing beneath the new brass four-poster bed. As she checked the gold Victorian alarm clock on the nightstand, an uneasy feeling spread through her. She couldn't imagine any of the few people—her agent and the *Brave* producers—aware of her recent move into the upscale Westwood apartment would come calling so early. Faith had been especially careful not to share her new address or unlisted telephone number with anyone from her past. This was her fresh start. She was a legitimate actress now. Old habits and old friends had no place in her new world.

When the knocking grew louder, Faith lifted herself from the bed, stepped into her fuzzy pink slippers, and walked out of the bedroom. She maneuvered her way carefully through the obstacle course of unpacked boxes crowding the hall, making a mental note to get completely settled by the weekend. The sooner she did, the sooner she'd start feeling like she truly belonged here.

Gingerly, Faith eased her eyes toward the peephole.

"I can see your shadow," the gruff voice said from the other side of the door.

Faith drew back quickly. She grew still, hoping the uninvited guest would go away.

"Come on, baby girl, don't leave me out here."

So much for hoping.

Faith bit down on her bottom lip. "What are you doing here, Lex?" she asked, her voice colored with displeasure and fear.

"Open up and I'll tell you."

The knocking on the door grew louder.

"Come on, open up."

Faith cursed under her breath. She should have known her ex-boyfriend would crawl out of his hole, reappearing just as her career was starting to take off. She could only imagine what one of her upwardly mobile new neighbors would think if they saw such a shady character standing at her doorstep.

What had possessed her to ever date such a jerk in the first place was beyond her. Well, that wasn't true. She knew exactly why she had gotten involved with Lex Martin. Besides his promises that he could get her meetings with top Hollywood agents—he never did—the man was great in the sack and could score some of the best cocaine in all of L.A. County.

"I'm not leaving!"

Faith knew Lex well enough to know that he wasn't kidding. Slowly she opened the door.

"That's a good girl." Lex kissed her on the cheek as he strutted confidently into the apartment. His jaw dropped as he spied Faith's new digs. "*Dayum*," he said. "Baby girl wasn't bullshitin' when she said she was going to live the high life one day." He turned to her. "You always said you were gonna make it to the big time."

Faith's porcelain-smooth face tightened. "Why are you here, Lex?"

"You still lookin' good, baby," he said, eyeing her breasts straining against the fabric of her pink satin nightie.

Faith folded her arms across her chest.

Lex moved toward her.

Faith stepped back. There was no way she was about to let this man charm his way back into her life. Lex was a jerk, albeit a very good-looking one. Faith could still recall the heat she felt when she first laid eyes on him two years ago at the Viper Room. There he was standing at the bar surrounded by a bevy of beautiful women all vying for his attention. The competitor in Faith demanded that she be the winner—the woman Lex took home that night.

"Don't I even get a hug?"

"How did you find out where I lived?"

Lex laughed. "I have my ways." He headed into the living room.

"You can't stay," Faith said, following him.

"This is nice—real nice," Lex said, fingering one of the crystal candlesticks atop the fireplace. He gave the space a sweeping once-over, then shook his head. "Shit, this room alone is twice the size of that dump you used to live in."

The memory of the tiny studio apartment she'd called home until four weeks ago made Faith cringe. Located in the absolute worst part of L.A.'s Wilshire district, the place was a dive in the truest sense of the word. It had puke green walls, so paper thin that Faith could hear everything her freak show neighbors were doing well into the wee hours of the morning. Overrun with roaches, the apartment always smelled of musty sex no matter how many times Faith scrubbed it down with Pine Sol. She would never forget the joy she felt as she placed the last box into her Honda Civic and drove away.

Lex took a seat on the red sofa.

Faith rolled her eyes as he lifted his scuffed boots onto her new smoked glass coffee table.

"I could get used to this."

"Well, don't." .

Ignoring his inhospitable hostess, Lex reached into his pocket and removed a plastic vial. "Let's celebrate your newfound success."

"I don't do that anymore."

Lex's crooked grin showed how much he believed her. "How 'bout we use a fresh twenty-dollar bill?"

As much as she craved a line, she fought the urge. "A lot has changed in the year since we broke up."

Lex gazed at her, trying to judge whether she was serious, then finally placed the vial back into his pocket. He rose to his feet, giving her a lascivious wink. "Some things never change, baby girl."

Faith backed up as he approached. "My life is different," she said, as much for her sake as his. "I've turned a new page."

"You're still as beautiful as ever, though," Lex said, reaching to stroke her cheek.

"Don't," Faith said, pushing his hand away. She studied him as he stood there, casually resting his weight on one leg. Even unshaven he was still dangerously sexy. "You need to go."

Lex smiled as he inched closer. "Come on, baby girl. You gotta admit, we did have some good times together."

Faith shuddered as he pressed his stiffening manhood against her. "I have to get to work." Her knees were threatening to buckle. Finally, she took a slow, steadying breath and backed away.

Realizing that his chosen approach was getting him nowhere, Lex pulled up short. He gave the place another sweep, then whistled. "You must be making crazy bank now."

Faith couldn't help but chuckle. How silly of her not to see this coming.

The cocky arrogance with which Lex had walked in with drained away. Pensively, he lifted his hand to his forehead and took a nervous breath. "Look, Faith, I've gotten myself into a little trouble . . . *financially*."

Faith shook her head. Some things never changed.

"I need to borrow five thousand for a few weeks," Lex said, approaching her again. "Just until I can get back on my feet."

Faith extended her arm to separate them. "You still owe me the twenty-five hundred I loaned you to make that demo tape two years ago."

Lex took her hand. "This time I'll pay you back, I promise," he said, raising her fingers to his lips to kiss them.

Faith pulled her hand back abruptly. "I don't have that kind of money."

"How much do you have?"

"I don't feel good about—"

"Please, baby girl, I need your help."

"I can't help you," Faith said, motioning toward the door. "Now, if you don't mind, I need to get to the studio."

Lex lurched toward her, grabbing her wrist. "You know," he shouted, "if the tables were turned and I was rolling in the dough, I'd do it for you!"

Faith flinched. The last time he'd gotten this angry, she'd wound up with a black eye.

Noting the look on her face, Lex softened his tone. "Come on, baby girl. After all we've meant to each other, you can't leave me hanging like this."

Fearful that whatever she said might set him off, she remained silent.

Lex lowered himself to one knee. "Please, Faith," he said, sounding desperate. "Do this for me and I promise never to bother you again."

Faith thought for a moment. If this was the price of final freedom, maybe she should just pay up and be done with it. "Wait here," she said, then stalked out of the room.

Lex breathed a sigh of relief when she returned with a check. "I promise I'll pay—"

"Don't make promises we both know you won't keep," Faith said, cutting him off. She handed him the check. "If you ever try to contact me again, I'll call the police. Understood?"

"Sure, baby girl," Lex said, nodding. He blinked at the amount written on the check to make certain it was real. "Consider me a ghost."

Faith walked over to the front door and held it open.

"Thanks."

"Good-bye, Lex," Faith said, praying that this time it was for good. If he ever showed up at the studio, all the progress she'd made would be lost. With her big break, she'd moved beyond grifters. A nice man with good manners and deep pockets—that's the kind of dream she was chasing now.

5

* * * * * * * *

Give and Take

"Were you able to set up the audition with the producers of the Harrison Ford movie?" Angel asked her agent before taking a quick bite of her corned beef sandwich.

"No, I wasn't," Helen said in her faux British accent. "I really don't think you're what they're looking for."

Angel rolled her eyes. How many times had she heard this refrain? She lifted her leg from the coffee table and leaned forward on the sofa in her dressing room. "Is that what they told you?"

"Not exactly," Helen said tentatively.

"Well, what did they say . . . *exactly*?" Angel tensed as the realization hit her. "You didn't even call them, did you?" she asked. "What possible reason could you have for not wanting me to get that audition?"

"No one's trying to keep you from auditioning," Helen said, a bit too condescendingly for Angel's taste. "I just think going out for this project would be a waste of our time."

Angel sucked on her teeth, recalling her conversation with Ben the other night at the Sunset Room. He would have gotten her the audition. He didn't mind wasting time on his clients.

"There is another movie role, however, that I think you may be better suited for," Helen continued. "Now, I know you said you'd never consider playing a maid or a prostitute, but—"

"And I don't plan on considering it today," Angel said, cutting her off before she could finish. "I expect you to do the job I give you ten percent of my money to do," she said curtly. "Call the producers of that movie and get me an audition," Angel instructed. "And from now on, you let me decide what is or isn't a waste of *my* time."

"I'm your agent, Angel. It's my job to advise you, and help direct your time and energies appropriately," Helen said. "There are only three female speaking roles in that movie, and none of them was written with a black actress in mind."

Angel erupted in agitated laughter. "This is Hollywood. No part is ever written with a black anything in mind."

"That's my point," Helen said as her cell phone rang. "Listen, honey," she said with practiced smoothness, "I've gotta take this call. We'll talk later."

"You bet we will." Angel snatched out her earpiece, and sat back roughly on the sofa. She lifted the sandwich to her mouth, then dropped it back onto the Styrofoam plate. "Heffa made me lose my appetite." She was still stewing when she saw the door of her dressing room open slightly. "Come in."

Gingerly, Lucien poked his head inside. "Got the script revisions."

"Just drop them over there," Angel said, pointing toward the makeup table on the opposite side of the room.

Lucien placed the stack of pages on the table, then realized Angel seemed upset. "You okay?"

She looked up and smiled weakly. "I'm fine." Angel waved her hand tiredly. "Sometimes I just . . . never mind," she said. "I'm sure you've got enough of your own drama to deal with. You don't need me bothering you with mine."

"That's not true," Lucien said, trying to be helpful. He took a hesitant step forward. "Sometimes listening to other people's stuff helps put your own into perspective. Or at the very least," he added, smiling, "it reminds you that other people are just as screwed up as you are."

"Good point," Angel said with a faint chuckle.

Lucien took another step forward. "Really, talk to me."

Angel studied him carefully. She didn't really know the new

writer, but from what she'd seen, he appeared to be a straight shooter. And she could use a sounding board.

"It's just that my agent, of all people, is trying to pigeonhole me," Angel said. "Tramp thinks I should be giddy just to have a steady acting gig. You know, seeing how I'm black and all."

Lucien knew that tune. "I see."

"I'm not naïve," Angel said. "I am acutely aware of the numerous double standards that exist in this ass-backward industry, but damn, you'd think my agent, at least, would think me capable of playing more than crackheads and whores."

"I feel you, Angel," Lucien said sympathetically. "Look, if she can't see outside the box, fire her butt and find an agent who can."

Angel looked at him like he was crazy. "I'm with *Brawner*," she said. "Do you know how many black actresses—hell, any actress— would kill to be represented by them?"

"Not if it means being stifled artistically," Lucien said.

Angel stared at him. Stifled artistically? She could see that this guy had a lot to learn about the business. "Trust me, Brawner—"

"Is a big lily-white agency," Lucien said, cutting her off. He shook his head, disappointed in her. "Black people need to stop with this 'If it ain't white it ain't right' crap."

"Excuse me?" Angel's brow furrowed. How dare he say that to her? Yet she caught herself before she spouted off. "You know what," she said, taking a calming breath. "Let's not even have this conversation." It was clear that Lucien was too much of a black militant to understand her bigger-picture point of view. And as much as she would love to *educate* him on the realities of showbiz, it wasn't worth the risk of alienating the show's newest writer. That was the best way to get herself cut out of scenes.

Lucien backed off too. "Listen, I'm not judging you."

Angel gave him an incredulous look.

Lucien unhinged his tightened jaw. "You are a good actress, with the potential to be a great one."

"Thanks," Angel said sarcastically. "I feel so much better now."

"Can you cut me some slack?" Lucien said. "I'm not trying to insult you here."

Angel clamped down on what she was about to say. She was the one who'd invited him into her problems. "Fine, I'm listening."

Lucien sat down in the chair. "I'm going to make a confession," he said. "But don't make more of it than what it is."

Angel leaned back on the sofa, mildly intrigued. What secret was this guy about to unload on her?

"The opportunity to write for an actress of your caliber was one of the things that sold me on this job," Lucien said, averting his eyes. "You are not just a good *black* actress, you're a good *actress*."

Angel was flattered. "Just not great yet," she said, teasing.

"You can be, but you gotta start demanding roles worthy of your talent," Lucien said.

Angel couldn't help but smile. "You do know how to spin the words, don't you?"

"Too bad the butt-holes who run this show don't appreciate it," Lucien said with a nod toward the door.

"Well, I appreciate it," Angel said sincerely. "There has been a marked improvement in the quality of our scripts since you came on board." She saw that he didn't believe her. "I'm not shittin' you."

Lucien tried not to beam with pride but was failing miserably.

"Before you got here, our characters were about as yellow as you could get without putting us in whiteface and blond wigs."

Lucien cringed at that image. "The producers of this show aren't interested in anything even close to the realities of black life in America." He rose to his feet. "This is John's old tight ass," he said, contorting his face the way the supervising producer did. Lucien mimicked: " 'That's some powerful stuff you've written there . . . er . . . Lucien, is it? Good stuff, Luscious. But we might . . . well, ya know . . . I hear what you're saying, Lucas . . . but . . . how can I put this? This script is just way too deep for a comedy format. It's a downer, ya know?' "

His imitation was perfect, making Angel bubble over with laughter. She jumped up from the sofa and high-fived him. "Oh, that is too dead-on."

"Like being black with their crazy white asses running things is a freakin' picnic for us," Lucien said, laughing himself.

"I know that's right!"

Faith knocked on the dressing room door, then peeked inside. "You guys having a party and didn't invite me?" she asked, trying for a joke.

"Hey, Faith," Lucien said, offering her a warm smile.

Angel eyed him curiously. For someone so pro-black, he was giving the white girl much love. Still, she had to admit she liked her too. Despite Erika's continued insistence that she was the blue-eyed devil incarnate, Faith appeared to be a genuinely sweet girl. "What's up?" Angel asked.

"I was hoping to treat ya to a quick lunch over at the commissary before rehearsal," Faith said. Her face fell as she noticed the corned beef sandwich and fries on the coffee table. "But I see you've already been."

"Rain check?"

Faith nodded. "Sure thing."

An uncomfortable silence descended on the three of them. They stood there unsure of what to say next.

"Well . . . uh, okay," Faith said, backing up toward the door. "I'll see you guys at rehearsal."

"Nice girl," Lucien said as the door closed.

"Seems to be, anyway," Angel said more cautiously. "Still not sure if she really is a ditzy blonde or just plays one on TV."

"I don't envy her position in all this."

Angel didn't respond, but only frowned. The conversation with her agent came back to her.

Lucien's attention suddenly shifted. Eyeing the remaining half of the corned beef sandwich, he said, "You gonna eat that?"

Angel slid the tray across the table. "Have at it." She walked over to the mini-fridge on the opposite side of the sofa. "Cranberry juice or mineral water?"

Lucien sat on the couch. "Mineral water, please," he said as he began devouring the sandwich.

Angel handed him the water, then sat back down. "What don't you envy?" she asked. "Looks to me like Faith is the big winner in this mess. She's taking the industry by storm . . . on the cover of every magazine. I wouldn't think she'd have a care in the world."

"But taking on a role that most people assumed would go to a sista. It can't be easy for her."

"Why should it be?" Angel said coolly.

Lucien did a double take. "What do you mean?"

"They don't make it easy for us," Angel said. "Black actresses can't catch a break as it is. What chance will we have once they start giving what few decent parts they write for us to white girls?"

"May I play devil's advocate?"

Angel looked at Lucien askance. She would have assumed someone that obviously Afrocentric would be in full support of her viewpoint. "Be my guest."

"You want the industry to, whenever possible, do color-blind casting?"

"Well, yes, but—"

Lucien raised his finger. "Let me finish my point," he said. "Wouldn't that make Faith's hiring, in theory at least, a positive step forward?"

Angel leaped up from the sofa. "Oh *puh-leease!* That's complete bullshit, Lucien, and you know it!"

"I don't know that," he said evenly. "If you want the chance to play parts that might normally go to white actresses, isn't it only fair for them to expect the same?"

"Ah . . . no," Angel said curtly. "That's like saying white folks should get the added support of affirmative action simply because black people do. Throughout our history *we* have been systematically excluded from opportunity. *They* can't just wake up one morning and say, 'Okay, everybody's even now,'" she said. "It doesn't work like that."

"Good point."

Angel's mouth fell open. "Good point?"

Lucien placed the plastic wrapper in the bag, then tossed it into the garbage. "Well, I better get back to work," he said, standing up.

Angel sat speechless as she watched him make his way to the door. Even his walk reeked of overconfidence. Lucien Alexander was proving more enigmatic—and interesting—with every passing day. Just when she thought she'd pegged him, he did something to surprise her. One minute preaching black power, the next expounding on the virtues of reverse affirmative action. "We're not finished . . ." she said, hesitating when she heard the knock at the door. "Come in."

"Great, I can kill two birds with one stone," the production assistant said as he stepped into the dressing room. He turned to Angel. "You're needed on the set in five for final walk-through."

"Thanks," she said distractedly, her eyes burning a hole in Lucien's back. Angel could tell from the arrogant way he was standing—jeans that hung just so over his high, firm butt, tight shirt clinging to every muscle—that he thought he'd gotten the better of her.

"And John wants to see you in his office."

"Okay," Lucien said, continuing toward the door. He glanced back at Angel. "See you on the set," he said, then walked out with the production assistant.

When she realized what Lucien had just done, a smile spread across her face. That man didn't honestly believe that white people deserved to benefit from reverse affirmative action. He was simply supporting the argument to see if Angel had the courage of her convictions when challenged.

Angel smirked. "Round one to you, Mr. Alexander."

*   *   *

Angel and her two make-believe roommates held their positions on the living room set of their make-believe apartment. The space was much smaller in size than it appeared on the television screens of the eight million people who tuned into WBN's top-rated show each week. Exquisitely decorated, it was far more attractive than anything three struggling twenty-somethings living on a shoestring budget in New York could ever have hoped to call home—in reality anyway. But this brave new world wasn't reality. It was a world where the rooms had three walls instead of four, and the camera peering through the window wasn't considered an invasion of privacy. In this world you could travel from your front door to your Wall Street office in approximately twelve seconds, and solve major life problems in just under twenty-three minutes.

Erika slammed her script down on the table. "Who put this line in here?"

Angel squirmed in her chair. So much for the drama-free day she had hoped for.

Placing a hand on her hip, Erika glared over at the group of writers warming the first row of bleacher seats. That's where a new studio audience sat each Friday night during the show's twenty-two-week season. "*Hello* . . . ? I asked a question."

"Let me guess," Lucien said, making his way onto the set. "You have a problem with that line too."

The *Inside Entertainment* crew on hand to cover the taping of phenom Faith Molaney's first show aimed their camera toward them. Aware that she now had an audience, Erika was more than happy to give the people their money's worth.

"*We* don't say that anymore," Erika said. "Maybe you were lusting for those white girls on *Sex and the City* when you wrote it."

Lucien was unmoved. "That's why the line is funny."

Angel glanced over at Erika, her every instinct telling her that her costar was about to meet her match in Lucien.

Erika barked right back, "Well, I'm not saying it."

Lucien pushed his hand through his dreadlocks. Shrugging, he gave Erika a bemused smile, then turned to Angel. "Do you mind picking up the line?"

Angel wanted to laugh. "Sure," she said, ignoring the look Erika was shooting her way.

"Thanks," Lucien said, relieved. He started to walk off the set, then hesitated. "Better yet . . . take everything from 'Welcome to New York' on down to the offending 'You go, girl' line," he instructed.

Angel marked the changes on her script, trying to keep a straight face as Erika picked her cracked one up off the floor.

"We should have given it to you in the first place," Lucien said. "You deliver punch lines better anyway." He shot Erika a bright smile. "There, problem solved?"

Angel studied Lucien as he made his way back to the bleachers. That brotha was proving more impressive by the minute.

"All right, people," the director yelled from off-set. "Let's take the scene from the top."

Erika took a bitter breath, then said her lines—what remained of them, anyway—as written. She'd be having no more *problems* today.

✳   ✳   ✳

During their next break, Erika tapped her Ferragamo-fitted foot irritably against the concrete floor as she eavesdropped on the latest conversation between Randall and Faith.

"Mr. Hunter, I don't think that would be such a good idea."

"Call me Randall."

Faith smiled. "Okay, Randall. I don't think dinner—"

"You do eat, don't you?"

"Well, yes," Faith said, twisting a lock of hair around her fingers.

"And I eat as well," Randall said smoothly. "I'm just suggesting that we eat . . . together."

Faith let out a flirtatious chuckle. "Mr. Hun . . . Randall, I am well aware of your legendary reputation."

"Are you listening to me?" Victoria yelled into the cell phone.

"Yes, Mother," Erika said in a distracted whisper as she eyed Randall and Faith huddled together in the back of the studio. She wanted to march over there and slap that silly grin off her perfect little face. It was bad enough that Faith had taken a role that should have gone to a sista. Now she had the gall to be putting her claws into Erika's man.

"Don't let that girl upstage you any more than she already has," Victoria instructed. "You take control of that interview. . . ."

Erika continued watching Randall put the moves on Faith as her mother rattled off up-to-the-minute instructions.

"What would your wife . . . and *Erika* think of us having dinner together?"

"My marriage is more a business arrangement than a love affair," Randall said evenly. "As for Ms. Bishop, whatever she and I *might* have had is long finished."

Erika wanted to explode. "You lying bastard," she hissed.

"What?"

"Nothing, Momma," Erika said, glaring at Randall. Maybe he'd been avoiding her the past few weeks, but the two of them were still very much together. Randall was simply saying whatever he had to in order to charm Faith's panties off. Erika could recall a time not that long ago when he'd done the same to her.

"This is your show. . . ." Victoria hesitated. "Erika?"

"Huh?"

"Girl, are you listening to me?"

One of the production assistants approached. "They're ready for you."

"Thank you," Erika said. "Mother, I have to go."

"Don't forget what I said."

Erika flipped the cover of the cell phone. Victoria needn't worry. She had absolutely no intention of letting Marilyn Monroe Lite hone in on her turf.

Moments later Erika joined Angel and the bane of her existence on the set for a group interview with the *Inside Entertainment* reporter. As Faith started gushing about the generosity of the staff and the show's fans, it took everything Erika had not to punch her in the mouth.

How 'bout I climb up that ladder and generously drop one of those spotlights on your bottle-blond head? Erika thought as she sat smiling for the rolling cameras.

The reporter turned to Angel. "Two years ago you were the new kid on the block, having just been hired to replace Cassandra Douglass. You successfully made the transition from 'replacement' actress to Emmy-nominated one. What advice would you give Faith as she tries to accomplish the same feat?"

"I would tell her to simply trust in her talent," Angel answered. "Faith has great comedic timing and is one helluva good actress. Fans of *Brave* will embrace her because they appreciate real talent."

Faith blushed, surprised by her costar's kindness. "Thank you, Angel." She turned to the reporter. "I can't tell you how much I'm learning about the craft by watching Angel work," Faith said. Then after a beat, "Erika too."

The reporter turned to Erika. "Yesterday on *The Tom Joyner Morning Show* you stated that you questioned the producer's decision to replace Khandi Long—a black actress—with a white one," the reporter began. "Do you believe Faith's hiring is in some way an insult to black actresses and the black viewing audience as a whole?"

Randall's head snapped toward the show's producers, standing behind him.

Erika took a measured breath, then waited. She leaned back casually in her blue canvas chair. Everyone on the soundstage held their breath.

"Faith is a sweet girl, and I have nothing against her personally," Erika lied. "But I don't recall anyone bending over backward to add black faces to the cast of *Friends*. I guess there was no flava in *their* New York."

Randall inched toward the stage, readying to yank Erika off the set if she didn't reel herself in.

"Now that I think about it," Erika said, "I don't think I ever saw one regular cast member of color on *Seinfeld*, or *Cheers*, or—"

Randall barged through the group surrounding his three stars. "I'm sorry, but we need to get Erika to her next appointment," he said, snatching her up from the chair. "Feel free to continue the interview with Angel and Faith."

Maintaining a vicelike grip on Erika's arm, Randall hurried her past the slack-jawed crew and down the long corridor leading to the dressing rooms.

"Take your hands off me," she snarled.

"Shut up and keep walking," Randall said through a tight smile.

He pushed her inside her dressing room, slamming the door shut behind them. "What the fuck were you trying to pull out there?"

Erika sauntered over to her brightly lit mirror and took a peek. "I don't know what you're talking about."

"Bullshit!" Randall shouted. "I've got enough on my hands right now without having to worry about you creating a new public relations nightmare for this show."

Erika adjusted her tight-fitting black jersey skirt, then strutted over to the bar. "The reporter asked me my opinion and I gave it to her," she said as she poured herself a glass of water. "There's nothing in my contract that precludes me from doing that. Is there?"

Randall marched over to her. "Don't push me."

Erika lowered the glass onto the counter, then slithered to within inches of his face. "Or what, Randy? You'll fire me?" she asked, thrusting her pelvis against his midsection. Erika rubbed herself slowly against Randall, her lips grazing the reddened tip of his left earlobe. "I have a five-year deal . . . pay or play. Short of my untimely demise, you couldn't get rid of me if you wanted to."

Randall's breathing intensified as Erika's hand eased toward the crotch of his gray Hugo Boss slacks. Yet before she could undo the zipper, he pushed her away.

"I know I was bad," Erika said playfully. With a few nimble twists her skirt fell to the floor, exposing the black French-cut lace panties she was wearing. "Let me make it up to you."

"Put your clothes back on, Erika," Randall said hoarsely.

"Come on, baby," she said, grinding herself against him. "Let me make it all better."

"I'm not in the mood."

"Oh, you're always in the mood."

Finally Randall pulled away. "Will you please show a modicum of self-respect?" he said coldly.

Erika snatched for air as if he'd just sucker-punched her. She flinched when she caught a glimpse of her half-naked image in the mirror. For once Randall was right. She was disrespecting herself for a jerk who wasn't even that great in the sack.

"You know what?" Randall said. "This is all getting a little too heavy for—"

"Save it," Erika said, cutting him off. "And please spare me the 'it's not you it's me' dribble, okay?"

"Come on. We both knew going into this that even great sex had a limited shelf life," Randall said as he straightened his tie.

Erika smirked. "Don't fool yourself—it wasn't so great."

"Bitterness doesn't look good on you."

Stung, Erika pointed toward the door. "Get out of my dressing room."

Randall nodded, then obliged.

After the door closed, Erika pulled up her skirt, stepped back into her shoes, then walked over to the mirror. Defiantly, she wiped away the single tear streaming down her cheek. Randall wasn't worth crying over. If Faith wanted him, she could have him.

With head held high, Erika walked out of the dressing room. She didn't cry over snakes.

6

* * * * * * *

Here Kitty, Kitty

Randall leaned back in his custom-made mahogany leather chair, clasping his hands behind his head. A big smile inched across his tanned face. The first episode of *Brave*'s new season had aired, and the show remained the most watched television program in black households. More important, his pet project had increased its white viewership by more than twenty percent over the previous season's average. His instincts had been on target. Faith had star power and American audiences—white and black—would adore her. Surely this latest success would quell any lingering speculation within the industry about the true reason behind the thirty-six-year-old's meteoric rise up the Wellington Broadcasting ladder.

Seven years ago, Randall had packed everything he owned into the back of his old Ford pickup truck and made the trek from Youngstown, Ohio, to Hollywood, intent on becoming the next Robert Redford. Three years and three soft-porn cable movies later, Randall had found the going anything but easy. To make ends meet, he took gigs working as a server with a company that catered private Beverly Hills parties. It was at one such party that he met Jasper Wellington, the founder and president of Wellington Broadcasting. The wealthy media tycoon took an immediate liking to him. Within a month of that meeting, Randall was working in WBN's mailroom. When Savanna, Jasper's pampered only child, laid eyes on him at a network party, she decided then and there that Randall Hunter was going to be her next husband—her third. The two exchanged vows six months later. Upon his return from their five-week Caribbean honeymoon, Randall started his new job in Wellington Broadcasting's program development department.

From the small black box on the desk, the executive assistant's voice buzzed: "Mr. Hunter, your wife is on line two."

Randall tugged at his earpiece, then pressed the flashing button. "Savanna . . . kind of busy here," he said briskly.

"I won't keep you long, my love," Savanna said. "Serge is planning dinner, and I was hoping to have him prepare for two."

With firm fingers Randall worked the tension forming at the base of his neck. "I'm under the gun—"

"We haven't sat down for dinner together in weeks, Randall."

"Savanna, you know how crazy things are at the beginning of a new season."

"I know, darling, but try anyway."

Randall swallowed his disdain for her. "I'll see what I can do." He glanced up at the door of his office, promising himself that he'd promptly give his assistant a bonus check if she'd walk through it and offer him an excuse to get off the phone. "I'll call you back when I know for sure, but no promises . . . okay?"

"Okay, my love," Savanna answered, grateful for a response that at least offered hope. "I'll have Serge make your favorite: filet mignon, garlic-roasted potatoes, asparagus."

When he saw his assistant appear in the doorway, Randall almost leapt up from his desk. "Yes, Heather?"

"Mr. Halverson is on line four," she announced apologetically. "He assured me that you were expecting his call."

"Yes, I am expecting his call," Randall said loudly. "Savanna, I've got to take this. I'll get back to you later."

"I'm so pleased that you'll be home—"

Randall disconnected the call before Savanna could finish. He waved Heather away as he pressed the flashing button. "Has the delivery been made?"

"Yes, Mr. Hunter. I saw to it personally."

Randall grinned like a lion readying to devour his prey. "Good. We'll talk soon." He pressed another button, then dialed up the number he'd been waiting to call all morning.

"Hello."

"Hello, yourself."

"Randall, the bracelet is beautiful."

"Not as beautiful as the lady wearing it."

"But I don't understand. It's not my birthday or anything."

"Do I need a special occasion to show you how much I think of you?"

There was a slight pause at the other end of the line. "You have been so wonderful to me," Faith said sincerely. "I wouldn't even know how to begin to thank you."

Randall looked down through his glass desktop, grinning devilishly at the rising excitement between his legs. "You can thank me by letting me take you out to dinner tonight."

"We've already talked about—"

"I'm just asking for dinner."

Faith hesitated for a moment. "Sure . . . okay. Why not."

"How does the Four Seasons in Beverly Hills sound?"

"The Four Seasons Hotel?"

Randall laughed—a low, mischievous growl. Faith's uneasiness only served to make her that much more of a turn-on. "They have a great restaurant," he said reassuringly.

"Oh . . . okay," Faith said, relieved. "Then the Four Seasons it is."

"Looking forward to it," Randall said. "Good-bye for now, Faith Molaney."

"Good-bye, Randall Hunter."

After Randall hung up, he reclined in his chair, gently stroking his stiffened manhood. The groundwork had been laid expertly on his part. He had gained the trust of the new ingénue. Now it was time to collect his latest prize.

"Wellington-Hunter residence?"

"Put my wife on the line."

Randall and Savanna's marriage was one deeply rooted in love— hers for him. Theirs was a union of mutually agreed upon but never spoken understandings between two people desirous of what the other had to offer. Randall performed admirably in the role of handsome, virile, doting husband in front of Savanna's uptight society friends, and she afforded him old-money respectability and fast-track career success. It was further understood that red-blooded Randall would, from time to time, seek elsewhere the stimulation his prim, frigid fifty-year-old wife couldn't supply him. As long as he remained discreet, she looked the other way.

"How does Black Forest cake with raspberry mousse sound for dessert?"

"Ah, looks like I'm going to have to work pretty late, after all. I'll probably just sleep in town tonight."

Sharp disappointment rang through her voice. "All right."

"I'm sorry about this, Savanna."

"Don't be, my love . . . I understand."

*   *   *

Faith sighed as she spied the driver through the glass divider. This was the life she'd always imagined for herself. The evening had been perfect thus far. When she walked out of her apartment to begin their date, Randall was standing in front of the black Mercedes limousine holding a single red rose. It was just like the scene from that movie with Julia Roberts and Richard Gere. Faith glanced over at Randall. He looked a little like Richard Gere. But Randall was cuter, and he had the most beautiful gray eyes Faith had ever seen.

"Did you enjoy dinner?"

"Very much," Faith said. "Thank you." No matter what his true intentions were, she appreciated the fact that Randall had treated her like a real lady tonight, not some potential conquest. Though it was obvious that he found her attractive, he had remained respectful. Not once during dinner had he brought up the subject of sex. To be honest, Faith wouldn't have been offended if he had. She knew what men like him wanted.

Randall reached into the breast pocket of his sports jacket, pulling out a small vial. "You game?"

"Sure," Faith said hesitantly, eyeing the white powder as he poured it onto the small mirror. She had sworn off the stuff ever since getting the job on *Brave*. Yet if her own boss was indulging, she guessed she could make an exception.

"Ladies first," Randall said, handing her the rolled-up hundred-dollar bill.

"Thank you." Faith pulled her hair back as she leaned forward. In one fluid movement she inhaled a line of the cocaine.

"I see you've done this before."

"Once or twice." Faith rolled her head from side to side as the drug began to work its magic. "Hmmm, that's nice."

"You're just full of surprises, aren't you?"

Faith eased her tongue teasingly across her perfectly painted red lips. "You think so?"

"Oh, yes."

Faith handed him the makeshift straw. "Your turn."

Randall snorted one line of the power, then another. "*Ahhh.*" He lifted his head, a dazed smile spreading across his face.

A spark shot up Faith's spine as he raised her hand to his lips, gently kissing her fingers. She closed her eyes and sighed. It all felt like a dream.

Faith reopened her eyes as the limo came to a stop in front of her apartment complex. The driver got out and walked around to the passenger-side door. "Well, I guess this is good-night," she said, more a question than a statement of fact.

"Guess so," Randall said, finally releasing her hand.

Faith thanked the driver as he helped her out of the limo. She turned back to Randall. "Thank you for a wonderful evening."

"You're very welcome," he said.

She stood there waiting for Randall to call in the marker, assuming the diamond bracelet on her wrist was a down payment for sex. And as down payments went, the two-and-a-half-carat bauble was a pretty sizable one. Faith had given herself away for far less in the past.

Randall smiled but said nothing.

"You sure you don't want to come in for a nightcap?" Faith prodded.

"No, I think I better call it a night."

Faith gave him a curious look. "You sure?"

Randall nodded. "I'm sure."

Thoroughly confused, Faith leaned into the window, placing a soft kiss on his cheek. "Well, good-night, then."

"Good-night."

Faith walked up the sidewalk to her apartment, trying to make some sense of what had just happened. Why didn't Randall come up? Was it possible that she had misread the signals? Maybe he wasn't interested in her sexually after all. Maybe he was simply being a good boss, taking his new star out to dinner as a gesture of goodwill. Faith chuckled at the absurd thought. Randall was a man. He wanted her.

She walked into her bedroom, slipped off her slingbacks, then reached for the ringing telephone. "Hello."

"Did I mention I had a great time tonight?"

Faith blushed. "Yes, you did."

"Okay, just thought I'd make sure," Randall said softly. "Well . . . good-night, Faith Molaney."

"Good-night, Randall Hunter." Faith lowered the phone back into its cradle, a smile overtaking her face. She stepped out of the pale blue silk dress and tossed it onto the chair. Her cat, Jade, appeared at the door of the bedroom, giving her mistress an 'it's about time you brought your happy ass home' look.

"Hi, baby," Faith said, reaching down to stroke the cat.

Jade's purr told her that all was forgiven.

"You won't believe how wonderful this night has been." Faith made her way over to the dresser. She removed the tennis bracelet, carefully placing it back into the aqua-blue Tiffany box. "Randall Hunter wasn't at all what I had expected."

Faith lifted an oversize T-shirt from the chair. "You know, I was a little leery about accepting his dinner invitation at first," she continued as she pulled the makeshift nightgown over her head. "But I must admit I really did have a good time."

She walked into the bathroom shaking her head. "Randall is either a sincerely sweet guy or one really good actor. He didn't even try to kiss me," Faith said, then smiled. "Well, not on my lips anyway."

Jade watched Faith from the foot of the bed as she stood at the bathroom basin, removing her makeup with cold cream.

"Randall played it perfectly," Faith said, reentering the bedroom. "But I know he wants me," she said, winking at the cat.

Jade began to lick her paw, lapping away.

"Yes, I know he's married." Faith smiled guiltily as she stepped into her pink slippers. "But it's not like I'm pursuing him," she said, heading for the door. "And besides the fact that he's gorgeous, charming and very powerful, Randall is responsible for all the good things starting to happen in my life," Faith called out from the kitchen. She walked back into the bedroom holding a black and gold coffee mug with the *Brave New World* logo emblazoned on it. "And he treats me like a lady," she said, then took a few sips of green tea. "No man has ever done that before."

Faith placed the mug on the nightstand. "This may all be for naught." She shook her head, trying to shake off the hope that something might develop between her and Randall. "He probably won't even ask me out again."

She reached for a bottle of lotion. "Women married to men like Randall can't possibly expect them not to stray from time to time," she said as she rubbed the lotion into her hands absentmindedly.

After a pause Faith turned to Jade. "So we're agreed. If he asks me out for a second date, my answer is yes."

Jade purred softly.

Satisfied, Faith reached over and turned off the light. She lowered her head onto the pillow and closed her eyes as her feline curled into a ball at her side..

*   *   *

Jimmy Snow leaned back in his tattered La-Z-Boy staring up at the life-size picture of Faith taped to the wall. He had fashioned the place into a virtual shrine to the "it" girl of the moment. Photographs, videotapes, newspaper and magazine clippings featuring Faith filled every available inch of the tiny studio apartment. Now if he could only muster up the courage to tell her how much she meant to him, his sad, invisible life would finally have meaning.

Jimmy made his way over to the photo. Tentatively, he placed his fingers against Faith's lips, then against his own. Turning on the television, he returned to the worn and tattered La-Z-Boy.

For the next thirty minutes Jimmy watched in awed silence, not daring to make a sound. Each time Faith appeared on the screen, his eyes fluttered, the energy shooting through his aroused manhood, causing him to twitch. She was so perfect, so unattainable, and yet he woke up every morning with the belief that this would be the day the two would meet face to face.

When the closing credits of *Brave* began rolling across the screen, Jimmy quickly hit the REWIND button. He walked over to the VCR and removed the tape, placing it carefully in the box. His heart racing, he placed another tape marked "Faith in the Red Dress" into the player. He returned to his seat, and with the same morbid attention began watching the season premiere of *Brave*. Whenever Faith was on the screen wearing the red dress, Jimmy hit the PAUSE button and watched the scene again.

He reached into the brown bag on the floor beside the chair, pulling out a dress exactly like the one Faith was wearing. As he continued watching the television, Jimmy began rubbing the dress against his acne-scarred face. With his free hand, he reached back into the bag, pulling out a bottle of Shalimar perfume—Faith had told *People* magazine it was her favorite scent. He sprayed the perfume on the dress, inhaling it greedily. For the next hour Jimmy watched and rewatched the show. Tentatively he lowered his hand toward his dingy blue jeans. His narrow hips gyrating, Jimmy bit down on the dress and whispered, "I love you, Faith."

Once he had recovered from his climax, Jimmy turned off the player. He leaned back in the chair, closing his eyes. Maybe tomorrow would be the day he'd meet his Faith.

7

* * * * * * *

Thicker Than Blood

Angel flopped over to the other side of the bed to answer the telephone. "Hello," she said sleepily.

"Do not tell me your triflin' behind is still in bed."

"And good morning to you."

"Uh, thanks," Jill said sarcastically. "But it's afternoon."

Angel yawned as she glanced over at the clock. It was 12:15.

"How are you doing on this beautiful day the Lord has made?" Jill asked.

Angel yawned. "I'm doing just ducky."

"Girl, where'd you toss my drawers?"

Angel lifted her finger to her mouth to silence Tristan as he stepped out of the bathroom wearing only a wife-beater and a smile. "My best friend," she mouthed, pointing at the receiver.

"Oops." He put a hand up to his mouth.

"Just ducky, huh?" Jill asked. "And how is *he* doing?"

Angel let out a silent scream as she tossed a pillow at the supermodel standing at half-mast before her.

Tristan dodged the satin-covered missile, then pointed toward the spot on the bed where the pillow had rested. "You found my drawers," he whispered.

"Don't be all silent now, girl," Jill said. "Is that Kenanu boy over there?"

"It's Keenan," Angel corrected her. "And, no."

"Well, well," Jill said demurely. "How cute is this one?"

"Cute enough," Angel said, handing the underwear to Tristan.

He frowned. "Cute enough?"

"And how is he in the sack?"

"Jill!" Angel squealed, embarrassed.

"Don't be acting all prissy now." Jill chuckled. "We both know you've taken the car out for a test drive. I'm just askin' if it's worth buying."

Tristan fastened the belt holding up his baggy jeans, then leaned over to kiss Angel on the cheek. "I gotta get to the gym."

Angel placed her hand over the receiver. "Have a good pump," she said with a coy grin.

Tristan smiled. "Already did."

Angel tossed another pillow at his head. "Get outta here."

"I'll call you when I get back in town next week," Tristan said, heading down the hall.

"Who is in your house, girl?" Jill demanded.

"Tristan," Angel answered. "Remember the guy who came over to our booth at the Sunset Room?"

"Oh, right," Jill said, then hesitated. "Color me confused, but I thought we agreed that you weren't going to sleep with him."

Angel's brow wrinkled. "I don't remember agreeing to that."

"Mm-hmm," Jill said. "Wait a minute. Isn't Tristan the same model who was on the show last year?"

"Yes, I told you that when you met him the other night."

"I thought you said he was gay."

"He's bi."

"Angel!"

"What?"

"He sleeps with men," Jill said.

Angel shrugged her shoulders. "That has nothing to do with me."

"The hell it doesn't," Jill snapped. "That boy could be carrying that virus for all you know."

"I'm very careful, Mommie Dearest," Angel said, rubbing her forehead to stave off the headache she could feel forming. "Besides, these so-called straight men are just as likely to be carrying something."

"Which is exactly why you need to settle down with one man," Jill said. "What happened to Keenan? At least he knew which team he was playing on."

"That wasn't serious," Angel said. "Just good booty." She laughed, trying to break the tension.

"Listen to you," Jill said, relenting. "You should have brought your fast little tail to church with us this morning."

"Already had a bedside service," Angel said. "Tristan made me call out God's name at least twice."

"My Lord!" Jill squealed. "You horny little heathen!"

Angel laughed. "Pray for me, girl."

"Hang on a sec," Jill said. "Yes, Jasmine?" she answered her daughter. "I'm talking to her now."

"Is that my baby?" Angel asked.

"Ms. Lady wants to know what time you're coming over today," Jill said, then answered Jasmine. "She'll be here around three."

"Excuse me, but I don't think I answered yet."

"You have your sexually promiscuous little self over here by three," Jill said.

"You need to recognize that I ain't scared of you," Angel said, laughing.

"And you need something more than a side of booty on your plate if you ever want to be truly satisfied."

Angel sighed. "My plate is full to overflowing."

"I just want you to know the love of a good man," Jill said.

"Like my mother knew it?" Angel asked with sudden, sharp bitterness. "No, thank you."

"Your mother isn't dead because—"

Angel cut Jill off. "I don't wanna talk about it."

"You need to talk about—"

"No, I need to jump in the shower," Angel said. She waited a beat, using a worried tone she knew would make her friend laugh. "Otherwise, some old lady is gonna kick my butt."

"I got your old lady," Jill said. "See you at three."

                    *   *   *

"Hop, step, brush, toe, step," Angel instructed Jasmine. "Hop, step, brush . . . yes!"

Jill sat in the lawn chair grinning from ear to ear as she watched her daughter execute the tap combination. "I think we have another star in the family."

"I think so too," Angel said proudly.

"I got it!" Jasmine jumped up and down. "Thank you, Auntie Angel."

"My pleasure, sweetie," Angel said. "You're very good."

Jill applauded as she made her way toward Jasmine. "My baby is so talented."

"Momma!" Jasmine cringed, wiping the spot on her face where Jill kissed her.

Jasmine turned to Angel. "Did it look okay . . . *really*?"

"You tore it up, girl," Angel said.

Jasmine sat down on the concrete patio, pulling off her tap shoes. "I can't wait to show Ashley," she said excitedly. "She's just gonna die 'cause I learned it before she did."

Angel and Jill exchanged bemused grins as Jasmine went on talking a mile a minute.

"Ashley thinks she's the best in the class 'cause—"

"Because," Jill corrected her.

Jasmine made a face. "*Because* she took tap at summer camp last year," she continued. "Wait until she finds out that I learned the new combination." Jasmine rose to her feet. "She's gonna . . . *going* to die!"

"Maybe instead of rubbing her face in it, you can teach her the way your Aunt Angel taught you," Jill said.

Jasmine was already on her way inside the house to find the phone. "I will," she yelled back. "After I rub her face in it."

Jill shook her head. "That little girl," she said. She made her way over to the picnic table, pouring two glasses of iced tea.

Angel sat down on the lawn chair. "She's not so little anymore," she said, tightening her ponytail. "And when did she get those breasts?"

"I swear, every day she wakes up she looks more like a woman," Jill said, handing Angel the glass.

"Thanks."

"Her father almost had a sugar stroke when he picked up the phone the other day and some boy was on the other end." Jill laughed as she turned the steaks on the grill.

Angel stepped into her sandals. "Calling for Jasmine?"

"Mm-hmm," Jill said, rolling her eyes.

"Is this a boyfriend?"

"Hell no." Jill reclosed the grill. She picked up her glass of tea from the table, then went to sit with Angel. "There will be no boyfriends until she's sixteen," she said flatly.

Just then Glen Jr. raced out the patio door. "Daddy, go long!"

Jill's head spun around. "I know you two are not playing football in my house."

Angel chuckled because she knew how particular her best friend was about her home. Jill had decorated every inch of the five-bedroom Tudor with painstaking attention to detail. From the original Varnette Honeywood, Shirley Woodson and Gordon C. James paintings hanging on the walls to the oak wood kitchen table where she and her family sat for breakfast each morning, Jill had created a living environment for her family that was both practical and beautiful.

The senior Glen gave his wife an innocent smile. "We were just coming outside," he said.

Jill gave her guilty-looking husband the eye.

"You wanna play with us, Aunt Angel?" Junior asked.

"No, that's okay, baby," she said. "I'll just watch."

Junior nodded, then ran toward the opposite side of the backyard. "Throw it, Daddy!"

"Thought you were going to keep an eye on the steaks."

Glen picked up the ball, then gave Jill a quick peck on the cheek. "I can do both," he said, tossing the ball to his son.

"Liar." Jill smiled as she watched her husband throw a perfect spiral.

Angel leaned back in her seat, a look of melancholy falling across her face.

Jill reached over and took her hand. "You okay, sweetie?"

"Yeah." Angel sighed. "You have a great life."

"So do you," Jill said.

"I know," Angel said unconvincingly. "I just wonder sometimes if it really means anything . . . you know, in the grand scheme of things."

Jill turned to face her. "Do you have any idea how much I envy you?"

"You envy me?" Angel asked.

"Yes, I do," Jill said. "You are so beautiful and talented. And, despite everything that's happened in your life, you never gave up."

Angel blushed.

"And on top of all that you have the nerve not to be stuck up," Jill said with mock arrogance.

Angel laughed. "Don't hate . . ."

"Appreciate," Jill said, completing the thought. She took a sip of iced tea. "I won't lie, I love my life," she said, glancing over as her husband mock-tackled her son to the grass. "But to be able to move people the way you do," Jill said, "that's truly something special."

Angel shrugged. "It's not all—"

"Don't you dare," Jill said, cutting her off. "What you have, my dear, is truly a gift," she said, looking Angel squarely in the eye. "And I know how hard you've worked, and how much you've sacrificed to perfect your craft."

Angel gave her an air kiss. "Love you," she said playfully.

"I love you too," Jill said, then sniffed. "Oh, shoot, I'm burning the steaks!" She raced over to the smoking grill. "Glen!"

"Sorry, baby," he said, rushing over to help her.

Jasmine walked out onto the patio. "Well, my Aunt Angel said I did it flawlessly," she said, the phone glued to her ear. "She's right here . . . ."

"Get off that phone and help me," Jill instructed her chatty daughter.

Jasmine smacked her lips.

Angel rose from her seat. "I can help," she said, winking at Jasmine. "Thank you, Auntie."

"I still want you off that phone in one minute, young lady."

"Yes, Mother," Jasmine said, frowning. "I do not like Malik," she said into the phone.

"Baby, will you get the potato salad out of the 'fridge for Mommie?" Jill asked Junior as she set the plastic plates around the table.

He bolted toward the door. "Yes, ma'am."

"No running!" Jill yelled after him, then turned Jasmine. "Say good-bye now or I will for you."

"Ashley, I gotta go," Jasmine said in her standard bored monotone.

Glen put the steaks on the table, then eyed his pouting daughter. "Young lady, didn't your mother tell you to get off that phone?"

"Sorry, Daddy," Jasmine said. "Girl, I gotta go."

Angel grinned as she removed the foil from the potato salad. Her goddaughter was indeed a daddy's girl.

"Auntie Angel, are you going to stay and watch your show with us tonight?" Jasmine hollered, still holding the phone to her ear.

Angel continued making Junior's plate. "Yep."

Jasmine looked over at Jill. "Momma, can Ashley come over and watch *Brave* with us tonight?"

"Not if you aren't off that phone in exactly three seconds," Jill said, then began to count.

"You can come . . . bye." Jasmine hung up, then grinned at Jill. "With a second to spare."

Once the entire family had gathered around the table, Glen led them in prayer. "Lord, thank you for this meal, and for the beautiful hands that so lovingly prepared it for our consumption," he said, his eyes meeting Jill's. "Father God, we ask that you continue to keep a watchful eye over this family . . ."

As Glen continued, Angel glanced up at the blue August sky, whispering a silent thank-you to the heavens. She may not be connected to these four people by blood, but they were very much her family, and for that she was grateful.

8

Muse

"Did you get this from the flea market in Compton?" Toya asked, pointing at one of the African masks hanging from the wall.

Lucien glanced over the railing. *A flea market?* "I bought it in Ghana," he said.

"Africa?"

"Uh-huh."

"Wow," Toya said, impressed.

Lucien shook his head as he continued printing out the pages of the screenplay.

Toya continued nosing around the two-thousand-square-foot, bilevel loft. She fingered through the CD collection that featured the likes of Miles Davis, Sarah Vaughn, Jill Scott and Eric Benet. "No rap music?"

"Not that big a fan."

"You look a little like Eric Benet," Toya said, holding up the singer's CD. "Before Halle made him cut off his dreads."

Lucien said nothing as he placed the pages into a three-ring binder. The sooner they got to work the better.

"Man, your place is nothing like I expected it to be," Toya said, making her way around Lucien's downtown L.A. home.

"How's that?" he asked.

"I just figured you were a little more . . . you know," she said with a nervous chuckle.

Lucien exited the space that served as his home office. "No, I don't know."

Toya gave him a weak smile as he appeared at the railing. "Hard," she said.

He gave her a curious grin. "Hard?"

"You dress like a thugged-out homeboy," Toya said, eyeing him in his oversized jeans and Sean John T-shirt. "But you talk like a white boy," she said. "And this place looks like it belongs to some middle-class—"

"Just goes to show that you shouldn't judge a book by its cover," Lucien said. He'd resisted the urge to do the same with Toya when he met her for the first time at the gym. Unfortunately, she opened her mouth and proved his initial assessment of her correct.

"It's all good, though," Toya said, ascending the spiral staircase.

Lucien raised his hand to stop her. "I'll come to you." He had invited her over for one reason and one reason only: to have his words brought to life by an actress.

"We can have more fun up there," she said salaciously.

Lucien handed Toya the script as he passed her on his way down the stairs.

Stopping cold in her tracks, she watched him continue into the living room area, taking a seat on the black leather sofa. "*Oookaay.*"

Lucien could tell from the sour look on Toya's face that she'd come there today with other ideas in mind. That was her problem, because he had been very clear when he'd invited her that this was to be a work session.

Toya stood in front of the sofa, holding the pages of the screenplay like they were a hundred-pound weight.

"Let's take it from the top of Giselle's monologue," Lucien said, ignoring her attitude. "Page seventy."

Reluctantly, Toya thumbed open the binder, making a big show of reading the page, as if she was letting it infuse her soul. She cleared her throat, then began: "We owe it to these children to fight for them. How can you sit there and allow this to happen? . . ."

Lucien bit down on his lower lip. Toya was reading so fast, none of the words had any emphasis.

Toya glanced up at him, then stopped reading. She shifted her weight, her hand rising to meet her hip. "Is something wrong?" she asked in a tone daring him to tell her that her reading was anything less than perfection.

"You're rushing through it a little," Lucien said. The pissed expression on Toya's face didn't change. He took a breath, trying to go easy. "What I mean is that this is a pivotal scene in the movie," Lucien said, softening his tone. "Giselle is steadfast in her belief that exposure to the arts—music, dance—has a positive impact on the lives of the students at the inner-city school where she works," he explained. "The school board is about to cut the music program, and Giselle is fighting to save it."

Toya nodded as if what he was saying was actually registering.

"She's got to make these people see that by cutting the arts programs, they are risking . . ." Lucien said, then hesitated. He eyed her carefully. "Toya, are you chewing gum?"

"Helps me concentrate," she said, smacking away.

Lucien sighed. *Not worth the fight,* he thought. He pushed the dreads from his face. "Giselle is a passionate woman," he explained patiently. "I need you to communicate her love for these kids."

"Got it."

"This monologue has to communicate—"

Toya cut him off. "I said, I got it."

"Okay," Lucien said, backing off. "Let's try it again from the top."

Toya looked down at the script.

"Take your time . . ." Lucien said

Toya shot him a glare.

"Sorry."

Toya twisted from side to side as if summoning up the talent hiding deep inside her. "We owe it to these children to fight for them."

Lucien frowned as she began racing through the monologue once again.

"There are myr . . . mirror . . ."

"Myriad," Lucien supplied.

Toya looked at him as if he were speaking in tongues.

"Numerous . . . countless . . . many," Lucien said, no longer able to mask his annoyance. "Pick one."

Toya sucked on her teeth to make it clear that she didn't appreciate his tone. "There are . . . *a lot* of reasons not to take this gift away from these students."

Lucien's temples started to pound as she continued reading. Clearly, things like periods and commas meant nothing to Toya.

"I implore you not to turn your collective backs . . ." Toya said, then stopped. She looked at Lucien. "Is this girl black?"

"Yes, Giselle is African-American."

Toya gave a little flick of her hair. "She talks awfully proper to be a sista."

"Giselle is an educator," he said carefully.

"That doesn't mean she has to speak so sadity."

On a good day, Lucien was a shoot-from-the-hip kind of guy. "The fact that Giselle has a firm grasp of the King's English doesn't make her sadity."

Toya rolled her eyes. "Well, it just don't sound real to me," she said. "She sounds like a stuck-up bougie." She smirked. "Just like your girl Angel."

"Angel's not my . . ." Lucien said, then caught himself. He rose from the sofa. He'd dedicated the last eight months of his life to this screenplay. "You know what? I don't think this was such a good idea."

Toya cocked her head arrogantly. "I'm just offering you some input," she said. "That's the kind of actress I am."

Lucien chuckled as he placed the binder on the coffee table. "Thanks," he said.

"Are you mad at me?"

"Nope," Lucien said, taking a seat on the sofa.

Toya sat down beside him. "I'm willing to help you work out the kinks in your script."

"Oh, no," Lucien said, trying not to laugh. "You've helped quite enough."

Toya eased closer to him. "I know something else I could help you with," she said, her hands easing toward his crotch.

Lucien jumped to his feet. The last thing he was doing was getting more involved with this woman than he already was. "Do you want a glass of wine?" he asked as he made his way toward the kitchen.

Toya eased her bare feet up onto the sofa. "You got any beer?"

Lucien sighed as he eyed the bottle of merlot in the rack, then retrieved a Heineken from the refrigerator.

"Thanks." Toya smiled as he handed her the bottle.

Lucien took a seat on the opposite end of the sofa. He glanced down at his watch, then picked up the remote from the steel-gray steamer trunk that served as his coffee table.

"Ugh," Toya said as the main titles for *Brave New World* appeared on the screen. "We not about to watch this, are we?"

"I write for this show," Lucien said, looking directly at the screen. Though he didn't make it a practice to watch *Brave*, he would gladly make an exception tonight, if for no other reason than to get a thirty-minute reprieve from Toya's grating voice.

As the show went on, he found himself fixating on Angel. Toya's opinion notwithstanding, he could see why everyone, including the male model jocking her at the Sunset Room, was so drawn to her. She had that special something that made her stand out. Since the night he'd watched her dance, Lucien had been finding it difficult to get her out of his head.

While he was engrossed with the show, Toya rose from the sofa. "I need to get going," she said in a huff.

"Thanks for coming," Lucien said, not bothering to turn from the TV screen.

Toya stepped into her silver mules, then marched toward the door. "Bye." When he didn't bother looking over, she sighed loudly and left.

When the final credits rolled across the screen ten minutes later, Lucien hit the remote. With his beer in hand he headed upstairs to his office. Sitting at the computer, he pulled up the file titled "Mad." As he typed feverishly, he thought about Toya's comments. Though her opinion meant donkey squat to him, she had made one good point—though she meant it to be an insult—regarding the actress best suited for the role.

Lucien smiled as he continued typing. "Angel *is* Giselle."

9

* * * * * * * *

If I Were You

Victoria Steinberg had always dreamed of becoming a famous actress. Not two weeks after graduating high school the young starlet-in-waiting bought a one-way ticket to New York, intent on landing a part in a Broadway show. Never one for naïveté, Victoria understood that she'd have to pay her dues; settle for a few chorus parts before securing the once-in-a-lifetime role that would propel her career into the stratosphere. She was prepared to bide her time—two years, tops—until some powerful producer took notice of her talent, and/or the female lead she was understudying *accidentally* broke her leg. Either way, Victoria was going to be a star.

Five years and a slew of less than noteworthy roles later, she found herself growing more and more unsure of not only her talent, but of the probability that her dreams of fame would ever be realized. Victoria's fading hope was renewed when she met Erik Williams. The young playwright had written a new piece that everyone in the know was heralding as the next big black thing to hit the Great White Way. When she learned that the producers were looking to cast the female lead with an unknown actress, Victoria called upon the one asset that she could always count on to get her what she wanted—her looks. With the power that her firm breasts, "good" hair, and fair-complected skin wielded over the weaker sex, Victoria knew that if she could get the man, she had the job.

By insinuating herself into an actors workshop led by none other than Erik Williams, Victoria was halfway to achieving her goal. When the actress scheduled to perform a scene from *Purlie Victorious* was a mysterious no-show, Victoria—who just happened to have the scene memorized—closed the deal. Selflessly, she stepped in and performed the part. The very handsome and very married Williams took notice of the confident twenty-two-year-old's ample *talents*. In the end Victoria got the job . . . and the man.

A year later, *How High the Moon* had closed not six days after it opened, and Victoria was reeling from piss-poor reviews and an unwanted pregnancy. Accepting that her own dreams were dead, she pledged herself to ensuring that her only child would someday achieve the fame that had eluded her.

Victoria begged, brokered, and bulldozed in order to get young Erika the training and support typically reserved for the children of the rich and famous: headshots taken by the best photographers, instruction from the most sought-after ballet instructors and attendance at the most prestigious acting workshops.

Even her marriage was the result of a steadfast commitment to her daughter's success. Fearful that another girl was about to beat out Erika for the part on *Momma Knows*, Victoria once again utilized the "get the man, get the job" approach. Six months after *Momma Knows* premiered, Victoria and Chuck Steinberg, the show's executive producer, were wed. She didn't love the Jewish man, thirteen years her senior, but she did love her child. Erika would become what Victoria had so desperately wanted to be—a star.

Erika rushed over to the table at they restaurant where they often met. "Sorry I'm late."

Victoria gave her a quick air kiss.

"I'm famished," Erika said, taking her seat.

Victoria gave her daughter a visual once-over. "Are you wearing your hair like that on purpose?"

Erika sighed. "Mother, please."

"What?" Victoria asked innocently.

"Do you think you could give me a minute to catch my breath before you start ripping me apart?"

"I don't know what you're talking about," Victoria said, pulling her Palm from her purse. "If I had a piece of spinach hanging from my teeth, wouldn't you tell me?"

Erika didn't bother to respond.

"I'll call José and make an appointment for you," Victoria said, tapping the electronic appointment keeper with the stylus. "You can't be on the cover of *Black Hair Magazine* looking like that, for goodness sake. The shoot's on Friday, by the way."

"I thought we decided against doing that," Erika said, surprised.

"That was before *Goldilocks* started showing up on the cover of every damned magazine in America," Victoria said, dropping the Palm back into her purse.

The waiter approached the table. "Good evening, ladies."

Victoria brightened at the sight of the hunk. "Well, *hellooo*."

Erika cringed.

"Are you ladies ready to order?" the blushing waiter asked.

Victoria winked at him. "What I'm interested in isn't on the menu."

"Mother . . . please."

"Fine," Victoria said demurely. "I'll pick something from the menu." She gave him a smile. "Let me have a small broiled-chicken salad . . . and another gin and tonic."

The waiter turned to Erika. "And you, ma'am?"

"She'll have a small broiled-chicken salad as well," Victoria said, eyeing her client. "You can afford to drop a few."

Erika looked up at the waiter. "And a big glass of vodka . . . straight."

He gave her a nod of sympathy. "I'll be right back with your drinks."

Victoria stared at his backside as he walked away. "I've still got it," she said. Turning to Erika, she added, "You, on the other hand, are in danger of being upstaged by the white girl."

"I'm not worried about Faith," Erika said dismissively.

"Well, you should be," Victoria said. "Do you know she had two and a half more minutes of screen time than you on last night's show?"

Erika shifted uncomfortably. "I'm sure it just seemed like it, Mother."

"No it didn't just *seem* like it," Victoria said. "I counted." In the twisted world of entertainment, two minutes amounted to an eternity. "You can't let that girl come into your house and just take over like that."

"She's not taking over."

Victoria leaned back in her chair, crossing her arms over her chest. "So that was you *People* magazine chose as one of its fifty most beautiful," she said with a taunting smirk. "And you on the cover of this week's *Celebrity Weekly*."

Erika slumped like a five-year-old being scolded.

"It's bad enough Angel got an Emmy nomination for your damned show," Victoria said with disgust. Her face softened as the waiter approached. "Thank you, darling." She smiled at him as he hastily retreated. "But at least she's in the *family* . . . and she lost."

Erika listened helplessly. These belittling scenes with her mother happened frequently.

"But this Faith girl," Victoria said, stabbing her fork into the salad. "Now, she's a pain in the ass of a whole different color. If you're not careful, they'll be renaming that show *Faith and Those Two Black Girls* before you know it."

"I'm doing the best I can, Mother," Erika said tightly.

"Do better," Victoria said. "I mean, look at you." She motioned toward the T-shirt and ripped jeans Erika was wearing. "You're dressed like a bum."

"I'm coming from rehearsal," Erika defended. "Did you expect me to be wearing a formal gown?"

"Don't get flippant with me, young lady," Victoria snapped. "You have a responsibility to your public to always look your best. If I were you—"

"But you're *not* me, Mother," Erika said, cutting her off. "This isn't your career. It's mine."

Victoria lowered her glass to the table. "You're absolutely right," she said, glaring at Erika. "This is *your* career. I'm just the person who sacrificed everything so you could have it."

Erika swallowed. "Mama, I do appreciate everything you've done for me."

Two women approached the table, smiling nervously. "I'm sorry to bother you," one of them said. "Are you Erika Bishop?"

"Yes," Erika said, though not friendly enough for Victoria's taste.

The woman turned to her friend. "I told you it was her!" she said excitedly, then turned to Erika. "I'm such a big fan of yours."

Victoria watched the exchange, brimming with pride. Moments like these made all her hard work on her ungrateful daughter's behalf worthwhile.

"I watch the reruns of *Momma Knows* on BET, and I never miss *Brave New World*."

Erika offered her a tight smile.

The woman shoved a pen and paper in her face. "Could I have your autograph . . . *please?*"

"Of course she'll give you her autograph," Victoria said for her daughter. "Anything for a fan."

✳   ✳   ✳

Erika walked into her kitchen, tossing the carry-out bag on the table. The moment Victoria had dismissed her, she had her driver take her straight over to Roscoe's so she could get some real food.

"Maria, you still here?" Erika poked her head into the hall. "Maria?" The last thing she needed was for her housekeeper to report back to Victoria that she'd caught her stuffing her face. Erika had fired her two previous two employees for similar violations. Unfortunately, when given the choice of who they least wanted to cross, most people chose Victoria.

Once Erika was certain she was alone, she walked back over to the table and removed the food from the bag. As she sat there inhaling the waffles and chicken, the sheer preposterousness of what she was doing struck her. Here she was, a thirty-two-year-old woman sneaking a meal in her own house.

Holding a piece of fried chicken, Erika stood up from the table. She walked over to the stainless steel refrigerator—the one Victoria had insisted she purchase. She reached around the grapefruit and orange juices retrieving a bottle of coke. Erika took another bite of the chicken as she raised the bottle to her lips.

"Excuse me," she said aloud as a burp escaped her lips. Erika glanced around the room, sighing gratefully. She was in fact alone.

As she sat back down at the table, she replayed the conversation she'd had with her mother earlier. It had taken everything she had not to react as Victoria rubbed Faith's annoying successes in her face. Though she had every right to, Erika hadn't dared remind her mother that as her manager it was her job—one for which she was paid a small fortune—to get her some of the photo shoots, interviews and magazine covers Faith was getting by the truckload. Doing so would have implied that Victoria was less than perfect, which of course was totally unacceptable—to Victoria.

A devious grin spread across Erika's face as she finished off the last of the three waffles. Victoria would have had a coronary if she saw her daughter stuffing her face like this. Doing things behind her mother's back brought Erika strange comfort. That desire for furtive rebellion was what had motivated her to pursue Randall. Knowing Victoria would hit the roof if she ever found out her daughter was sleeping with a married man made it all the more attractive. When she did find out about the affair, however, Victoria didn't pop a blood vessel as Erika had expected; instead she congratulated her daughter for making a smart career move. "Nothing says job security like banging the man who signs your checks," were her loving mother's words.

Feeling bloated and thoroughly unattractive, Erika lifted herself from the chair. She carried the white bag containing the remnants of her secret meal over to the trash. After glancing back over her shoulder to make sure she was still alone, Erika opened the can. She lifted the top layer of trash with one hand as she pushed the white bag deep into the can with the other. Carefully she replaced the top layer of garbage, then resealed the lid. Erika sighed in relief.

Making her way upstairs to her bedroom, Erika walked into the master bath and headed directly for the black marble toilet. She lowered herself to the floor, then stuck her finger down her throat. Once she'd finished purging, she stood slowly to her feet. When she spied her reflection in the full-length mirror attached to the door of the walk-in closet, Erika shook her head in disappointment.

Removing her clothing, she methodically inspected her body. Maybe her four visits to the gym each week should be increased to five. Her stomach and thighs had always been problem areas in need of dedicated attention—a combination of thirty minutes on the

StairMaster and three hundred crunches daily—but now both seemed determined to increase no matter how hard she worked to stop them.

Erika took a final critical look at herself, then walked back over to the toilet. She stuck her finger down her throat again.

10

* * * * * * * *

He Is

The only child of media tycoon Jasper Wellington, Savanna Wellington-Hunter was a privileged, reserved woman with a deep affinity for protocol and tradition. Though considered handsome by most who knew her, she was acutely aware of the fact that she was no natural beauty. She had, however, learned to take full advantage of the vast array of enhancement tools her family's money afforded her. By way of liposuction, a little nipping here, some tucking there, along with thrice-weekly visits from her personal trainer, Savanna had made the most of her limited attributes. Unburdened with a nine-to-five job, she used her limitless free time fashioning herself into a rather accomplished runner. In a few weeks she would start training in preparation for her fifth appearance in Los Angeles' annual marathon.

"Where is your husband?" the old man growled.

"That'll be all, Carlotta," Savanna said, waving the maid away from the patio. She looked across the table at her father, smiling pleasantly. "He's working late at the office."

Jasper eyed his daughter severely. "I just left the office," he said. "Randall is not there."

Savanna hid her response by taking a bite of her salad. "I'm sure you just missed each other."

"Missed each other, my ass," Jasper snarled. "Vanna, you need to get your husband in line."

"Daddy—"

"Silence!" Jasper yelled.

Savanna drew back in her seat. She hated confrontations with her intimidating father.

Jasper composed himself. "Vanna, I turn a blind eye while your husband fucks his way through greater Los Angeles County," he said, not touching the Texas-sized steak Savanna had had the cook prepare especially for him. "But I will not tolerate tackiness," he said through clenched teeth. "People are starting to talk."

Savanna sat stone-faced as her pulse pounded like a drum in her throat.

"Your husband's increasingly public infidelities are becoming an embarrassment to this family," Jasper said. "The whole incident with the black girl was simply distasteful."

Savanna leaned forward. "Erika?"

"Khandi Long," Jasper said. "I had to pay that girl almost a million dollars to keep her from going public about her tawdry affair with your husband," he said, disgusted. "Do you have any idea how much damage that would have caused to the Wellington reputation?"

Savanna twisted the heavy cloth napkin resting in her lap. It came as no surprise to her that many within her circle considered her marriage to Randall Hunter as little more than a business arrangement— Daddy's gift to his only child. She didn't care. Randall was everything she had ever wanted in a man: charming, good-looking, a bit dangerous. She would continue to ignore the affairs, endure the lukewarm indifference, and withstand the alienation of affection, so long as Randall never left her.

"I'm not perfect myself," Jasper said. "But I have enough respect for your mother not to let my private *business matters* become public." He took another sip of his drink. "Now, whatever agreement the two of you have is your business, but I expect it to remain private."

Savanna nodded. "I'll handle it, Daddy."

"See that you do."

✳   ✳   ✳

Randall opened the door attired in black raw-silk pajamas. When she saw his handsome face, Faith smiled. She kissed him softly on the cheek, then stepped inside the apartment.

"Make yourself at home," Randall said, walking over to the wet bar. "Brandy?

"Yes, thank you." Thanks to Erika, she'd experienced one of those days best forgotten as soon as it ended. The only thing that had made it bearable was knowing that tonight she would be having her second date with Randall.

"So how was your day?" Randall asked as he handed Faith a glass. He sat down beside her.

She took a sip of the brandy and sighed. "I thought this was quite possibly going to be the worst one ever," Faith said. "But things turned out pretty okay . . . thanks to Angel."

"What happened?"

"Erika had been riding me all day," Faith said, slipping out of her copper-colored slingbacks. "But Angel has been nicer." She smiled. "I really think we're going to get along."

"I've always liked Angel," Randall said as he lifted Faith's feet from the floor and placed them in his lap. "I'll have a talk with Erika."

"No, don't do that," Faith said. "That'll only make matters worse."

"You don't have to put up with her shit, you know," Randall said. "You're hotter than she is right now. I could probably break her contract after the season ends and nobody would even notice," he said, warming to the idea as he spoke it. "Build the show around you and Angel."

Faith lowered her glass onto the coffee table, then crawled into Randall's arms. "I appreciate how you've been looking out for me, but women like Erika are everywhere in this industry," she said. "I've learned how to coexist with them."

"As long as I'm around, you don't have to learn how to coexist with anybody."

Faith tilted her head up to kiss him. "Thank you."

Randall was pleased by her forwardness. "I've got just the thing to get your mind off your troubles," he said, rising to his feet.

"Really?" Faith asked, wondering if he was referring to cocaine. A part of her hoped he was.

Randall helped her up from the sofa. "A few somethings, actually."

Faith worked to keep cool as he led her down the hallway. She sensed that this was it. This was the night Randall was going to make his move.

Faith gasped as she stepped into a candlelit bedroom. Her gaze wandered from the rose petals forming a trail to the garment bag and boxes lying atop the king-size bed on the opposite side of the room over to the bottle of Dom chilling in a bucket, finally coming to rest on the white powder shaped into four neat lines atop a square mirror.

Floating toward her bounty, Faith reveled in the experience of being treated like a princess. "You're going to totally spoil me."

"Open the garment bag first," Randall instructed as he poured two glasses of champagne.

Faith removed a full-length jet black mink coat. "Oh my goodness!" she squealed. "This is simply too much."

Randall placed the two glasses onto the coffee table, then sat down on the loveseat. "No, it's not."

Faith gave him an incredulous look. "Why?"

"Why what?"

"You could have almost any woman you want," Faith said, studying him intently. "Why me?"

"Because you're special," Randall said simply.

Faith shivered as a chill shot up her spine. No man had ever told her she was special before. Could he possibly mean it?

"Come here."

Faith lowered the fur onto the bed, then slinked over to Randall, her every step oozing with sexuality.

He leaned back on the loveseat as she approached. "Damn."

Faith kissed him softly on the lips. "Thank you, Mr. Hunter."

Randall smiled. "You're welcome, Ms. Molaney."

Easing herself between his spread legs, Faith pressed against his chest. She could feel his heart racing. Was he nervous? She exhaled as another shock wave rippled through her body.

Randall kissed her neck, his awakened manhood straining against his pajamas as he did.

Faith stroked his flushed face, then lowered her head toward the powder. Coughing as she resurfaced, she flung her hair back. "Mmm," she moaned, brushing the white residue from her nose. "That's nice."

"Only the best, baby," Randall said. He dipped his pinkie into the remaining powder, rubbing the cocaine-coated finger across his top gum.

"Go try on the rest of your gifts," he said.

Faith smiled as she made her way back over to the bed. She was more than happy to let him run the show. The one thing she had learned about men was that even when they weren't in charge—which was most of the time—the smart woman let them think they were.

"Open the larger one first," Randall instructed.

A devilish grin spread across Faith's face as she removed the red lace panties and garter. "Aren't you the dirty boy?"

Randall stroked his hardness as he watched her change into the lingerie.

Faith turned to him. "What now, Daddy?"

"Put the fur back on, then open up the other box."

Faith did as told. After stepping into the three-inch red stiletto pumps, she started to make her way back over to him.

"Stay there," the deep baritone voice demanded. "Dance for me . . . slow and easy."

Randall's breathing intensified as she followed his instructions. "Touch yourself while you move."

"You like that," Faith asked, her finger disappearing inside the panties.

Randall leaned forward. "Oh, yeah," he croaked, manipulating his johnson to its full eight inches.

Faith closed her eyes as she massaged her aroused nipples, losing herself in the enjoyment of self-exploration. When she felt his strong hands spreading her legs apart, she reopened her eyes. With a raised brow she spied Randall's bobbing head as he gnawed on her crown jewels like a hungry beaver. After enduring the abuse for a few seconds, Faith grabbed his head.

Randall looked up at her. "What's wrong?"

Not wanting to tell him that he was giving her about as much pleasure as a Pap smear, Faith used visual aids instead. She stuck her upwardly pointed tongue out, moving it in a circular motion. "Do it like that for me . . . *Daddy*."

The devilish grin on Randall's face made it clear that she had used the right approach.

Faith licked her lips as he resumed. "Oh, yes, Daddy," she said, impressed. "Slow . . . mm-hmm . . . that's it," she groaned. "To the . . . ooh, right there, Daddy."

Finding his way back to her clitoris, Randall suckled it gently like the tip of a sweet Hershey's Kiss. Faith pressed her pulsating midsection into his face, her knees threatening to buckle beneath her as an orgasm powered its way through her body.

"Oh, yes . . . yes . . . *yes!*" she squealed in ecstasy.

Randall lifted her into his arms and carried her over to the bed. "You are so fucking beautiful," he whispered in her ear.

Faith blinked quickly, the heat of his breath threatening to send her over the edge again. She took slow, steadying breaths as she watched Randall struggle to get out of his pajama bottoms. When he'd finally freed himself, Faith gasped.

"I'll be gentle," Randall assured her.

Faith edged back on the bed. "I've never been with a man as big—"

"Shhh." Randall placed his finger to her lips. "I won't hurt you," he assured, carefully mounting her.

Faith pressed her hand against his chest, her eyes locked on his. "Promise?"

Randall nodded. "I promise."

Gripping the sheets with her hands, Faith braced herself to receive his rock-hard manhood.

Sensing her trepidation, Randall pulled back. "You gotta relax, baby," he said gently.

Faith nodded her head. "Okay." She closed her eyes as he reentered her, this time allowing her body to freely accept him. As initial discomfort quickly gave over to intense pleasure, she placed her hands on his firm backside, prodding him farther inside.

Randall's thrusts, at first slow and easy, increased in speed and intensity. "You're blowing my mind, baby."

"Deeper . . . yes . . . oh yes," Faith said, moaning.

Balancing his weight with one hand, Randall grabbed Faith by the hair with the other. "I'm gonna . . . Faith, I'm—"

"Yes!" she squealed. "Me . . . me too!"

Randall's face contorted, his entire body seizing wildly. "Oh, Faith!"

*   *   *

Faith studied Randall as he slept beside her. Tentatively, she extended her hand toward him, tracing the outline of his chiseled face with her fingers. He was a beautiful man. Everything about him—his muscular chest with just a dusting of hair, the small scar on his right thigh, his pedicured size-ten feet—was perfect in her eyes.

Faith's thoughts turned to Savanna. Was she aware how wonderful her husband was? Did she too lie awake at night, entranced by every inch of this magnificent being? Did Randall's touch make Savanna shudder with ecstasy as well?

The brutal reality of her situation swept over Faith like a gust of cold air. The man who had just brought her to pleasure the likes of which she'd never known before was, in fact, married. He belonged to someone else. Another woman laid claim to his touch, his smell, his smile. And no matter how much she tried to make herself believe that it didn't matter, Faith knew that it did.

"Hey, you," Randall said, waking.

"Hey."

Randall's sleepy eyes filled with concern as he raised himself against the headboard. "What's wrong?"

Faith wiped away the tears from her cheek. "Allergies," she said, sniffing.

"Do you want me to go out and pick up something?" Randall asked, though it was obvious from the look on his face that he wasn't buying her excuse for the waterworks.

"No, I'll be okay."

Randall cupped Faith's chin, looking tenderly into her tearstained eyes. "Tell me what I can do to make it better."

"Hold me?"

Randall lowered himself back onto the bed, pulling her into his embrace. "For as long as you want me to."

Faith exhaled softly. Tonight she wouldn't worry about being another notch on his belt. She just wanted this man to hold her.

* * * * * * * *

11

Dirty Rotten Liar

Erika stuffed another Cheez Doodle into her mouth as she read the current issue of *Celebrity Weekly*. "Give me a waffle-thin break," she muttered, loudly enough to be overheard by the others in the makeup suite.

Angel ignored the verbal outburst, continuing her conversation with Ernesto. "How was Rage last night?"

"Chica, let me tell you," Ernesto said as he continued dressing Angel's face, "those queens were being *sooo* nasty."

Angel frowned. "That's too bad."

"Oh, no, Chica," Ernesto said, shaking his head. "Nasty in a good way."

"Yummy," Angel said with a devilish grin. "Do tell all, darling."

While Ernesto covered the highlights of his evening at one of the hottest gay clubs in West Hollywood—WeHo to the locals—Erika flipped loudly to the next page of the magazine story. "This heffa is good at pouring it on," she said. "I'll give her that much."

Angel cut her eyes at Erika but didn't take the bait. "So, how did Jackson like it?"

"He like it okay," Ernesto said. "Papi Chulo was looking so sexy in he little overalls," he said proudly. "He so big . . . *everywhere.*"

"I take it things between you and Mr. Policeman are progressing nicely?" Angel asked.

Ernesto grinned. "I think he the one, Mommie."

"If memory serves me correctly, you also thought Dean was the one . . . and Orlando . . . Zack and—"

"No, *lissen*," Ernesto said, waving his hand. "I know I said it before, but this time is different. Last night we finally got . . . you know . . . sexual."

Angel's lips curled into a devilish grin. "All right, now."

"We were doing it and everything was good, yes?"

Angel eased forward in the chair, hanging on his every word.

"Then all of a sudden, he flip me on my stomach and, well . . ."

"Well?" Angel asked eagerly.

Ernesto blushed. "He took me to heaven with his—"

"That lying skank!" Erika bolted up from her chair almost sending the woman working on her hair into cardiac arrest. "Okay, that's it!"

"Girl, what is wrong with you?" Angel said, clutching her chest.

Erika threw the magazine onto the makeup table. "I can't believe that *bitch* has the nerve to be lying like this!"

"Who?" Ernesto asked.

"Faith!" Erika said, burning with anger. She turned to Angel. "Do you wanna know what she told them?"

"Not particularly."

"She told them she was a damned orphan!" Erika snatched up the magazine, pointing at the cover photo of Faith. "America's newest sweetheart here claims that both her mommy and her daddy are dead," she snorted. "That heffa's parents are about as dead as I am."

From what Angel knew of Faith, she couldn't imagine her lying about something like that. "How did they die?"

"Her parents are not dead, Angel," Erika said, pissed. "Both of their TPT asses are probably sitting in matching lawn chairs somewhere guzzling down forty-ouncers as we speak."

"What is a TPT?" Ernesto asked curiously.

"Trailer park trash," Erika answered. "And believe me, the hick don't fall too far from the hick tree either."

"Erika, no matter what you may think of Faith, you really should cut her some slack on this," Angel advised. "I doubt that she'd lie about such a thing."

"She would if it meant getting more press than you and me," Erika said, growing defensive. "How much you wanna bet that girl—"

"Hi, everybody," Faith said brightly as she strolled into the makeup suite.

Erika spun around, her lips twisting. "Well, speak of the devil."

Faith ignored the jibe from her costar. "Sorry I'm late, Ernesto," she said, sitting down in the chair next to Angel.

Ernesto smiled. "No problem, Mommie."

Faith turned to Angel. "Would you mind running lines with me when we're done here?" she asked. One of the makeup artists tied her hair back and began applying foundation to her forehead.

"Sure," Angel said, giving Erika a dirty look. "I'm having trouble memorizing this week too."

"I usually get them down at least a day before taping," Faith said with a weary sigh. "But things have been so hectic this week."

"Memorizing all those *lies* can be tricky," Erika said.

Faith stiffened. "What do you mean?"

Erika picked up the magazine. "So, the parents are in the big trailer park in the sky, huh?"

"Erika . . . don't start," Angel warned her.

Faith recognized the magazine and what she'd said in it. "If you mean, are my parents deceased . . . the answer is yes."

Ernesto and Angel tensed, but remained silent, hoping Erika would realize she was going too far.

"You poor thing," Erika said, reeking of mock sincerity. "How did it happen?"

"It's in the article," Faith said tightly.

Erika shook her head agreeably, but didn't let it go. "Did they drive off a cliff . . . go into the ocean?" she asked. "Hit a tree? Get crushed under a beer truck?"

Faith tightened her grip on the handles of the chair. "I really don't want to talk about it," she said weakly. "It's all too painful to revisit."

"I'm sure it must be, but—"

"Leave it alone," Angel said.

"It all sounds so movie of the week," Erika pressed. "Maybe you should work up a screenplay and ship it to Warner Brothers."

Faith drew a breath through clenched teeth, the look in her eyes a combination of anger and gut-wrenching sadness.

"I mean, it's all so convenient—"

"Convenient!"

Angel recoiled as Faith's shout echoed off the walls around them.

"Ay-yi-yi," Ernesto said, lowering his head.

"I assure you, Erika, my mother being dead is anything but convenient."

Erika tried to appear unimpressed by Faith's newly found backbone, but she drew back. "*Look*—"

"No, *you* look!" Faith cried. "How dare you speak badly of my mother . . . and father—"

"I'm just saying—"

"I'm not finished!" Faith barked.

Angel's eyes widened. Sitting between the two women, she leaned forward ever so slightly in her chair, ready to intercede should either one reach for the neck of the other.

"I overlook the eye rolls and the 'accidental' kicks to the chin," Faith said, her cheeks red, her eyes blazing. "I play stupid when scripts mysteriously disappear from my dressing room. I even ignore the racist insults spat at my back when you think I'm just out of earshot, but I will not tolerate you sullying my mother's memory."

Angel swallowed as Faith stood up and moved toward Erika.

"Don't ever speak of my mother again," Faith said, standing directly in front of Erika's chair.

Erika cowered, not saying a word.

Faith marched toward the door. "I'll come back later," she said in a cracking voice.

Ernesto nodded reassuringly. " 'That's just fine, hon."

When Faith was gone, Angel glared over at a slack-jawed Erika. "You just don't know when to quit, do you?"

Erika looked surprised. "Guess Barbie has a little backbone after all."

✳   ✳   ✳

Angel knocked on the door and waited.

"Who's there?"

"It's me, Angel."

There was a pronounced pause. "Come in."

As she stepped inside the pink-accented dressing room, it dawned on Angel that she hadn't visited there since it belonged to Khandi. Over the past eight weeks she had spent on average twelve hours a day, five days a week with Faith and hadn't once stepped inside her private space. What few conversations the two had shared were microscopic in length and almost always centered on script changes or rehearsal notes.

Angel glanced at the four teddy bears propped on the sofa, then over at the knitting supplies piled in one of the chairs. She studied the photos hanging from the walls and set atop the makeup table, each capturing what Angel could only assume were important moments in Faith's life. She had absolutely no clue who this woman really was, or what she had to do to get here.

"Would you like to have a seat?" Faith asked, wiping her swollen eyes with a tissue.

"I don't want to intrude."

Faith appealed to her with a pitiful smile. "I could really use some company right now."

Angel nodded, then took a seat in the empty chair. "Listen, I am so sorry about what happened in there," she said. "Erika had no right to do that."

Faith flinched but remained silent.

"Anyone with any human decency wouldn't have dared question the veracity of your story . . ." Angel hesitated. " 'Story' might be the wrong word."

"It's the right word."

Angel was certain her ears were playing tricks on her. "I'm sorry?"

"Erika was right," Faith admitted. "To a degree anyway."

Angel's brow furrowed. So now she was about to learn that Faith was lying all along? "I suggest you start at the beginning."

Faith let out a long breath, then began revealing her shameful background. "The reporter caught me completely off guard when he asked me about my parents. I purposely make no mention of them in my bio," she explained.

"Please tell me that your parents are dead," Angel said firmly. "Dead as a doorknob dead."

"My mother is," Faith said.

"And your father?"

"I never knew who my father was, so for all intents and purposes, he's dead as well."

Angel studied Faith's body language closely, uncertain whether or not this woman she hardly knew was telling the truth or simply covering old lies with new ones. "So your mother died in a car accident?" she asked skeptically.

Faith nodded her head in the affirmative. "I was only six at the time. The authorities didn't notify my grandmother until a week after it had happened." Noting the look of confusion on Angel's face, Faith explained, "My mother had changed her name from Loretta Molaney to Sarah Storm. The police spent five days looking for the Storm family. I found out I no longer had a mother three weeks later . . . on my birthday, of all days," Faith said with a strained giggle. "Happy birthday to me, huh?"

Angel could feel dark clouds rising around her, filled with bitter memories of her own childhood. "So your grandmother raised you?"

"If you can call it that," Faith said. "My grandmother got pregnant when she was sixteen. Even as a child, I remember she was cold and distant to my mother, blaming her, I guess, for stealing her youth. When my mother got pregnant at seventeen, Gram kicked her out of the house, damning her for repeating her mistake," Faith said, wiping a newly formed tear from her eye. "Needless to say, raising her daughter's child was about the last thing my grandmother was interested in doing. She reminded me of that fact on an almost daily basis."

Angel cringed inside as the image of a man brutally striking his wife leapt into her mind. She hardly heard Faith as she went on.

"But at least she was willing to put a roof over my head and a hot meal in my stomach," Faith said. "Things were pretty decent until I was sixteen," she continued as she walked over to the mini-fridge. "Mineral water?"

Angel pulled herself out of her vivid memory. "Scotch on the rocks would be better," she said dryly.

Faith laughed. "You're very funny," she said, pouring some water for herself. "I have learned so much from you about timing—"

"Yeah, thanks," Angel said, cutting her off. "So what happened when you were sixteen?"

"I told her that I wanted to be an actress," Faith said. "She just about blew her top."

Angel leaned back in the chair, concentrating on the story.

"You have to understand that Gram was a Bible-thumping Southern Baptist," Faith explained. "As far as she was concerned, my being an actress was tantamount to doing a slow dance with the Devil himself." Faith chuckled nervously. "She absolutely forbade me from stepping foot on a stage."

"So what did you do?"

"Told her I wouldn't . . . then took acting classes and auditioned for shows behind her back, of course." Faith laughed.

"That's one approach," Angel deadpanned.

"I was able to keep the charade going—for a while anyway. Then one day the local paper ran a picture of me performing in my high school's production of *42nd Street*." Faith paused, her eyes lowering to the floor.

"What happened?"

"She kicked me out and told me to never come back," Faith said disconsolately. "I haven't seen her since."

Angel was staggered by what she was hearing. It amazed her how people could carry on what appeared on the surface to be normal, happy lives, all the while secretly dealing with such damaging heartaches. There were so many people in the world who suffered in quiet shame, believing their pain was unlike anything ever experienced by anyone else. Angel knew, because she was one of them. Feeling utterly alone, she had somehow carried on after the tragedy that had changed the course of her life forever.

"My mother's dead too," Angel said quietly.

Faith's eyes widened.

"She was beautiful, my mother. Sweet, funny, smart," Angel said, struggling to keep in check the sadness and anger that lived deep inside her. "I miss her so much sometimes."

Faith knelt down in front of Angel, taking her hands in her own. "I had no idea," she said. "I'm so sorry."

Angel looked into Faith's tearstained eyes. "And I'm sorry for you," she said, then managed a weak smile. "Well, I guess since we know each other's painful secrets, we have no other choice but to be friends." Angel wiped Faith's face with the sleeve of her blouse. "Only friends can swear each other to secrecy, right?"

"Right." Faith nodded eagerly. "Only friends can do that."

12

* * * * * * * *

You're a Shining Star

*B*rave's supervising producer, John Weisenthal, rushed into the makeup suite. "Has anyone heard from Faith?" he asked, concerned.

Erika continued her self-admiration session in the mirror, ignoring the question.

Angel looked worried. "She hasn't signed in?"

"Sorry I'm late," Faith said, dashing into the makeup suite. "I overslept."

John let out a relieved sigh, then turned for the door. "Please have yourself in makeup and wardrobe in time to shoot the affiliate promos," he said over his shoulder as he walked out of the room.

"Sorry, John . . . it won't happen again," Faith called after him. She sat down in the chair and pulled off her sunglasses. "What time is it?"

Ernesto looked down at his watch. "It's eleven thirty," he said, then resumed applying makeup to Angel's face.

"Oh, shoot," Faith said tensely. "I'm gonna be late."

"Relax, Mommie," Ernesto said, motioning for his assistant to tend to the disheveled hair surrounding Faith's colorless face. "The taping's not for another thirty minutes. We got time."

Angel glanced over at Faith, then turned to Ernesto. "I can do my own lipstick," she said. "Why don't you go ahead and get started on Faith's makeup?"

"I'm so sorry about this, guys," Faith said, almost in tears.

"Never you worry," Ernesto said reassuringly. "I'll have you looking good as new in no time."

Feeling left out, Erika stewed quietly in the corner until a production assistant entered the room carrying a crystal vase filled with three dozen roses. "Those must be for me," she said, standing to receive her bounty. "My agent probably congratulating me on my write-up in *Ebony*."

"No, these are for Faith," the production assistant said, placing the roses down on the counter.

"Oh," Erika said, stricken. She lowered herself back into her chair, embarrassed.

Faith pulled out the card and read it to herself. Her pale face brightened.

Ernesto raised his thumb and forefinger to his head. "Somebody has a *luvvaah*," he teased.

"Do not," Faith said, blushing. "They're just roses."

"Well, they are putting a smile on your face . . . so I like whoever sent them," Ernesto said.

Faith smiled. "Me too."

The stage manager poked her head through the door. "Angel, we need you on the set."

"Sure thing," Angel said, rising from the chair. She walked over to Faith and rubbed her shoulder. "You gonna be okay, honey?"

Faith nodded. "I'll be fine."

"Okay . . . see you on the set," Angel said, then left.

"Are you almost done with me?" Faith asked Ernesto. "I need to make a quick call before we tape."

Ernesto shook his head and smiled. "Go call your lover," he said, helping Faith up from the chair. "I'll finish you up on the set."

"Thanks," Faith said, picking up the vase.

Erika waited for a few seconds, then discreetly ducked out of the makeup suite. She followed Faith back to her dressing room, standing unnoticed outside the slightly ajar door.

"Randall Hunter, please. This is Faith Molaney calling."

Even though she had let him go—in theory anyway—the thought

of Randall sending roses to Faith awakened sharp pangs of jealousy in Erika.

"You're too good to me," Faith cooed. "What? What necklace?"

With growing anger, Erika watched Faith as she walked over to the flowers, noticing for the first time the Harry Winston box sitting on the table beside them. She almost screamed when she saw the necklace with a diamond pendant shaped in the form of a star.

"Oh, Randall, it's beautiful," Faith said, holding up the dazzling strand. "Roses and a diamond necklace. It's simply too much."

Erika's lips twisted into a snarl. Randall had never given her more than a happy meal and a clumsy lay. But the blond bimbo got flowers and a two-plus-carat diamond.

"You make me feel like a star," Faith said, smiling brightly. "Dinner would be great."

Erika felt a queasy spasm in her stomach as she backed away from the door. She'd been feeling a little off for the past few weeks, and she'd made a doctor's appointment for later that day. "Probably a severe case of envy overload," she muttered as she took a final look at the necklace. "This kinda shit would make anybody sick."

*   *   *

Erika glanced down at her watch as she paced the floor of the examining room. "Come on, already," she said impatiently.

Upon her arrival at the medical suite an hour and a half ago Dr. Benson had handed Erika a white gown and a plastic cup. Though she'd insisted that she only had an upset stomach, the doctor had run a battery of tests on her.

"Sorry about the delay," Dr. Benson said as she stepped into the examining room.

"I need to get back to work at some point today," Erika said rudely.

Dr. Benson motioned for her to take a seat. "Not so fast."

Erika gritted her teeth as she sat down. This was exactly why she hated coming here. Doctors always pulled this kind of stuff, and it always got on Erika's last good nerve. One more doctor with a God complex. Scare your patients into taking unnecessary and expensive tests, then take your sweet-ass time telling them that in fact they are *not* going to die.

"I found something interesting in your urine test."

Erika looked at her stone-faced. *Here we go.*

"When was your last period?"

"My cycle has always had a mind of its own," Erika said, rising to her feet. "Look, unless I have some terminal—"

"You're pregnant."

Erika was so stunned, she was barely aware that she dropped back down into the chair. She clutched the armrests. The room began spinning around her. Surely she hadn't heard the woman correctly. There was no way in hell that she was knocked up. Okay, she and Randall did have a spotty record of condom use, and that damned diaphragm never seemed to be within reach when she needed it most.

Erika took a deep breath. This couldn't be happening. Getting pregnant prior to the occurrence of her five-hundred-person wedding ceremony was not in the plan. She shook her head confidently. No, this simply was not happening.

"And I would strongly suggest that you seek immediate treatment for the bulimia," Dr. Benson said as she opened Erika's folder.

"What?" Erika asked, glaring at the doctor. "Who said I was bulimic?"

"You show all the classic symptoms of bulimia: inflammation of the esophagus, tooth decay—"

"I do not have a problem," Erika said flatly.

Dr. Benson handed her a pink slip. "Dr. Mariman is both a medical doctor and psychotherapist specializing in the treatment of eating disorders."

Erika stuffed the paper into her plaid Burberry purse. Maybe she was speaking in a foreign tongue or something, because she could have sworn she'd just told this woman that she didn't have a problem. And even if she did *sometimes* overindulge to the point of *needing* to purge, she damned well wasn't going to see a shrink about it. The last thing Erika needed right now—besides being pregnant—was for the media, or Victoria, to find out that she was bulimic, which, as far as she was concerned, she wasn't.

"I'm going to write you a script for some prenatal vitamins—"

Erika waved her off. "Keep 'em."

Dr. Benson leaned back, her face utterly bland. "Listen, Erika, I know the news of an unplanned pregnancy can be terribly unsettling," she said. "But as you are already fourteen weeks into—"

"I can't deal with this right now," Erika said, rising to her feet.

Dr. Benson stood from her desk, walking around to meet Erika. "Then take them until you decide one way or the other," she said, slipping the prescription into the pocket of Erika's cream suede jacket.

"Sure." Erika put on her shades, then headed for the door.

"I know this is a lot to take in," Dr. Benson said. "But we will need to make a decision soon."

Distantly, Erika said, "I'll call."

The instant she was in the limousine, Erika pulled out her cell phone.

"Randall Hunter's office," the voice answered.

Erika closed the phone, tossing it across the leather seat. She lowered her head into her hand. "Dammit!" she said. "How the fuck could I let this happen?"

The driver glanced up into the rearview mirror. "Is everything okay, Ms. Bishop?"

"Hell no!" Erika wanted to scream, but managed to get hold of herself. "Everything's fine," she said, pushing the button to close the smoked-glass partition that separated them.

In the silence, Erika played out various scenarios in her head, none of which offered a result she found remotely appealing. Forcing Randall into marrying her—assuming she could pry him from Savanna's liver-spotted hands—placed her into a loveless marriage with a man she'd never really wanted to be with in the first place. Being a single parent was simply out of the question; Victoria would kill her before she reached full-term.

Erika gazed out the window, her vision blurred by the tears burning her eyes. Her picture-perfect life was proving to be one big, cruel joke. Despite having a baby growing inside her, she felt emptier than ever.

"I'll be damned if I deal with this alone," Erika said, snatching up the phone. She didn't have a clue what she was going to do about the child, but she did know the man responsible for putting her in this situation needed to suffer.

"Randall Hunter," Erika said, cutting the woman off.

"Mr. Hunter is in—"

Erika cut her off again. "Tell him to call Erika Bishop . . . it's important," she said, not bothering to wait for a response before flipping the cell phone closed. An ironic smile came to her lips. If they'd pay Khandi $750,000 to keep quiet about an affair, the Wellingtons would cough up a nice chunk of cheddar to keep Randall's illegitimate, half-black baby from sullying their snow white bloodline.

The driver opened the door.

"Thank you," Erika said as he helped her from the limo.

"Will you be going back to the studio today?"

Erika shook her head as she continued toward the front door. "I'm not feeling well."

Once inside, she headed straight for the kitchen. She walked into the pantry, removing her private stash from the bottom drawer of the cabinet. Erika was certain her mother would never find her comfort food there, since bending down made her tight skirts wrinkle.

Sitting at the kitchen table, a prisoner of her own desperate solitude, Erika stuffed Twinkies and Oreos into her mouth. She wasn't particularly hungry—not for food anyway—but the sweets brought her comfort just the same.

Ten minutes later, when she was full to the point of nausea, she stood up from the table. She returned the bag of Oreos to the cabinet, then pushed the empty Twinkie wrappers down into the trash bin, careful as always to bury the evidence of her crime near the bottom.

Feeling like a beached whale, Erika made her way down the long hall. She lowered herself onto the white marble floor of the foyer. She looked up at the crystal chandelier, over to the Senghor Reid painting hanging on the wall, then down the hall that led to her elegantly appointed great room. She had amassed all of the things Victoria had assured her would make her happy: money, fame, and a truckload of material possessions. *So why in the hell*, Erika wondered, *was she miserable?*

"Ain't that a bitch?" she chuckled bitterly. All-knowing Victoria had been wrong about something.

Erika ran her hands across her full stomach, still unable to get her mind around the thought of being a mother. And, with a role model like Victoria, who could blame her? She thought about her fans. What would they think of her getting pregnant with a married man's child? God help her when they found out the daddy-to-be was a married *white* man. Erika's street cred would be shot straight to hell.

Getting wobbly, she took one more look around her "perfect" world before heading up the stairs. Once in the master bathroom she lowered herself to her knees in front of the onyx-colored toilet, slipping her index finger down her throat.

Erika pulled back. That might hurt the baby.

Tentatively, she removed her hand, rising to her feet. She turned to the mirror, studying her expanding stomach. A baby was growing inside her. Was that what she wanted? How was she supposed to know?

Finally Erika sighed and walked out of the bathroom.

13

* * * * * * *

Catch Me If You Can

Patrons of Beverly Hills' ultra trendy Pane e Vino Restaurant—a cozy, Mediterranean-influenced production of vine-covered apricot walls and terra-cotta tiles—stole glances at Angel as they passed her patio table. Those lucky enough to make eye contact blushed nervously as she gave them queenly smiles and friendly nods.

"When is Glen getting back from the conference?" Angel asked, taking a sip of her apple martini.

Jill sighed. "Tomorrow, thank God."

Angel grinned coyly. "Is Momma horny?"

"As a Catholic schoolgirl."

"I ain't mad at cha," Angel said, laughing. "Hey, have you heard from Ben this week?"

"Thank you," Jill said to the waitress as she cleared their plates. "I talked to him this afternoon. He's on a cloud because one of his clients just got the female lead in some new movie," she said, raising her glass of wine. "Apparently, every actress in Hollywood had been vying for the role."

"Cassandra Douglass?"

"No, this is a new client," Jill said. "Oh, what's that girl's name?" She rubbed her forehead in thought. "Short, dark-skinned sista with the pretty hair and freckles . . ."

"Michelle Wilson?"

Jill snapped her fingers. "That's her," she said. "Ben's all jazzed because it's Steven somebody or other's new movie."

"Steven Soderbergh?"

"Yeah . . . I think that's the one."

Angel snatched up her purse from the floor. "Son of a bitch!"

"What's wrong?" Jill asked.

"Benjamin Riley!" Angel barked into her cell phone. "Don't 'Hey, Boo' me."

"What is it?" Jill pressed.

"Hang on, Judas," Angel said, covering the phone. "That's the movie Helen told me to forget about because they weren't going to consider a black for the female lead."

Jill cringed. "Ahhh."

"Benjamin, I told you how much I wanted that role," Angel said into the phone.

"What role?"

"You know what role!"

"And as your friend, I told you how much I hoped you'd get it," Ben said.

"Then how could you have gotten it for—"

"But—"

"But what?"

"But I'm not your agent, Angel . . . I'm Michelle's," Ben explained. "As much as I may have wanted you to get the role, my *job* was to get it for her."

"Well, you still coulda . . ." Angel said, hesitating as the truth of what he was saying settled in. Ben was simply doing his job and doing it better than Helen was doing hers. She forced her lips into a tight smile. "Congratulations."

"Thank you," Ben said.

"I'm going to hang up now."

"Okay," Ben said easily. "Talk to you later."

Angel frowned at the phone. "Don't tell me that you're about to pass up a perfect opportunity to rub this in my face," she said. "Go on and tell me how the role might have been mine if you were my agent."

"Nah, I love you too much to do that," Ben said. "Besides, you know the door is always open. You'll walk through it when and *if* you want to."

Angel wanted to kick herself.

"Listen, I gotta roll," Ben said. "Love you."

"Love you too . . . bye." Angel closed the phone. She looked over at Jill. "Could you hear it from over there?"

"Who, Ben?"

"No, the sound of my ass tearing?"

"I'm sorry, girl," Jill said, trying not to laugh. "Maybe you should consider letting him . . ." she began, then stopped herself. "Not my business."

The waitress returned to the table. "Would you like more water, Ms. Hart?"

"Another apple martini would be better," she grumbled.

"Another glass of wine for you?" the waitress asked Jill.

"I'm good, thanks."

"Be right back with that martini."

Jill leaned forward in her chair. "Don't look now, but at three o'clock a tasty morsel of man candy is all up in your grille."

Angel turned her head. "Where?"

"Did I not just say *don't* look?"

"I know that guy," Angel said, waving. "He's a writer on *Brave*."

"Don't usually feel a brotha in dreads," Jill said, giving him the once-over. "But they work on his fine self." She raised her brow at Angel. "Have you done him?"

Jill's directness made Angel draw back. "Why would you even ask me something like that?" she asked feigning embarrassment.

"Save the innocent act for someone who might actually buy it," Jill said, studying the man as he sat alone at the table in the corner. "We both know you ain't no virgin."

The waitress returned with the apple martini. "Here ya go."

Angel smiled. "Thank you."

"What's he like?" Jill asked, returning her attention to Lucien.

Angel exhaled a frustrated sigh. "An enigma wrapped in a blanket of mystery."

"Translation: He hasn't fallen for your Mack Momma moves."

"Trust me," Angel snorted, "if I wanted him I could have him."

"Mm-hmm," Jill said. "He is a good-lookin' brotha."

"A little too serious if you ask me."

"Translation: He's deeper than the vapid pretty boys you usually screw," Jill said.

Angel gave her the finger. "And the horse you rode in on."

Jill smiled as only a friend being wicked could smile. She called the waitress over.

"Yes, ma'am?"

"That guy over there," Jill said, pointing at Lucien.

"Stop pointing."

Jill ignored Angel. "What's he drinking?"

"Grey Goose and cranberry," the waitress said. "The woman he was with left about twenty minutes ago," she added, giving Jill a conspirator's grin. "She didn't seem too happy."

"*Really*," Jill said, turning to Angel. "Is he straight?"

"As far as I know."

Jill turned back to the waitress. "Grey Goose and cranberry, you say?"

Angel tensed in her chair. "Do not send that man—"

"Have one sent to his table," Jill instructed the waitress. "And tell him it's courtesy of Ms. Hart here."

"Okay," Angel said, laughing. "I'll play along."

Angel and Jill played it cool as the waitress delivered the drink. When he caught Angel's eye, Lucien raised his glass and smiled.

"You are *sooo* predictable," Jill chuckled as Angel waved him over to their table.

Angel nudged her friend with her elbow. "Just having a little fun."

"Good evening, ladies," Lucien said as he approached.

"Well, hello," Jill said, even more impressed with him up close.

"Lucien Alexander," he said, extending his hand to her.

"Jill Prescott."

Lucien turned to Angel. "Thanks for the drink."

"You're very welcome," Angel said, her eyes flicking to Jill, wanting to see what she would do next.

"So Angel tells me that the two of you work together," Jill said, motioning for Lucien to have a seat.

"I'm a writer on the show," he said, sitting down. "Just started this season."

"So you're the man responsible for making my Angel so happy."

Lucien gave Jill a curious grin. "Sorry?"

"The marked improvement in the show's writing," she clarified. "You're responsible for that?"

"I'm just one of eight writers," Lucien said. "It's a team effort."

"Talented and modest," Jill noted to Angel. "And good-looking."

Playing it cool, Angel nodded sagely.

Lucien had no idea what was going on between them, but he plunged ahead. "You look familiar," he said to Jill. "Have we met before?"

"Unless you've been to peewee football or girls soccer, I sincerely doubt it," Jill said jokingly. "Besides, I'm sure I'd remember meeting such a lovely gentleman."

"The Sunset Room," Lucien said. "You were there with the agent?"

"Benjamin Riley," Jill said, surprised and pleased. "Yes, I was."

Lucien turned to Angel. "And if I recall correctly, you were there as well."

Angel allowed, "Yes, I was."

"I remember you had a good time on the dance floor."

"Yes, I did," Angel said. "Did you have a good time watching?"

Lucien licked his lips. "It was aiight."

Jill had no sooner thought she should slip into the background when her cell phone started ringing. "Excuse me," she said, reaching into her purse. "Hello."

"So how did the evening end?" Lucien inquired.

Angel demurred. "A true lady never tells."

Jill covered the phone. "She's using the word 'lady' loosely."

Lucien laughed.

"Ignore my friend," Angel shot back. "She's off her medication."

"And where exactly is your key, young lady?" Jill said into the phone, now the no-nonsense mother. She rose abruptly from her chair. "Will you two excuse me, please?"

"Sure." Lucien rose to his feet as she departed.

That was a nice touch, Angel thought as he sat back down. "So, you're all alone tonight?"

"I had a date."

"And?"

Lucien's lips twisted. "Let's just say I couldn't give her what she was looking for."

"What was she looking for?"

"A sponsor."

"That's too bad."

"It is what it is," Lucien said, raising the glass to his lips. "So the guy you were dancing with . . ."

"Tristan."

"He your boyfriend?"

"He's a friend."

Lucien nodded. "I see."

Angel cocked her head to the side. "What exactly do you think you see, Mr. Alexander?"

"It would only make sense that a woman like you would have a lot of 'friends.'"

Angel leaned back in her chair, offering Lucien a frosty smile. "I'm not sure if I should say thank you or slap you across the face."

Lucien feared he had stepped over the line. "It's not my goal to offend you."

"What is your goal with me?"

Lucien blushed. "You're a direct something, aren't you?"

"I find it keeps misunderstandings to a minimum."

Just then Jill returned to the table. "I'm afraid I'm going to have to get going," she said, retrieving her purse from the chair. "My daughter has managed to lose her key yet again."

"Well, it was nice—"

"No, you two stay and enjoy your drinks," Jill said, stopping Lucien before he could rise from his chair.

He looked over at Angel. "Is that cool with you?"

She remained perfectly sphinxlike. "Absolutely."

Jill leaned over to kiss Angel good-bye. "The panty rule still applies," she whispered in her ear.

"Still not wearing any."

Jill pinched her on the arm, then turned to Lucien. "It was a pleasure meeting you."

"You as well." Lucien watched Jill make her way back inside the restaurant. "She's good people."

"The best," Angel said warmly.

Jill's departure caused a lull in the conversation that Lucien finally filled. "Another beautiful night in the big city," he said, glancing up at the star-filled sky.

"Sure is." Angel's eyes lowered to the tree-trunk legs straining against the fabric of Lucien's fitted black slacks. The baggy jeans he favored around the studio only hinted at the delicious man-meat lurking beneath. But tonight the goodies were on full display. Her eyes eased up to his chest. The top three buttons of his royal blue shirt were undone, offering a *loverly* view of his hairy, well-defined pecs.

Lucien gave Angel an "I see you" wink as he took a sip of his drink.

She smiled, unembarrassed. "*Sooo*, Lucien."

He returned her confident smile. "*Sooo*, Angel."

"What you in the mood for tonight?"

Lucien maintained eye contact. "What are you offering?"

Her lips softened into an alluring smile. "I guess that all depends on what you can handle."

"I can handle whatever you got."

"Is that a fact?"

Lucien nodded his head confidently. "Oh, that's a fact."

The waitress approached their table. "Can I get you guys another round?"

"Absolutely," Lucien said, handing her his empty glass.

She turned to Angel. "Another martini?"

"No, I'm good."

"Be right back."

Lucien turned to Angel. "So where were we?"

"We were deciding how much you could handle," she said, crossing her stocking-free, baby-butt-smooth legs.

"Were we now?"

Angel extended her leg, allowing her foot to brush against Lucien's leg. "Mm-hmm."

"Why don't you make me an offer?"

"Here you go," the waitress said, placing the drink on the table.

"Thanks," Lucien said, not taking his eyes off Angel.

Angel waited until their server was out of earshot before continuing. Leaning forward, she looked Lucien dead in the eye. "One night of no-holds-barred, toe-curling passion," she said, stone serious. "Are you man enough to handle that?"

Lucien took a long sip of liquid courage. He lowered the glass to the table, then took Angel's hand. "Bring it on."

*   *   *

"Make yourself comfortable," Lucien said as he lifted the half-eaten bowl of cereal from the coffee table, carrying it into the kitchen.

"You've got a nice place."

"Thanks," Lucien called out from the kitchen.

"Did you get these in Africa?" Angel asked, eyeing the masks hanging on the wall. "These have to be authentic."

Lucien stuck his head out over the counter. "Yep," he said, impressed.

"Very nice, Mr. Alexander."

"Thanks again."

Angel walked over to the stereo. She held up the Jill Scott CD. "Do you mind?"

"Not at all," Lucien said, returning from the kitchen. "*Mi casa es su casa.*"

Angel chuckled lightly as she placed the disc into the tray. "I bet you say that to all the honeys."

Lucien settled onto the sofa. "Right, 'cause I got it going on like that."

Angel stirred her hips in time to the music. She extended her arms to him. "Come dance with me."

Lucien hesitated. "I'm not really a dancer."

"Then I'll lead."

"I suspect that's something you do quite often."

Angel kicked off her black Manolos as Lucien approached. "Nobody's complained yet."

"You something else, girl."

She narrowed her eyes at him. "You ain't seen nothin' yet."

A bolt of lighting shot through Lucien's midsection as he and Angel started dancing. Since the night at the Sunset Room he'd been fantasizing about the two of them sharing a moment like this together. The reality was proving far better than anything he'd imagined. In his dreams Angel was just a pretty girl with a bumpin' body and mad sex appeal. In the real she was all that plus funny, smart, self-assured and surprisingly down to earth.

They danced for a while, nice and slow. Grinding into him, Angel pressed her lips against Lucien's ear. "Where's your bed?"

"Umm . . . upstairs."

"Take me to it."

Another bolt of lighting.

Once in his bedroom, Lucien drew Angel into his arms, kissing her hard and full on the lips. Before long she was unbuttoning his shirt, applying gentle pressure to each of his nipples with her thumb and forefinger. His six-pack abs quivered as she lowered herself to her knees, tracing the line of hair leading down from his belly button with her tongue.

Pulling Angel up from the floor, Lucien kissed her neck. He removed the ribbon binding her hair, allowing her auburn locks to cascade down her back.

Angel stepped back, and Lucien blinked quickly as her pale blue dress fell to the floor, revealing a body that only God could have created. "Damn."

Bending before her, he circled the outlines of her erect nipples with his tongue before taking each of her firm, cantaloupe-shaped breasts into his mouth. She tasted like peaches ripened to perfection.

Angel exhaled a pleased sigh as she released his throbbing manhood from his Calvin Klein boxers. "And are we in good health?" she asked, heading southward.

"Perfect," he replied, gulping.

Lucien cupped her head as she teased the tip of his throbbing shaft. He bit down on his bottom lip, fighting the urge to scream Angel's name to the heavens as she played his johnson like a Stradivarius. When the rising pressure between his legs threatened to explode, Lucien jerked away. "Whoa . . . wait . . . wait."

Angel tightened her hold on his butt, refusing to release him.

"No . . . ooh . . . baby, wait," he pleaded, squirming. "You gon' make me come."

Mercifully, Angel freed him. She pushed him onto the bed. "Condoms?"

"In the . . . the . . . uh, nightstand."

Lucien struggled to catch his breath as she retrieved the rubber, sliding it over his flagpole-hard penis. He moaned softly as she climbed on top of him. There were no words to describe how good her body felt as it wrapped itself around him like a glove. Angel was a five-alarm fire, engulfing Lucien in her flames.

"What you doin' to me, girl?"

"You like that?"

Flipping her onto her back, Lucien drove himself deeper into Angel's creamy pleasure. "Hell yeah," he growled.

"Ooh, yes," she moaned, locking her legs around his waist like a vise-grip. "Harder, baby."

Lucien held onto Angel's waist, pumping into her.

Her body began to seize wildly. "Yes . . . yes . . . YES!"

The sounds of her pleasure urged Lucien toward his own climax. The muscles in his legs tightened as his toes curled. No longer able to fight it, he closed his eyes and allowed the orgasm to overtake him.

* * *

Lucien turned on the lamp.

"Sorry, didn't mean to wake you," Angel said as she dressed. "Go back to sleep."

"You don't have to go," he said, sitting up in the bed.

"I have an early morning," Angel said.

Lucien looked over at the clock on the nightstand. It was five a.m.

"What?" Angel asked, noting the look on his face.

"Nothing," Lucien said, trying not to sound hurt. "Do what you need to do."

Angel walked over and kissed him on the forehead. Drawing back, she gave him a frank look. "See ya, playa."

"Can I at least walk you to your car?"

"I can get to it fine on my own," Angel said breezily, waving over her back. "See you at the studio."

Lucien sighed as he watched her walk out the door. "Bye."

14

* * * * * * *

You Remind Me

Randall panted as he lifted himself off Faith. "Baby, you . . . are amazing," he said, struggling to catch his breath.

"You're not too shabby yourself," Faith said, her moist face smiling. She loved the moment right after they'd reached orgasm together. There was an almost childlike glee in Randall's eyes that let her know how much he genuinely enjoyed her.

"You thirsty?"

"A glass of water would be nice," Faith said, propping herself up against the headboard.

Newly energized, Randall jumped up from the bed. "Your wish is my command, my lady," he said.

Faith could feel another layer of the protective wall she fought to maintain around her heart melting. Her eyes were glued to Randall's naked form as he walked out of the room. The firmness of his hair-dusted butt, the monumental muscularity of his runner's thighs and the fullness of the manhood swinging between them. There was no denying his physical appeal. Somewhere along the way, however, Randall had become more than just a good-looking man who could help grow both her bank account and her career. She was almost afraid to admit it, but she was falling for him.

"Here you go, baby."

"Thanks," Faith said, accepting the glass. She took a long sip of the iced water, wondering if she should let him in on her thoughts.

Could he handle her growing feelings for him? Though his actions suggested he felt something deeper than carnal lust for her as well, Faith couldn't be certain. He was a married man after all. And despite his assertions to the contrary, Randall had pledged his heart—legally anyway—to Savanna.

"I got you something," Randall said, placing a red box dressed with a white satin ribbon before her. "Hope you like it."

Faith's heart sank.

Taking a step back, Randall said, "What's that look about?"

"Nothing," Faith said, trying to shake off her uneasiness.

"Go on, open it," he said eagerly. "I think you'll like it."

Faith reached for the box but stopped short. "Randall," she said, her voice pensive, "I really appreciate this, but I can't accept it."

The carefree smile on Randall's face morphed into one of confusion. Pulling the covers up over her breasts, Faith took an unsteady breath. She didn't want to hurt his feelings, but she had to make him understand how cheap the endless stream of gifts were starting to make her feel. It was as if Randall was paying her in diamonds for sex. That might have been okay in the beginning. But, when someone you cared for treated you like a commodity, it hurt.

Randall pressed her. "What's the problem?"

Faith shifted her weight on the bed. "It's not that I don't appreciate all these gifts," she said, biting down on her bottom lip to stop it from trembling. She forced her eyes to connect with Randall's. "I just don't want you to feel like you *have* to give them to me."

"I give you the gifts because I *want* to," he said, affronted. "If I didn't I wouldn't." Randall glared at Faith. "What's this really about?" His tone sent a shiver up her spine. "You don't want to do this anymore, is that it?"

"No, that's not it at all," Faith said. "I absolutely love being with you, Randall." She reached for his hand, but he pulled away. "It's just that the gifts are starting to make me feel a little . . . cheap."

Randall faltered. "Cheap?" he asked in shock. "Everything I bought you is top-shelf. Tiffany, Cartier—"

"That's not what I mean," Faith said quickly. "*I* feel cheap, Randall. *Me.*" Her eyes began to well up. "It's starting to feel like I'm a high-priced call girl being paid for her services."

"Ah, baby, you got this all wrong," Randall said, taking a seat on the bed beside her. Lifting her lowered head with his hand, he stared into Faith's eyes. "That's not what I'm doing. I promise," he said sincerely. "I bought you the bracelet and the necklace . . . and the earrings in that box to show you how special you are to me."

"Really?" Faith asked.

He nodded. "Yes, really." He kissed her tenderly, then picked up the box lying between them, tossing it across the room.

Faith's eyes widened. "What are you doing?" she asked, surprised.

"No gift for you," Randall said jokingly.

"I'm not saying I don't ever want you to give me a gift."

"And risk making you feel like less than a lady?" Randall said with feigned seriousness. "Never!"

"Don't do that," Faith said, hitting him playfully on the arm.

"You know this means I'm not buying you another gift until at least Christmas," Randall said, rising from the bed. He picked up the box and put it into a drawer.

Faith smiled softly. "You're gift enough."

Randall reached for the plastic vial on the desk. "If you won't take my diamonds, then maybe I can tempt you with a little candy," he said with a devilish grin.

"About that . . ." Faith said, wincing.

"What is it?"

"It's just that . . ."

"Come on, spit it out," Randall said defensively.

Faith took a breath. "I made a promise to myself that if I got the role on *Brave*, I'd give up coke for good," she explained. "Besides, those two times with you—"

Randall raised his hand. "I understand." He promptly dropped the vial into the garbage can beside the nightstand.

"What are you doing?"

"Supporting you," Randall said. He climbed back into bed, pulling her next to him.

"Thank you," Faith whispered.

Randall kissed her on the forehead. "Thank *you*," he said, then reached for the light.

Resting her head on his chest, Faith listened to the sound of her lover's heart beating. If there was indeed a point of no return, she had passed it. God help her, she was in love with another woman's husband.

✶   ✶   ✶

Randall opened his eyes when he felt the empty space beside him. He rose from the bed.

"Faith?"

Grabbing his slacks from the pile of clothes lying on the floor, he put them on and walked out of the bedroom. He made his way down the hall and into the kitchen.

"Faith, where are you?"

Noticing the open back door, Randall stepped out onto the porch. His worried face immediately softened when he saw her.

Dressed in his white shirt, Faith was standing barefoot on the beach, gazing up at the morning sky. She looked so serene and peaceful. There was something about her—besides the movie-star looks, firm ass and full breasts a plastic surgeon could only wish to take credit for—that got under his skin. Usually he could count on tiring of a woman's company around week six of their affair, but after two months of his relationship with Faith, Randall found himself more enchanted by her than ever.

"Good morning, beautiful."

Faith smiled when she felt his familiar arms wrap around her waist. "Good morning."

Randall kissed the back of her neck.

"This place is so beautiful," Faith said. "I can't believe you and your . . . wife are putting it up for sale."

"Savanna isn't big on the beach," Randall said, then quickly changed the subject. "Whatcha doing up so early?"

"Couldn't sleep."

Concern returned to Randall's face. "Is something the matter?"

Faith stiffened slightly in his arms. "Everything is perfect."

"Good," Randall said uncertainly.

Faith turned toward him, a look of mischief in her eyes.

"What?" he asked with a raised brow.

"Do you see that house?" she asked, pointing toward a property thirty yards up the beach.

"Yeah."

"I'll race you to it."

Randall chuckled. "*You* want to race *me?*"

"What, you don't think a girl can beat you?"

"Did I mention that I was an all-state track star in high school?"

"Then it'll be that much more fun to beat you," Faith said with a confident grin.

Randall proceeded to draw a line in the sand with his toe, motioning for Faith to stand at his side. "Okay, on my coun—" She bolted off. "No fair!" Randall yelled as he chased after her. "No head starts!"

When she reached the house, she jumped up and down. "I won!" she said excitedly. "I beat the track star."

Randall raced toward her. "Come here, you!"

Faith squealed as he tackled her.

"Gotcha." Randall pulled her into his arms, kissing her softly on the lips. In that moment he realized what it was about her that had captivated him. Faith reminded him of home. Like the girls he'd known growing up in Ohio, she was sweet and innocent. Faith still viewed the world in soft hues. She saw the good in everyone. Life in the big city had toughened her up, but at her core she remained a small-town girl. And when he was with her, he felt like a different man. The one he used to be.

Faith sighed wistfully as she gazed up at the sky. "My mom used to say that the start of a new day was like falling in love."

Randall wrinkled his forehead. "That's an interesting way of looking at it."

"Have you ever been in love?"

The question caught Randall off guard, which explained why he answered it honestly. "Once."

"Tell me about her."

Randall stared out at the waves crashing against the Malibu shore. "Her name was Bethany," he said tentatively. "We were high school sweethearts."

"Was she pretty?"

"She was no Faith Molaney."

Faith blushed.

"Everybody, our parents included, was certain the homecoming king and queen were destined to marry and have perfect little children together." Randall rubbed Faith's shoulders absentmindedly as he told the tale. "But when Bethany made it clear that she had no aspirations beyond the Ohio border, I broke things off with her."

Faith's eyes widened. "But you loved her."

"I hated that small town more," Randall said.

"Have the two of you spoken since?"

"I ran into her a few years ago when I went home for my father's funeral," Randall said, melancholy coloring his face. "Clinging to her arm was the most adorable little girl . . ."

Faith pulled his arms around her tighter.

"Everything turned out the way it was supposed to." Randall shrugged, emerging from the sad memory. "Small-town life would have driven me to distraction." He kissed Faith on the top of her head. "You probably had a whole army of potential suitors in high school," he said, wanting to shift the focus off himself.

Faith continued gazing at the ebbing tide. "No, I wasn't very popular."

"Come on," Randall said, genuinely surprised. "A beautiful girl like you?"

"I didn't go out on one date the entire time I was in high school."

"Get outta here!"

"I'm serious." Faith smiled weakly. "Not one date."

"The guys in Tennessee must be blind."

"Exactly the opposite," Faith said. "Problem was, the boys . . . and the girls . . . couldn't get past the blond hair and big . . ."

Randall grinned slyly. "Come on, say it."

Faith shook her head. "No."

"Come on."

"No, I won't say it!" Faith squirmed. "Stop it!" She laughed.

"Say it or I won't stop," Randall said, tickling her.

"Okay!" Faith cried out. "Tits!"

Randall spun her around to face him. "I'm gonna corrupt you yet," he said, easing his hands under her shirt. "Let me see them."

Faith eased back. "You gotta catch me first," she said, then dashed away.

"Cheater!" Randall laughed as he chased her into the house.

15

* * * * * * *

Meant to Be

My Beauty,
*   You were so amazing on the show last night. The girl who*
plays your half-sister was okay, but you stole the show, like
always. You really should wear more stuff like that sweater you
had on in the first scene. It accentuated your hourglass figure so
nicely, plus the color really brought out the blue in your eyes.
Your eyes are really pretty . . . so soft and warm. Sometimes,
though, even when you're smiling, I see a sadness in them that
makes me sad too . . .

Angel turned off South Doheny Drive, navigating her navy blue convertible Jaguar—a gift from WBN for her Emmy nomination—around the semicircular drive of the Four Seasons. Two valets stood at the ready, grinning broadly as she and Faith stepped out of the car, chatting and laughing their way into the hotel lobby and down the long marble hall leading to Café. After an afternoon of power shopping on Rodeo Drive in search of the perfect gowns to wear to WBN's Christmas party next week, Angel and Faith were looking forward to capping off the day with dinner and more girl talk.

"Do you know what you want to order?" Angel asked as she glanced over the menu.

"The chicken alfredo here is to die for."

Angel looked up askance. "I didn't know you'd been here before."

"A few times with Randall."

"So the rumors are true?" Angel asked disappointedly. "You know you're playing with fire, don't you?"

Faith lowered her eyes. "Randall is not the monster everyone makes him out to be," she said, taking a sip of her water. "He's really quite charming."

"Spare me," Angel said, groaning. "Randall Hunter is a lying cheater who should be put down like the rabid dog he is."

"That's a bit harsh, don't you think?" Faith said, surprised by Angel's sharpness.

"No, I don't," Angel said flatly. "Men like that are . . ." She caught herself. "That charming, *married* man you speak of with such sweet affection has had affairs with at least five people that I know of," Angel said. "And Khandi, the girl you replaced: Randall got her kicked off the show when she had the audacity to ask for more than being his whore."

The waiter approached the table. "Ms. Molaney, how nice to see you again."

Faith forced a smile. "Hi, Anderson."

"Shall I start you off with a cosmopolitan?"

"That would be great."

Anderson turned to Angel. "Welcome to Café, Ms. Hart," he said. "May I say that you are even more beautiful in person than you are on television?"

Angel gave a big nod. "You may. Thank you."

"Is this your first dining experience with us?"

"Yes, it is," Angel said.

"Well, we'll make sure it's a pleasant one," Anderson said. "May I start you off with a drink as well?"

"That cosmo sounds pretty good," Angel said. "How strong do you make those puppies?"

"I promise you won't be disappointed."

Angel grinned at the waiter. "Now, that's something I never get tired of hearing a handsome man say to me."

Anderson laughed as he stepped away from the table. "Be right back with those drinks, ladies."

When he was gone, Angel returned to the subject at hand. "Randall is trouble," she said.

Faith sighed. "Let's not ruin what has been a perfect girls' day out with talk of a man."

That pulled Angel up short. They'd truly had a fun day. She laid a hand on Faith's arm. "We've only known each other for a few months, but I really like you," Angel said.

"I like you too," Faith beamed. "You're like the older sister I never had."

Angel drew her hand back. "How much older?"

Faith laughed. "Just a little."

"That's better," Angel said, grinning. She waited a beat before getting in her last appeal to good sense. "Look, I'm really not trying to rain on your parade. I just don't want to see you end up like Khandi."

"I appreciate your concern," Faith said. "But I'm not Khandi."

*Other women wish they could be like you because you are so
beautiful. You're beautiful on the inside as well—I just know
it. Some guys might go for the Julia Roberts type, but not me.
I'd take you over her or any other woman any day. . . .*

"All right," Angel said, resigned. "I'll leave it alone."

Faith shook out her cloth napkin. "I really do appreciate your concern, though."

Angel smirked. "Yeah, yeah, yeah."

Anderson placed their drinks on the table. "You fabulous ladies ready to order, or do you need more time?"

"I'm ready," Faith said.

Angel gave the menu another look. "What do you suggest, Anderson?"

"Our spinach salad is delicious," he said. "All the actresses and models swear by it."

"That's nice," Angel said, eyeing Anderson. "Now tell me about the stuff you serve to the people who actually chew their food."

He gave her a knowing smile. "The stuffed flounder with rice pilaf is simply divine."

"Then stuffed flounder it is," Angel said, handing him the menu.

"And for you, Ms. Molaney?"

"It's Faith . . . and I'll have the chicken alfredo," she said. "No, wait . . . let me have the chicken fettuccine instead."

Angel considered that, then said to Anderson. "Could you switch my flounder for her alfredo?"

"You got it," Anderson said. "I'll be back to freshen your drinks shortly."

Faith smiled at Angel as he left. "This has been such a wonderful day," she said. "Thank you for inviting me."

"And thank you for coming," Angel said.

"Can I ask you something?"

"Sure."

"And be honest with me, okay?"

"Okay."

"Do you have a . . . problem with me being on the show . . . not me so much as a person," Faith said, struggling to find the right words. "I mean me the white actress on a black show?"

Angel took a long sip of her cosmo, then lowered the glass to the table. "To be totally honest with you, I did in the beginning," she said. "But then the reality hit me. *Brave* is not now, nor was it ever, a 'black show.' It's a show featuring three . . . now two black women," Angel said with a chuckle. "But the show is owned by a white network and run by white men."

Faith nodded, still uncertain of where she stood.

"You would have been a fool to turn down this job," Angel said emphatically. "If the tables had been reversed, I would have taken it in a New York minute." She leaned forward in her chair. "Now, I'm about to let you into the Negro inner circle for a minute, so you have to swear to keep what I say between us," Angel said in a hushed tone.

Faith raised her hand. "I swear."

"The combined spending power of black people last year was over five hundred and seventy billion dollars. Individually and collectively we buy a large amount of shit," Angel explained.

"Wow."

"That's a lot of shit, ain't it?"

Faith shook her head. "Heck yeah."

"The problem is this: black people don't leverage that power the way we should," Angel said. "We buy a lot of shit, but we own very little of it. Until we realize that it's equally important to have black asses in the owners' boxes and network suites and boardrooms as it is to have them in front of the cameras, or out on the playing fields, we have no right to throw a hissy fit when you white folk hire white folks for y'all's shit," Angel said, then laughed. "That was a no to your question, by the way."

Faith laughed. "Got it."

Angel waved her hand as if saying good-bye. "I'm climbing down off my soapbox now," she said. "Next topic."

"Ooh, I got one," Faith said, pulling a letter from her black Gucci purse and handing it to Angel. "Is that not the sweetest thing?"

At that moment her cell phone buzzed, and she retrieved it from her purse. "I need to take this," Faith said apologetically.

Angel nodded distractedly as she read the letter.

> *The first thing I do every day when I wake up is think about you and how much I wish you were lying right here by my side. If I had you I would surely be the luckiest son-of-a-gun in the world. I'd treat you like a queen too! I know that kind of think-ing is silly seeing how a woman like you could never be inter-ested in an average Joe like me. Still, I know you and I would be good together. I'm going to make you so happy. I can't wait to be next to you, touch you . . . smell you. I LOVE YOU. . . .*

Faith blushed. "You're too good to me," she whispered discreetly into the phone.

> *I saw you at Mann's National Theatre for the premiere of that movie a couple weeks back. I was too afraid to come up to you, so I just watched. You were there with your half-sister and some Mexican guy. Boy, what I wouldn't have given to be him putting his hand around your waist like that. WHO IS HE??? Whoever he is, one thing is for sure—he's NOT good enough for you. That guy doesn't deserve to breathe the same air you do!!*

"Of course I wanna see you," Faith cooed. "Do you wanna see me?"

You are so pretty and innocent. No one is innocent anymore, but you are, I can tell. People are probably clamoring to hang out with you and spend time in your presence, but just remember that none of them loves you more, or cares more about you than I do. Remember that.

I Love You,
Your Biggest Fan

"Okay . . . bye." Faith pressed the button to disconnect.

P.S. We were meant to be together.

Angel placed the letter on the table, shaking her head in disbelief. "You don't think this is a good thing, do you?"

"Well . . . I know he's technically my boss, and I'm twenty-four and he's thirty-six . . . and he's married, but Randall—"

Angel's eyes widened. "*Randall* wrote this?"

"No, that was delivered to the studio this morning. I don't know who sent it," Faith said. "But it's kinda sweet . . . don't you think?"

"If you're into the psychotic stalker type."

"It's just a harmless letter from a fan," Faith said. "I think that guy's sent me letters before. It's no big deal."

"Faith, love you like a play sister, but sometimes you are too sweet and innocent for your own good," Angel said, holding up the letter. "This here is neither sweet nor innocent. It's scary."

Faith was utterly baffled by Angel's concern.

" 'I love you . . . we were meant to be together . . . I wish you were lying by my side.' " Angel cringed as she read the letter. "And he basically implies that poor Ernesto is a dead man just for breathing your air."

"Don't you think you're overreacting a bit?" Faith asked nervously.

"No, I don't," Angel said. "You gotta remember that you're a famous person now, seen by almost ten million people every week," she explained. "Now, you might want to believe that every one of them is a wonderful human being, but the fact is, some of our so-called 'fans' are cuckoo-for-Cocoa-Puffs crazies who don't know how to separate the fantasy from the real.'" Angel motioned toward the letter. "This *flower* can't even seem to grasp the reality that I only play your half-sister on television."

The color drained from Faith's face. "You think I'm in danger?"

Angel reached across the table, placing her hand on Faith's trembling one. "No, I don't think there's anything to worry about," she said, softening her tone. "I'm just saying, in general, you need to be more be careful. You're not just anybody now . . . you're a star."

"I will," Faith assured her. "And thank you for being concerned."

"You're welcome," Angel said. "Speaking of concern . . ."

Faith sighed.

"Everything in my gut tells me that you're going to get hurt if you don't leave Randall alone."

"Angel . . ."

"I'll say this, then I really will leave it alone."

Faith sighed. "Yes, big sister?"

"Be careful, with Randall . . . and that fan."

Faith nodded. "I will."

＊　　＊　　＊

Pressing his acne-scarred nose to the window, Jimmy stared at Faith as she had dinner with Angel. Her blue eyes—twinkling like bursting stars as she spoke—mesmerized him. Being this close to Faith both excited and terrified Jimmy. Her smile could break his heart, then put it right back together again. She was magical, ethereal and always just beyond his reach. The power of Jimmy's love for her made him ache. Was it really so implausible to think that a woman so wondrous, so perfect could love him in return?

With his fingers Jimmy stroked the glass—fogged over from his hot breath—imagining it was Faith's soft cheek. She wouldn't recoil from his touch because she wasn't like all the other pretty women, the ones who averted their eyes and quickened their pace when they saw him. No, Faith was different. She would look past Jimmy's toadlike exterior, embracing the handsome prince that lived inside him. How could she not? Faith was perfect.

"Sir, may I be of some assistance?" a snooty voice asked.

Jimmy flinched when he sensed movement behind him. Without turning he shook his head, hoping that would send the voice on its way.

"Are you dining with us tonight?" the voice asked in a tone that made it clear Jimmy didn't belong there among the rich and beautiful.

Jimmy's eyes twitched.

"Sir, I'll have to ask that you leave the property." The man took a step forward. "Sir, you're going to have to—"

"Don't . . . touch . . . me," Jimmy growled, snatching his arm away. "I'm waiting for my wife."

"Is she an employee?"

Jimmy didn't respond.

"This is private property," the voice announced as two burly security guards hovering on either side of Jimmy inched toward him. "Now, you can either leave on your own, or these nice gentlemen here can physically escort you."

Jimmy took a final look at Faith. "Soon, my love," he whispered. "We'll be together soon."

16

* * * * * * *

Mr. Right Now

"Has Phallon found a dress for the party yet?"

"About the party—"

"Don't even say it," Angel said, cutting Ben off. "Do not tell me you two aren't coming."

"I'm sorry, babe, but Phal just found out this morning that she has to cover for the chief of neonatology."

"Shit," Angel said, disappointed.

"That doesn't mean that you can't still come," Jill said chiming in on the three-way call.

Ben clearly hadn't considered that possibility. "I don't really want to without—"

Angel interrupted him. "Hey, you can be *my* date!"

"Thought you were going with Devin?" Jill asked.

"He hasn't returned my page, so screw him," Angel said. "You snooze, you lose."

"Is Glen going?" Ben asked.

"Yes, he is," Jill said definitely. "There will be no repeats of last year."

Ben started laughing. "Man, you were so pissed."

Jill bristled at the memory. "Sometimes being married to a doctor is a pain in the—"

"Watch yourself," Angel said playfully.

"Show 'em whatcha workin' with," Ben chimed in.

"I'll show him, all right," Jill said, lightening up. "I told mister doctor man that if he stands me up again this year, I'll be withholding sex until New Year's."

"Raise him to your hand, Mrs. Prescott," Angel said, impressed. "Ben, maybe you should try that with—"

"Hell no," he said, not letting Angel finish the thought. "Y'all women may be able to turn that shit off and on like a faucet," Ben said. "But we brothas gots to get ours on the regular."

Angel and Jill laughed.

Ben chuckled uneasily. "Withholding sex . . . that's just crazy talk."

"Hold on a sec, somebody's on the other line," Jill said, then clicked over.

Angel took a seat on the dressing room sofa, adjusting her ear piece as she did. "Wear that gray Armani you wore to the Circle of Hope fund-raiser this summer."

"You ain't the boss of me," Ben said, trying to sound defiant.

"And get that bush of a mess you call hair chopped down too," Angel said as she flipped through the magazine on the coffee table. "You aren't in college anymore . . . Benjamin."

"Don't be treatin' me like I'm one of your little-boy bitches."

"Oh, you love it."

"True dat," Ben said with a mischievous chuckle. "Getting me a little excited south of the border."

"Ugh," Angel said, frowning. "Boy, you are so nasty!"

"I'm back," Jill said, returning to the line.

"Took you long enough."

"Don't you start with me, little girl."

"What you gonna do if I start?" Angel asked.

"Slap you so hard your ancestors will bleed," Jill replied.

Ben laughed. "All right, black peoples, I gotta get to a meeting over at CBS."

"Faith just arrived with lunch, so I need to roll too," Angel said.

"Layta, playas," Ben said.

"The limo will pick you up at six-thirty sharp," Angel said.

"Oooh, you really getting me hot now, girl!"

Angel shook her head. He was really too much. "Get a hold of your loins, freak boy."

"I'll let you do that on Saturday."

"You both need Jesus," Jill said. "Bye."

Ben laughed. "Bye."

Angel smiled. "Bye."

Faith picked up the photo of Angel, Jill and Benjamin on the dressing table. "You are so lucky to have such good friends."

Angel removed the earpiece. "Yes, I am," she said, eyeing the photo. "Don't know what I'd do without those two."

"How long have you guys known each other?"

"Jill and I have been friends since third grade," she said, removing the plastic wrap from her corned beef sandwich. "Ben moved into the neighborhood a few years after I did. At first Jill and I wouldn't give him the time of day 'cause he was two years younger . . . and a boy," Angel said with a wry smile. "But ever the dog with a bone, Ben stalked us for almost a year until we finally gave in," she said. "The three of us have been tight ever since."

Faith continued studying the picture. "He looks a little like that singer."

"Maxwell," Angel said. "Too bad he can't sing like him." She chuckled lightly. "I love that boy to Reese's Pieces, but Benjamin Riley is quite possibly the worst singer I have ever heard."

Faith looked up, curious. "You two ever date?"

"Who, me and Ben?" Angel asked, surprised by the question. "Good God, no," she said. "He's like a brother to me . . . a *little* brother."

"He's not so little anymore," Faith said with a coy grin. "And he's hot."

"And he's married to one of my dearest friends," Angel said.

"Oh." Faith lowered the photo back to the table. "What about Lucien?"

That shook Angel out of memory lane. "Lucien? What about him?"

"He's not married," Faith said. "And it's obvious that he's interested in you."

"I assure you Mr. Alexander is not interested in me," Angel said. In fact, Lucien had been going out his way to avoid her ever since she'd laid it on him a couple weeks back. "Now, will you please stop trying to play matchmaker and come eat your lunch."

Faith gave her a wink as she sat down in the chair. "You like him too."

Angel looked at her like she was crazy.

"Don't try to deny it," Faith said. "I see the way you guys look at each other around the set."

Angel tried not to blush. "How does he look at me?"

"Like a man who wants you to be his *girlfriend*."

"Oh, please!" Angel guffawed. "I know you're wrong."

"How do you know that?"

"I got it from the source."

"Lucien told you he didn't like you?"

"Not in so many words," Angel said, considering. Still, under the circumstances, not getting involved was the right choice.

"If he said it in any words, he's lying," Faith said confidently. "I have a sixth sense about these things."

"Whatever you say, my dear."

Faith wasn't letting up. "Deny as much as you want, but I know you're attracted to him."

Angel didn't respond. She'd never admit it aloud, but she was very attracted to Lucien. Since the night of white-hot passion they'd shared, she couldn't get the man out of her head. And though she had absolutely no interest in pursuing anything serious with him—despite the dark-chocolate good looks, great body, cool confidence, and thoroughly intoxicating intelligence—she was very interested in going another round or three under the sheets with him. Problem was, Lucien hadn't asked, and if his current standoffishness was any indication, he wasn't planning to.

"What are you wearing on Saturday?" Angel asked, changing the subject.

Faith shrugged as she picked up her fork. "I don't think I'm going," she said sullenly.

"Why not?"

"Randall's wife will be there."

"You knew he was married," Angel said. "Sooner or later you were bound to be in the same room with her."

"It's one thing to know the man you love—*care about* has a wife. It's another thing to stand in the same room with her," Faith said. "I never allowed myself to think of Savanna Wellington as a real person . . . it's easier that way," she explained. "But the fact is she's very real and I'm having an affair with her husband." Faith gave Angel a beseeching look. "You must think so little of me," she said with a depressed sigh. "I know I do."

Angel brushed a stray bang from Faith's face. "I think you are sweet and caring and learning as you go just like the rest of us," she said reassuringly. "You got swept away by Randall's down-home boyish charm. It's hard not to. What woman doesn't like to be showered with attention, affection and expensive gifts?"

Faith wiped away the tear pushing its way down her face.

"But none of those things are worth sacrificing your self-respect or long-term happiness for." Angel glanced over at the door. "Come!"

Lucien walked inside the dressing room. "Oh, I'm sorry," he said, embarrassed. "Hey, Faith."

"Hi, Lucien."

"Just dropping off script revisions for this week's show," Lucien said, already backing up toward the door.

Faith motioned him to stop. "No, you stay," she said, rising from the chair. "Angel was just mentioning that she wanted to talk with you."

Angel's head snapped back. "No, I didn't."

"Yeah, you did . . . remember?" Faith said smoothly.

"No, I don't," Angel said, not playing along.

"It'll come back to her," Faith said to Lucien as she headed for the door. "See you two later."

When the door closed, Lucien turned to Angel. "What's up?"

"Faith is just having . . ." she said, hesitating as an idea popped into her head. "Hey, do you have a date for the network Christmas party?"

"No . . . and yes," Lucien said, flashing the dimples.

"Yes what?"

"Yes, to whatever you're about to ask me."

Angel pursed her lips. "So you can read minds, can you?"

Lucien leaned against the wall. "I'm not saying I can read minds, but I am good at feeling out vibes," he said confidently.

"That is so great," Angel said with a wide smile. "So you'll ask Faith to be your date, then?"

"Huh?"

Angel rose from the sofa and approached a visibly shell-shocked Lucien. She'd address his eagerness to taking her to the party later. For now she was having too much fun busting his overconfident chops. "Thank you so much for doing this."

Lucien shook his head. "Wha—?"

Angel patted him on the arm like she would a buddy. "You really are one of the good guys," she said, reeking of mock sincerity.

"Who you going with?"

"An old friend," Angel said, trying not bust out laughing as she adjusted her baseball cap in the mirror.

"I like Faith, but I'm not interested in her like that," Lucien said, retreating toward the door. "Why don't you ask *your* old friend to take her?"

Angel could feel his eyes burning a hole into her backside. "Because he's already taking me, silly," she said coquettishly.

Lucien rolled his eyes.

"Don't think of it as a date-date," Angel said, turning to face him. "Think of it more like a friend-date. Like if you and I were to go out together."

"Is that the kinda date you're having with *him*?" Lucien asked, trying to appear unfazed but failing miserably. "A friend-date?"

"A lady never tells," Angel demurred.

Lucien smirked. "Your girl already established that you aren't one . . . remember."

"I remember every *inch* of that night," Angel said, sauntering over to him. "So will you do it . . . as a favor to me?"

"Why should I do you a favor?"

"I'll owe you one," Angel said, then whispered in his ear, "Anything you want."

Lucien brightened. "Is that right?"

"Mm-hmmm."

"And I can call in the marker whenever I want?"

"Absolutely."

"You really are a trip, girl."

Angel smiled. "Is that a yes?"

Lucien licked his lips. "*Aiight.*"

17

* * * * * * * *

Fairy Tales Seldom Come True

Popping flashbulbs greeted Angel and Faith as Ben and Lucien assisted them out of the black Mercedes limousine. As the foursome made their way up the red carpet, fans gathered on either side of the barricades cheered wildly, straining their necks to get a good look at the two celebrities and their dates.

Angel had already educated Faith on the routine—take a deep breath, adjust your gown for maximum visual appeal, then smile and wave your way up the runway like a seasoned Hollywood veteran. Lucien and Ben assumed their positions at the women's sides with the full understanding that for the purposes of this odd exercise in celebrity-media-fan synergy, they were little more than handsome accessories. Angel and Faith were the ones the people had come to see.

"Angel! Faith!" photographers called out in an attempt to get the ladies to pose in front of their lenses.

"I love you, Angel!" one fan shouted.

"Marry me, Faith!" another yelled.

"Look this way!"

"Over here!"

"Look here!"

"Faith!" someone else cried.

"Angel, turn around!" a woman behind the barricade insisted.

"Coming up the red carpet right now are two of WBN's biggest stars," the KCAL entertainment reporter said to the camera as she motioned for Angel and Faith to join her. "Ladies, can we get a minute with you?"

Ben and Lucien stepped into the background while Angel and Faith fulfilled one of the many unspoken but utterly necessary requirements of celebrity: satisfy the ferocious appetites of your adoring public, and act like you're having a good time doing it.

"Angel, congratulations on your Image Award nomination," the reporter yelled out over the screams of the crowd.

"Thank you so much," Angel said, acting as if she didn't notice the four television cameras now locked on Faith and her. "It's such an honor to be nominated."

"You look absolutely breathtaking," the reporter gushed as her cameraman zoomed in on Angel's body-hugging and—in direct light—translucent lavender gown. "Who are you wearing tonight?"

"Randolph Duke," Angel said.

"How many of you ladies at home wished you had the body to pull this dress off?" the reporter teased her viewers.

Angel spun around to give the camera a glimpse of the gown's severely plunging backside.

"Standing next to Angel is the equally gorgeous Faith Molaney . . . the lady in red." The reporter laughed, a bit too pleased by her own play on words. "Who designed that fabulous number?" she asked, pointing at the form-fitting halter bodice verging into a full, flowing skirt of ostrich feathers.

"Oscar de la Renta," Faith said. She wasn't going to mention she was wearing her first-ever designer gown.

"Well, you both look stunning," the reporter said, exposing every capped tooth in her mouth. "Have fun at the ball tonight."

Angel and Faith smiled like stars. "We will."

*   *   *

Faith stood awestruck at the entrance of the Beverly Hilton International Ballroom. Transformed into a winter wonderland, the room was a spectacle of glittery fabulousness, a tribute to the creative powers of a limitless budget and L.A.'s party planner of the moment, Marie Loren. Strategically placed faux snow covered the marble floors. Rotating spotlights bounced in colorful hues from the white powder onto the walls and ceilings to breathtaking effect. Gigantic red and green velvet ribbons cascaded down from the ceiling, and ice sculptures set atop illuminated glass pedestals extended up into the air for what seemed like miles. Set in the center of each of the twenty-five red satin-covered dinner tables—themselves exquisite arrangements of polished silverware, crystal goblets and sparkling china—were two six-foot candles nestled inside crystal votives, which sat on square mirrors encircled by four smaller candles. A twenty-piece orchestra filled the festive ballroom with glorious sound.

"This is absolutely incredible," Faith gushed.

"I told you you'd have to see it to believe it," Angel said.

Faith had resisted attending the party, but Angel pressed her until she finally relented. As painful as being in the same room with her lover and his wife was, Angel hoped seeing Randall and Savanna together would give Faith the strength she needed to walk away from the dangerous liaison—before things got really messy.

"Mademoiselle," Lucien said, pulling out the chair for Faith.

Faith half-curtsied. "Why, thank you, sir."

Ben teased Angel as she took her seat. "I see Paris, I see France . . ." he sang.

"Stop teasing me, boy," she protested. "How was I supposed to know this damned gown became invisible whenever light hit it?"

Lucien leaned back in his chair, trying to cop a free peek.

Angel noticed the move. "If you want a better view, I could bend over and grab my ankles."

Lucien looked away quickly. "Nah, I'm good."

Erika and her date approached them.

"Gentlemen." Erika smiled at Ben and Lucien as they stood. She turned to Angel. "I'm hating you for that dress."

"Thank you for hating," Angel said with a chuckle. "How you livin', girl?"

Erika flung her hair with dramatic flair. "Like the diva I am," she said, her gaze making its way over to Faith. "Well, aren't you looking especially blond tonight?"

"Thank you," Faith said through a plastic smile. "And you're looking . . . well fed."

Ben whispered to Lucien, "She shoots."

Lucien grinned. "She scores."

Erika smiled coolly. "I see Angel's bringing you along nicely," she said, impressed. "Pretty dress, by the way."

Faith's jaw dropped. "Thank you," she said, taken aback.

"You're welcome," Erika said, acting as if she always handed out compliments so freely.

"Hi there," Jill said as she made her way to the table.

"You made it!" Angel said, happy to see her best friend. "Where's Glen?"

Jill rolled her eyes. "Hospital."

Angel sighed.

Ben smirked. "Dead brotha walking."

Jill gave him the eye, then turned to Lucien. "Good to see you again."

"Same here," he said. "You look wonderful."

Jill's face softened into a smile. "Thank you."

"Allow me to take care of the introductions," Angel said, turning to Erika's date. "I'm Angel Hart," she said, forcing his prying eyes off her gown by extending her hand toward him. "And you are?"

The six-foot-two-inch banker smiled sheepishly. "Joseph Pratt."

"Nice to meet you, Joseph," Angel said. "This fabulous beauty standing beside me is my best friend in the whole wide world, Jill Prescott."

"Nice to meet you, Jill."

"You as well."

"The gentleman to my right is Lucien Alexander," Angel said as the men exchanged nods. "And the beautiful lady to Lucien's right is Faith Molaney."

Joseph's eyes widened. "Hello."

Erika tightened her grip around his arm. "Down, boy," she growled under her breath.

"And this bum is Benjamin Riley," Angel said, popping him on the head.

"Sup, playa," Ben said with a nod.

Erika made her way around the table toward him. "I think you're the only one here of whom I haven't had the pleasure," she said flirtatiously.

"Then how can you be so sure it would be?" Ben asked as he kissed her hand. "A pleasure, that is."

Erika laughed wildly. "Handsome and a sense of humor," she said, holding his hand a little longer than needed.

Joseph pulled out the chair for her.

"I think I'll sit here instead," Erika said, taking the seat directly next to Ben. "I get the feeling you and I should know each other better, Mr. Riley," she cooed.

Ben cocked his head to the side. "I like your style, Ms. Bishop."

"Most men do," she said with a playful wink.

"Hello, beautiful people," Ernesto called out as he and Jackson reached the table. "My beauty, you came!" he said, surprised to see Faith sitting there. "I'm so glad."

Faith stood to greet him. "Angel didn't give me much choice."

"Look at you giving all that fifties glamour," Ernesto said, admiring her dress. "Spin around, let me take it all in."

Faith complied, giggling.

Ernesto turned to Angel, grinning broadly. "And who dat sexy lady over there?"

"It's me!" she said enthusiastically. "Hey, Action Jackson."

Jackson kissed her on the cheek. "Do you look amazing, or what?"

Lucien's jaw tightened.

Ben leaned over. "He's Ernesto's new *friend,*" he said in a whisper.

Lucien nodded as if he didn't care.

Ernesto smiled at Jackson. "I tell you I work with the most beautiful women in TV," he said, then added, "and Erika."

"Don't you start."

Ernesto blew Erika a kiss. "You know I just kid," he said, then waved at Jill.

"Hey, Ernesto."

Once Angel finished repeating the introductions, everyone took their seats except Jackson, who excused himself to go to the men's room. Ernesto turned to Angel. "Where's Benjamin's wife?" he asked in a whisper.

"Had to work."

Ernesto sighed longingly as he watched Ben talk with Erika. "God is testing me."

Angel glanced over at Lucien. "Me too."

"I love Jackson, I love Jackson, I love Jackson."

Angel laughed as she took her first bite of antipasto. "You just keep reminding yourself of that."

*   *   *

"Jasper wishes he could be here tonight, but Savanna and I are delighted to welcome you on his behalf," Randall said to the two hundred and fifty assembled guests, Savanna standing at his side. "WBN is a family . . ."

"A big, back-stabbing, incestuous family," Angel whispered in Jill's ear.

"We think of each of you as members of that family . . ."

Faith stood from the table. "Will you excuse me, please?" she said weakly.

Angel looked at her with concern. "You okay?"

"I just need to get a little air," Faith said, then bolted for the door.

"This night is our little way of saying thank you," Randall said with well-rehearsed sincerity.

Lucien looked over at Angel. "Cash would have been just fine, thanks," he murmured.

Angel mouthed back, "Hello!"

"Tonight's your night," Randall said, raising his glass into the air. "So eat, drink and be merry."

Erika's eyes tightened as she watched him and his wife exiting the stage together. She rose from her chair. "I need to speak with someone," she said to Joseph, then dashed away.

"Think I need another drink after that," Lucien said, rising to his feet.

Ben pushed back his chair. "I think I'll join you."

"You ladies want anything?" Lucien asked.

"I'm good," Jill said.

"Me too," Angel said. "But bring back a cosmopolitan for Faith. I think she's gonna need it."

"You got it."

"I like him," Jill said, watching Lucien make his way over to the bar with Ben. "Splain to me again why you won't date him?"

"He isn't into me."

"The hell he isn't," Jill said. "That boy has been watching you so hard tonight, I'm getting bruises for you."

"I hadn't noticed," Angel said with nonchalance.

"And it's obvious that you like him," Jill said more pointedly. "So why you not giving him any love?"

"He isn't my type," Angel said.

"Why not?" Jill persisted.

"He just isn't." Angel toyed with her glass uncomfortably. "Now, can we talk about something else, please?"

Jill gasped as a light went on in her head. "You're afraid of him, aren't you?"

"When," Angel asked with a nervous chuckle, "have you ever known me to be afraid of any man?"

"My point exactly," Jill said, eyeing her intently. "There's only so far you can go emotionally with all these bi-boys you date . . . you do know that, don't you?"

"My mind is on my career," Angel said with conviction. "I have neither the time nor the inclination to get involved in anything too intense."

"You're protecting that cold-ass heart of yours by keeping it in a lockbox, and I know why."

Angel gave her meddling friend a tolerant smile. "You so pretty."

"Whatever," Jill said, giving her the hand. "At some point you're going to have to put what happened behind you and trust a man enough to let him love—"

Angel cut her off. "This has nothing to do with my mother," she said, becoming agitated. "I just . . ." she said, then hesitated. "Lucien's too heavy."

"Ooh, your weak-ass excuses wear me out," Jill said. "He's too heavy, he don't move me . . . his peter's too small—"

"Hold up now," Angel said, interrupting. "I ain't never said nothin' 'bout *that* being too small."

Jill's brow lifted. "Just how *not* small?" she said, then caught herself. "We'll come back to that some other time," she said. "For now let's stay on point."

"And what exactly is the point?" Angel asked.

"The point is, you are just making up excuses for why you won't date Lucien," Jill said. "I've been talking with him tonight, and the man is absofreakinlutely adorable. He's smart and funny and actually has opinions about things . . . loves his momma," she said, impressed. "As far as I can tell, Lucien is a massive improvement over those bi-curious, gay-friendly me-so-confused boys you like to waste your time with."

"Then *you* date him," Angel said snappishly.

Jill flashed the three-carat diamond perched on her ring finger. "Got a good man already, thank you very much."

Angel laughed.

"His workaholic ass ain't here," Jill said with mock anger. "But he *is* a good man."

"That he is," Angel said.

"The thought of Lucien sneaking under your skin scares you something awful," Jill said, challenging her. "I dare you to tell me I'm wrong."

Angel sighed tiredly. "Jill, please."

"Okay, I'll leave it alone," she said. "Just let me say this—"

"Saying stuff like just let me say this is not leaving it alone," Angel put in.

"Really, this is the last thing I'm gonna say on the subject . . . I promise."

Angel slumped against her chair back. "Say it."

Jill placed her hand on Angel's, looking her straight in the eye. "You might think you want to go through your entire life never knowing love, but trust me, you don't," she said. "Love is the one thing that makes all the rest of this shit worthwhile. Love isn't just something . . . it's *everything*."

"Hey, lady."

Jill spun around in her chair when she heard the voice that could still make her heart skip a beat. "Glen!" She leapt to her feet. "You made it."

"Thank God," Angel said, relieved. "Take your wife . . . *please*."

Glen leaned over and kissed Angel on the cheek. "Hey, superstar."

"Hey, doctor," Angel said, nuzzling his cheek. "My, don't you clean up well?"

"You looking mighty fine yourself, young lady," Glen said, then turned to Jill. "So do I get a dance with the most beautiful lady in the joint or what?"

Jill blushed. "You get every dance."

"All right now." With a flamboyant sweep Glen reached for his wife's hand and led her toward the dance floor.

Angel smiled as she watched them. It was amazing how after two years of dating and eleven years of marriage, Jill's eyes still lit up whenever Glen walked into a room. The two of them had been through so much together—disapproving parents, the pregnancy senior year of undergrad, the lean medical school years—but they'd survived it all, fortified by the sheer magnitude of the love they shared for one another. From time to time Angel would daydream about meeting a man and taking a chance on love the way Jill had. In reality, however, she didn't dare take such a risk with her heart.

"Penny for your thoughts?" Lucien asked, returning from the bar.

"Not important," Angel said, shaking herself. "Just a momentary flight of fancy." She smiled at Lucien. "I'm back now."

"Have I mentioned how amazing you look tonight?"

"No, you haven't," Angel said, blushing. "You look great too."

"Thank you." Lucien extended his hand toward her. "Dance with me."

"I don't really—"

"Please."

Angel exhaled, then stood to her feet. She placed her hand in Lucien's and smiled. "Lead the way."

*   *   *

"We need to talk."

Randall flinched as he turned around. "You scared the hell out of me," he said, looking startled and extremely guilty.

"Why haven't you returned my calls?" Erika asked, her words laced with hostility.

"I've been really busy," Randall said unconvincingly.

"Well, you need to get unbusy."

Randall glanced around the room nervously. "This isn't a good time—"

Erika cut him off. "Trust me, time is the one thing we don't have that much of, Randall," she said in an annoyed whisper. "Call me tomorrow at home, or I'll call you tomorrow . . . at yours." She waved at the couple passing them. "Tomorrow, Randall," Erika said, then walked away.

Savanna watched the intense exchange between her husband and Erika. Once she was certain that Randall was moving toward the bar, she rose from her chair and followed Erika into the powder room.

The attendant smiled pleasantly. "Good evening, ma'am."

Savanna ignored the gray-haired black woman as she walked over to the vanity mirror. She didn't deal with the little people.

Erika glanced over at her former lover's wife as she freshened her lipstick. What was this? Had the old battle-ax come in looking for a fight?

Savanna pulled a silver compact bearing the Chanel logo out of her clutch and began applying powder to her face with the satin-backed pad. "Fucked anyone's husband lately?"

Erika lowered the tube of lipstick onto the counter, blotting her lips with a tissue. "Only yours."

"I wouldn't get too cocky if I were you, dear," Savanna said, eyeing her through the mirror. "You are little more than a diversion for my husband. Men like Randall may be inclined to take a trip to the dark continent . . . they seldom build homes there."

Easing back her black sequin jacket, Erika smiled. "Never say never . . . dear."

A look of horror spread across Savanna's surgically enhanced face as she eyed Erika's protruding midsection. "You bitch, I'll kill you!"

The attendant gasped as Erika caught the hand rushing toward her face in midair.

"Old lady, you must be out of your freakin' mind," Erika sneered as she squeezed the vein-lined hand inches from her cheek.

"Let go of me!" Savanna demanded, struggling to release herself from Erika's grasp.

"Do not . . . I repeat . . . do not let all this glamour fool you,"

Erika said, outlining her frame with her free hand, while maintaining a death grip on Savanna with the other. "I have no qualms kicking off these Manolos, hiking up this Ungaro, and whippin' your ass like you stole something," Erika growled. "Don't you ever raise your hand to me again. Now, get your Cruella De Vil–lookin' ass outta my face," she said, flinging the hand away.

Savanna glared at Erika, her eyes burning with hatred. "I'll kill you with my bare hands before I allow you to have that baby," she hissed.

"Now, is that any way to speak to a lady in my condition?" Erika said, returning Savanna's menacing stare.

"You're no lady."

"Maybe not," Erika said, unmoved. "But I am the bitch carrying your husband's baby."

"Someday, somebody is going to give you exactly what you deserve."

"Ole girl, please," Erika said with a scowl. "You aren't nearly *woman* enough to handle me . . . or your man, for that matter," she said, then picked up her clutch from the counter and headed for the exit. Reaching the door, Erika glanced over her shoulder at Savanna. "Oh, and for the record . . . I was Randall's second trip to the motherland. Khandi played hostess the first go-round. The young blonde has the honors of fucking his brains out this year. I'm thinking he might want to build a home there," she said, then strutted out.

Savanna glared at her enraged, heavy-breathing reflection in the mirror. Steadying herself against the countertop, she took a few calming breaths. She raised her hand toward the stray lock of hair that had fallen into her face, returning it to its original position behind her ear. Once she had regained the composure and class so important to her, Savanna turned on her heels and walked out of the powder room as if nothing had happened.

＊　　＊　　＊

"These rich people are too much," the attendant said to herself as she returned to folding hand towels. Assuming she was alone, the woman jumped when the door to the last stall squeaked open behind her. With all that had transpired in the last five minutes, she hadn't noticed that the person who'd entered the powder room just moments before Erika and Savanna had never departed.

"Are you all right, ma'am?" the attendant asked the crying woman who emerged. "Maybe you should sit down," she suggested as she helped the blonde over to the velvet sofa next to the door.

Faith sat down with an awkward thump, unable to stop the tears streaming down her face.

The attendant took a seat next to her. "There, there, honey," she said, rubbing Faith's trembling arm. "Why you crying like somebody just died?"

"Because someone just did," Faith said, her voice aching with sadness. "Me."

18

* * * * * * *

Laying the Foundation

"I guess this is good-night," Angel said as the limo came to a stop.

Lucien exhaled a disappointed sigh. "Guess so."

"Thank you for escorting Faith tonight," Angel said. "She really appreciated it."

"So much so that she skipped out early," Lucien said with a chuckle.

"She didn't leave because of you," Angel assured him. "No woman in her right mind would—"

"Would what?"

Angel could feel the heat rising inside her. "I should say good-night now."

"Why don't you come up?" Lucien suggested. "For coffee."

"It's a little late for coffee," Angel said, playing hard to get. "I need to be getting into bed soon."

"I have a bed."

"Yes, you do," Angel said, trying not to blush. "I remember it fondly."

"It misses you terribly."

Angel gave him a look of mock concern. "Then I would be remiss if I didn't come in and say hello."

Lucien nodded his head. "Terribly remiss."

"Will you be needing me to wait?" the driver asked Angel as she and Lucien stepped out of the limo.

"No, I'll take it from here," Lucien said before she could respond.

The driver gave him a sly grin, then nodded to Angel. "Good-night, Ms. Hart."

"Good-night."

As soon as they were inside the loft, Lucien pulled Angel into his arms, kissing her passionately on the mouth. "I've been wanting to do that the past couple of weeks," he said when he finally released her.

Wonderingly, Angel ran her fingers slowly across her moist lips. "That was some kiss, Mr. Alexander."

Lucien drew her back into his arms. "I can do better," he said, kissing her again.

Angel moaned softly as his hot tongue intertwined with hers. The touch of his strong hand against the small of her back made her quiver. Lucien had a thoroughly masculine energy that was both powerful and terribly sexy. Every inch of Angel's body pulsated with aching desire. She snatched off his jacket, tossing it to the floor. Never had she wanted a man as badly as she wanted this man to-night.

Before Angel could unbutton his slacks, Lucien stopped her. "Let me be the man tonight," he said with gentle but undeniable firmness.

Angel exhaled as she stared into his tender brown eyes. Any other guy would have gotten a swift kick in the nuts for saying such a thing to her. But from Lucien's deliciously full lips, the suggestion only served to advance the moisture between Angel's legs to flood levels. She said simply, "Okay."

*   *   *

Yawning as she sat up in bed, Angel glanced over at the clock on the nightstand. Instead she noticed a note card across which her name was written in bold letters, followed by:

Went to get b-fast . . .
DON'T LEAVE!!

Angel chuckled as she returned the card to the stand. She reached toward the foot of the bed. Perched atop a T-shirt and drawstring pants was another note:

> *High fashion it ain't, but I think you'll find them more practical than the dress . . . which you looked amazing in—and out of—by the way.*
> —*L*

Angel blushed as she dressed. She read the note again, then headed out of the bedroom. It hadn't been her intention to be at Lucien's place when the sun rose, but after the lovemaking he put on her last night, she had neither the strength nor the desire to go home.

Lucien smiled when he spied her coming down the stairs. "Good morning, beautiful."

"Morning," Angel said sleepily as she walked into the kitchen. "Mmm, something smells good."

"I hope pancakes, bacon and eggs are OK?"

Angel's stomach growled. "Bless you, young man," she said gratefully. "I'm so hungry I could eat this chair."

"Why don't you pop a squat in it instead?" Lucien said as he removed the two white containers from the bag.

"Here, let me help."

"Woman, sit back down," Lucien said, waving her off. "I got this."

Angel settled in, willing to be pampered. "Such a man."

"I wasn't sure whether to get you pancakes or an omelet," Lucien said as he retrieved the container of orange juice from the refrigerator. "Then I remembered that time I saw you eating pancakes at one of the table reads." He smiled. "Figured I'd go with what I knew."

Lucien set a glass of juice in front of Angel. "Coffee should be ready in a minute. You like coffee, right?"

"Love it," Angel said.

Lucien chuckled as he took his seat. "I guess you would, the way you chug it down at the studio," he said, then jumped up from the chair. "Almost forgot the silverware."

Angel studied him as he opened the drawer. For someone who

went out of his way to appear uninterested, Lucien sure seemed to know a lot about her habits.

"Here ya go."

"Thanks," Angel said, taking the fork and knife.

Lucien began stuffing his face with food. "You a native Angeleno?" he asked between chews.

"No, I was born in Cleveland."

"Your parents move here for work?"

"Something like that," Angel said, pretending to concentrate on her food. "What about you?"

Lucien's brow wrinkled. "Oh, hell no."

Angel laughed as she took a bite of bacon. "Where is home?"

"Chicago."

"Oh? That's a great city."

"With three-dimensional people and four real seasons," Lucien said proudly. "If it wasn't for this job, I'd be on a plane back home today."

"L.A.'s not quite your cup of tea, huh?"

"Too artificial for me," Lucien said, frowning. "This place is a straight-up bizarro world populated by the artificial and emotionally vapid," he said. "It's sick the way people here treat themselves and others as commodities to be bought and sold."

"Please, don't hold back," Angel said, laughing. "Tell me what you really think."

"I'm sorry," Lucien said with a sheepish grin. "It's just that sometimes I get fed up with all the games people play out here."

Angel nodded emphatically. "I feel you on that."

"So, tell me something about yourself, Ms. Hart."

"About me? What would you like to know?"

"Let's see," Lucien said, rubbing his chin thoughtfully. "Do you have any siblings?"

"I'm an only child," Angel said. "And you?"

"I have a younger sister, Vanessa. She's in law school at Northwestern."

That was impressive. The sister must be as smart as he was. "Are the two of you close?" Angel asked.

"We're real tight." The intent look in Lucien's eyes confirmed his words. "My entire family is close-knit, actually. They're the most important thing in the world to me."

Angel's eyes lowered to her plate in shame. "You're very lucky."

"Yeah, I am," Lucien said with a genuineness that struck Angel. "I imagine you and your parents are close too, seeing how you're the only child."

"No, we're not," Angel said as she got up. Moving so he couldn't see her face, she asked, "You want some coffee?

"Nah, I'm good," Lucien said. "Why aren't you and your parents—"

"Long story, best left for another day," Angel said, feigning a light tone. She turned around, smiling brightly. "You sure you don't want any? It's very good."

"Ah, yeah . . . I'm sure," Lucien said, perplexed. "Can I ask—"

Angel silently thanked God when she heard the muffled ring of her cell phone. "I better get that," she said, hurrying over to retrieve her purse on the counter. "Jill will send out a search party if I don't answer," Angel said as she flipped open the phone. "Good morning, Mrs. Prescott."

"Where are you?"

"Huh . . . hey . . . what's that you say?" Angel asked, playfully dodging the question.

"Don't 'huh' me," Jill said, undeterred. "You heard what I asked." she said, then hesitated. "Are you at Lucien's?"

"No, I'm not," Angel said unconvincingly. "I'm at home."

"I'm so happy!"

Angel's eyes rolled back in her head. "Climb down out of the tree, crazy lady."

Lucien chuckled as he walked out of the kitchen.

"My gut told me that he was right for—"

"Don't say it," Angel said, cutting Jill off.

"Don't say what?"

"Whatever it is you were about to say next," Angel ordered her. "And before you start planning my wedding, let me assure you that what Lucien and I have is at best a casual thing," she said, tapping her bare foot nervously against the floor. "We're just two consenting adults partaking in some good . . . great sex."

"Yeah, well, you can call it whatever . . ." Jill said, then caught herself. "How great?"

"The man should be a plumber," Angel whispered into the phone. " 'Cause he knows how to lay the *pipe*."

"Oooh-wee," Jill said breathlessly. "I think it's time you bring him to dinner so he can meet the family."

Angel pulled the phone from her ear and stared at it. "Have you been listening to me at all?"

"I heard what your mouth said," Jill responded. "But I can hear your heart beating from here."

"My breakfast is getting cold," Angel said, covering as Lucien walked back into the room carrying a folder of some sort.

"You cooked breakfast?" Jill cackled.

"No, Lucien was kind enough to—"

"Oh, my *Gawd!*" Jill said. "Now, you listen to me, girl . . ."

Angel blushed as Lucien winked at her. There was no denying that the man was soothing on the eyes. She was barely listening to Jill as she watched him finish off his breakfast. When he let his guard down, Lucien could be charming and caring. Even in his homeboy gear he had an air about him that made it clear he was a proud, intelligent man who stood for something. Were Angel even remotely interested in pursing a serious relationship with a man—which she wasn't—Lucien would certainly be a viable candidate.

"Angel Hart, are you listening to me?"

"Huh?" Angel asked, surfacing from her thoughts.

"I said, you should give Lucien a chance."

"Sure, sure. I'll see you at three."

"You got a good man there, so don't you—"

"Layta, playa," Angel said, then hit the END CALL button. She turned to Lucien. "Hands off my food, man."

He grinned guiltily as he eased his fork back across the table from her plate. "Oh, I thought you were finished."

"Uh-huh," Angel said, giving him the eye as she sat down at the table. "Gon' get yourself hurt trying to steal my food."

Lucien laughed as he drank the rest of his orange juice.

"What's that?" Angel asked, pointing at the folder.

"It's a screenplay I've been working on."

A screenplay? This man just got better and better. "Do you mind?" Angel asked, sliding her hand over.

"Please."

Angel opened the folder. *"The Mad Season,"* she said, liking it. "That's a provocative title."

Lucien cleared his throat. He looked vulnerable as he asked, "I was wondering, if you had some time, maybe you wouldn't mind taking a look at it?"

"You want me to read your screenplay?"

"But if you don't have time, I understand," Lucien said, reaching for the script.

"I'll make time," Angel said, snatching it away from him.

"I'd appreciate it."

"It's my pleasure." Angel stowed the folder next to her purse. "Hey, is it okay if I take a quick shower before I go?"

"Absolutely," Lucien said. "Clean towels are in the closet at the top of the stairs."

Angel returned to the table to clear her mess.

"I got that," Lucien said, stopping her before she picked up her plate. "Go take your shower."

"Thanks," Angel said, making her way out of the kitchen. When she reached the stairs she hesitated. "Hey, Lucien?" she asked in a too-innocent voice.

"Yep?"

"I could really use some help with those hard-to-reach places."

A goofy grin spread across Lucien's face as he jumped up from the table, racing out of the kitchen. "I'm on the way!"

19

* * * * * * *

No Way Out

Randall studied Savanna as she placed the napkin across her lap. Catching his eye, she smiled demurely, pleased to have him at her side dining together like loving husbands and wives do. For his part, Randall would have preferred to be sharing the meal with Faith, with whom he hadn't been able to connect since before the Christmas party.

The butler held up the bottle of merlot, waiting for Randall's approval before filling the gold-rimmed wine glass. Unless something was spilled, undercooked or otherwise less than perfect, Savanna ignored the presence of the hired help. Her singular focus was Randall.

As he sat there at the head of the elegantly appointed mahogany table that seated twenty—centered in a dining room that could easily hold a hundred—all Randall could think about was Faith. When he'd invited her to dinner three months ago, he had done so with the intention of getting in her panties. But after hours of surprisingly pleasurable conversation, bedding the young beauty—though still an enormously attractive idea—was no longer his principal goal. Faith's innocence, her smile, the needy way she looked at him, had awakened feelings in Randall that had lain dormant for years: feelings of tenderness and caring . . . and love.

"How's your steak, dear?" Savanna asked.

"It's fine," Randall said. He had to really search his mind for things he loved, or at least appreciated, about the woman he had married. To her credit, Savanna didn't ask him about his nights away. She shared her wealth and powerful resources with him without question. And, despite the fact that she was fully committed to her vegan diet—last year it was no-carbs, the year before that, cabbage— Savanna still had the cook prepare animal products for him.

Randall shuddered inside. The fact that she let him have steak was a good reason for being married? He took a long sip of his wine, wishing that liquor could somehow make his marriage more bearable, but knowing full well it couldn't. This was the life he'd created for himself. The choice to trade happiness for wealth had been his.

Shaking off the image of Faith as quickly as it reappeared in his head, he reached for Savanna's hand. She preened at his touch. He tried hard to reflect the look of love being projected at him.

Four years, three Jaguars, and a senior vice presidency later, Randall had become a man trapped in a life he had willingly helped create. He had amassed all the material trappings he thought he wanted more than anything else in the world. He had also gained a wife he didn't love, and a marriage contract that seemed unbreakable. Or was it? Now that he had some legitimate successes under his belt— including the mega-hit nighttime soap *Charleston* and *Brave*—maybe he could leave Savanna behind.

"Don't answer it," Savanna said, tensing when she heard the cell phone ringing.

"It could be work," Randall said, raising the phone to his ear. "Yes?"

"What part of 'call me tomorrow' did you miss?" the voice on the other end of the line asked.

Randall twisted in his chair. "Can this wait until tomorrow?"

"Did your wife tell you?"

"Tell me what?" he asked, spying Savanna out of the corner of his eye.

"I can't believe it," Erika said, feigning shock. "Ol' girl didn't share the blessed news with you?"

Randall took a breath, trying to maintain his composure. "What news is that?" he asked smoothly.

"I'm pregnant," Erika said.

Randall's head turned slowly toward Savanna. She offered him a pleasant smile.

"I'll give you one guess who the father is."

His voice was tight and thready. "Are you sure?"

"That I'm pregnant or that it's yours?"

"Both."

"Oh, I'm quite sure . . . *Daddy*."

Randall swallowed. "Let's discuss that—"

"Today," Erika said before he finished. "Let's discuss *our* baby today."

"Meet me at the office in an hour." Randall placed the phone on the table, then reached for his wife's hand. "I'm sorry."

"It's work," Savanna said with a weak smile. "I understand."

*   *   *

Victoria stood at the bedroom door watching her daughter as she lowered the phone to its cradle. "What have you done?"

Erika whirled around. "Mother, what are you doing here?"

"Why don't you answer my question first?" Victoria asked, staring at Erika's stomach in the mirror. She laughed bitterly. "You have either completely lost your mind, or you're the most brilliant bitch I know . . . besides myself, of course."

Erika ignored her as she walked over to the closet. "As usual, *Mother*, I have no idea what you're talking about."

Victoria sat down in the chair, crossing her legs. "How far along are you?"

Erika cringed as she removed the dress from the hanger. She vacillated for a few moments before wisely choosing not to try to outwit her mother. "Just over sixteen weeks," she said in a barely audible whisper.

"Good," Victoria said, relieved. "That still leaves time to end it if Randall refuses to leave his wife and marry you. What approach are you going to take?"

Erika poked her head out of the closet. "What?"

"You've got to be careful not to push too hard. Randall is a Wellington after all," Victoria said, musing. "Not blood, but a

Wellington just the same. The last thing we want to do is fuck up our relationship with that family."

"Mother, I'm not trying to get that man to marry me."

Victoria glowered at Erika. "Then why are you still pregnant?"

"I haven't decided whether or not I want to have the baby," Erika said, avoiding eye contact with her mother.

"And . . . ?" Victoria asked deliberately.

"And what?"

"What smart, cunning, or otherwise logical reason do you have for not getting rid . . . ?" Victoria hesitated. "Please tell me you have a better reason than 'I don't know if I want to have the baby.' "

Stung by her sarcasm, Erika said, "Well, there isn't."

"Oh, but there'd better be," Victoria said, slithering out of the chair. She marched over to her daughter. "Give me a reason and give it to me *now!*"

"I don't have one," Erika said, fighting to keep her voice from trembling. "If you'll excuse me—"

"Girl, have you lost your fucking mind?" Victoria asked, grabbing her daughter by the arm.

"Let go of me," Erika said, snatching her arm back. "In case you haven't noticed, I'm an adult—"

"Then goddammit, act like one!" Victoria shouted. "You are not about to screw up everything I've worked to create because of some twisted maternal instinct."

"Mother, please—"

" 'Please,' my ass!" Victoria barked.

Erika stepped back. "Will you calm—"

Victoria stalked closer. "Shut up and listen."

Erika cowered as her mother pressed her back against the wall.

"When you meet with Randall tonight, you will assure him that you'd never do anything to embarrass the Wellingtons . . . the people who write the fat checks that keep your dumb ass living in the lap of luxury," Victoria said, blocking Erika's retreat. "And make sure he understands that at the very first opportunity you will be taking care of this."

A tear trickled down Erika's cheek.

"Don't waste your tears on me," Victoria said coldly. "Save them for where they will do you some good . . . with Randall." She took a step back, her tense face softening. "Now, darling, I trust that you will go and handle this so we can put it behind us, and move forward with our lives."

Erika stiffened as Victoria kissed her on the cheek. Without saying a word to her mother, she walked out of the room.

20

* *   * *   *   *   *

Stranger in My House

As soon as Faith was inside her apartment, she slumped back against the door and cried. Though it seemed like she'd already shed a lifetime's worth of tears in the past two days, they continued falling just the same, each leaving her feeling more empty and alone than the last. She knew very well what pain and disappointment felt like; they had been the main ingredients of her childhood. Still, nothing in her past came close to the bitterness of what she was experiencing right now.

Guided only by the light of the full moon beaming through her living room window, Faith made her way down the hall and into her bedroom. It had taken everything she had not to break down at the studio today. Now all she wanted to do was crawl into her bed and sleep until the bitter aching in her heart subsided.

Supporting herself against the doorway, Faith pulled off her shoes, tossing them angrily into the blackness surrounding her. She reached back behind her neck to unfasten her dress, but decided the effort more than she was willing to expend. Dropping her hands to her side, Faith fell forward onto her bed.

The cool sensation of glossy paper against her cheek caused her to flinch. Carefully she raised her hand up toward the foreign object, running her fingers along its perimeter. Realizing it was only a magazine, Faith exhaled a sigh of relief only to flinch again as a pungent odor filled her nostrils. She reached over to turn on the lamp, blinked as her eyes adjusted to the light, then looked back down at the bed.

"Oh, my God!"

Lying next to an issue of *Celebrity Weekly* magazine turned to her photo was an assortment of her panties, all stained with a familiar-looking white substance. Faith reached toward the items, but stopped before touching them. She looked down at her trembling hands, then jumped up from the bed and raced into the bathroom.

Frantically, she turned on the water faucet, snatched the bar of soap from its gold holder, and began scrubbing her hands. Once she was certain no sign of her uninvited guest's calling card remained, she turned off the water. Only then did she see the cryptic message written out in lipstick on the medicine chest mirror.

We Will Be Together . . . SOON.

A chill drenched her spine as she eyed the open door of the bath-room. What if he's still in the apartment? she wondered. The man responsible for riffling through her lingerie drawer and leaving his sex on her bed might still be out there ready to jump out from a dark corner and attack her at any moment.

Fighting against the growing urge to give in to tears, Faith edged toward the door, poking her head out into the bedroom. She gazed nervously around the room, then tiptoed over to the closet and looked inside. Satisfied that she was the only person in the room, Faith ran over to the bedroom door and locked it. She backed up slowly toward the telephone, almost screaming when she heard the dial tone. Frantically she dialed Angel's cell.

"Talk to me."

"Someone's broken in to my apartment!" Faith shouted into the phone. "He left his . . . he came on my bed and my picture . . . my panties—"

"*What?*" Angel said in shock. "Okay, sweetie, calm down."

Faith whimpered.

"Did you call the police?"

"I called you!" Faith twisted the phone cord around and around her hand. "What if he's still here? Oh, my God, I'm so scared, Angel!"

"Someone broke in to Faith's place," Angel said to someone on the other end. "Where are you?"

"In my bedroom," Faith answered. "Oh, my God . . . where's Jade?"

"We'll worry about the cat later," Angel instructed her. "First, lock the door."

"I did."

"Go check the closet and—"

"I already checked," Faith said quickly.

"Just try to stay calm."

Faith could hear a male voice in the background telling Angel that he was going to follow her. "Where are you?"

"I'm pulling out of the studio lot now," Angel said. "Lucien and I will be at your place in less than ten minutes."

"Should I hang up and call the police?"

"No, Lucien's doing that now," Angel said. "Don't hang up until you see my face."

"Oh, God!" Faith screamed. "I hear something!"

"What? Is he outside the door?" Angel asked nervously.

"I don't know!" Faith cried.

Meow.

"Pick up something you can hit him with." Angel instructed. "Like a stick or a bat."

Faith reached down and picked up one of her rhinestone shoes, then thought better of it. She dashed over to the closet to retrieve a mini-bat Lex had once won at a county fair. "I've got a baseball bat."

There was scratching at the bedroom door. *Meow!*

Faith looked up. "Jade?"

"Where is she?" Angel asked.

"On the other side of the door."

"And that's where she stays until we get there," Angel demanded. "If anyone so much as sticks a toe inside that door, I want you to whack it like you're Barry fuckin' Bonds . . . you hear me?"

Faith nodded eagerly.

"You just stay cool," Angel said. "Help is on the way."

Faith took a few quick breaths, tightening her grip on the bat. "Stay cool," she exhaled. "I can do that."

*   *   *

Lucien yawned as he saw the women were settled in. "Well, ladies, I'm going to get out of here."

Faith gave him a meek smile. "Thank you . . . for everything."

"Don't mention it," Lucien said, placing a gentle kiss on her forehead. "Try to get some rest?"

"Okay."

Angel came over to them. "Let me walk you out," she said, escorting Lucien to the door. "Thank you for sticking around."

Lucien waved his hand. "Don't mention it," he said, giving her a quick peck on the cheek. "Call me if you need anything."

"Will do."

Faith gave Angel an appraising look as she returned to the sofa.

Angel explained, "We're just friends. Here, let me take out some of that tension."

"Oh, that feels so good," Faith moaned as Angel began rubbing her shoulders.

"So how you holding up?"

Faith said, discouraged, "I just can't seem to get it right."

Jade jumped onto the sofa and twisted herself into a ball at Faith's side.

"Don't beat yourself up," Angel said, continuing the massage.

"Someone was in my house . . . in my bed," Faith said, struggling to make sense of what she'd experienced. "Why would someone do such a thing . . . to me?" she asked, her eyes filling once again with the tears that never seemed to be more than a breath away. "It has to be me. I must be sending out some kind of freaky signal that tells people it's okay to screw me over."

"You are doing no such thing," Angel said resolutely. "No one has the right to violate you that way. You didn't give your keys to that psycho asshole and say, 'Hey, why don't you come on into my home and jack off on my panties', now did you?"

Faith shook her head.

"No, he decided to do that crazy shit all on his own," Angel said angrily. "He chose to mess with your stuff, and for that he should be caught by the police and punished," she continued. "As for the married asshole who messed with your heart—I trust Savanna Wellington will see to it personally that he receives an appropriate punishment."

Faith winced when the visual of Randall and his wife formed in her mind's eye. Intent on shaking the painful image, she jumped up from the sofa and walked over to the glass door that opened onto the terrace. She loved the view from Angel's Hollywood Hills home. The world looked prettier from up here. The moon seemed to shine more brightly, the stars more abundant.

"Do you think you'll ever have children?" Faith said, staring out at the city of angels below.

"No," Angel said, a trace of sadness in her voice. "My career is my focus. I made that choice a long time ago."

"I'd give mine up like that in order to start a family," Faith said. "Randall and I talked about children. He wants a large family too."

Angel remained silent.

"I really thought he was the one."

"Faith," Angel said uneasily.

"I know, but—"

Angel stopped her. "But nothing," she said, going over to Faith. "Please listen to me. You have to end this affair with him."

Faith leaned her forehead against the glass. "But I love him," she whispered, half hoping Angel wouldn't hear her, or at least would choose not to respond.

Angel grabbed her by the shoulders, shaking her like a ragdoll. "Snap out of the fantasy, Barbie!" she said firmly. "Randall is not the prince in shining armor that's going to save you from the big bad world. He is a *married* man, cheating on his wife. Erika is carrying his baby, for goodness sake!"

Faith felt her knees weakening. "God help me," she said, sliding down onto the floor. "I love that man, Angel, and no matter what he's done in the past, I know he loves me too."

Angel wasn't listening to any more of this crap. She sat down beside Faith on the polished hardwood. "Let's assume for a moment that in some warped, self-serving way, Randall actually does loves you," she said, trying not to choke on the words. "Let's also assume that he's not a duplicitous, devious snake in the grass. The fact that he's married is reason enough for you to end this."

The words stabbed Faith like freshly sharpened knives. Despite everything Angel was telling her, she wasn't willing to end the relationship.

"Maybe falling in love with me will change him," Faith said, desperate to cling to the dreams. "Maybe if I just give him a little more time—"

"What, maybe he'll get a divorce?" Angel asked, interrupting.

"Yeah."

Angel snorted. "And maybe I'll win an Oscar," she said sarcastically. "Randall would sooner kill himself, or his own mother . . . hell, he'd kill you before he'd risk losing his place in the Wellington empire." In one smooth motion Angel popped to her knees, then to her feet. "And if he leaves Savanna, that's exactly what he'll be doing."

"Fine, maybe he won't marry me," Faith said back. "I still don't think I can give him up."

Angel went to the kitchen and returned carrying a bottle of Belvedere. "See, that's what you don't seem to get," she said, retaking her place on the floor. "This is going to sting, so brace yourself." Angel handed the bottle to Faith. "Be it a business arrangement or not, the fact remains Randall already has a wife, so he never belonged to you in the first place." She waited for Faith to take a long swig of the liquor before delivering her next dose of painful truth. "It also means that he isn't yours to give up now," Angel said. "You don't have any more claim on the man than any of the other slew of women he's fucked before you."

Faith made a face as she sucked down the vodka.

"The only people with any real equity in all this are Savanna Wellington . . . and Erika."

"I didn't set out to fall in love with a married man," Faith said defensively.

"But for some self-destructive reason you did have an affair with one."

Faith ran her hands pensively through her pulled-back hair.

"You deserve better than this," Angel said. "You deserve to love someone who can give his whole heart to you. Until you stop dishonoring yourself this way, you will never be open to receiving the kind of love you so desperately desire, and truly deserve."

Faith shot up from the floor, as if to put some distance between herself and the cruel truths Angel was serving up. "You don't understand," she said. "This is not about me being self-destructive. Randall and I share something special. I can't just turn my back on that."

"Oh, give me a stiff break," Angel spat out. "You are not that damned naïve, so stop acting like it."

Faith's eyes widened.

"You are not Juliet, and Randall most surely ain't Romeo," Angel said. "What the two of you share isn't some unique, once in a lifetime thing. It's an adulterous fling between a married man and his mistress. At least be honest enough with yourself to see this for what it is."

Faith spun around. "You are such a hypocrite!"

Angel rose to her feet. "Excuse me?"

"What about you?"

"What about me?" Angel asked, not seeing a connection.

"Do you see your relationships with men for what they are?" Faith asked.

"What the hell are you talking about?"

Faith started laughing like she'd just heard the funniest joke in the world. "Looks like I'm not the only one in denial here," she said. "I'll take, 'Women who only date men they can never have' for five hundred."

Angel snatched the bottle out of Faith's hand. "You've had enough."

"Wanna know what I think?"

"No, I don't."

Faith expelled a most unladylike belch as she followed Angel across the room. "I think you really like Lucien, but you keep him at arm's length because you're afraid you might fall in love with him."

Angel stopped in her tracks.

Faith moved to the door, blocking it with her body. "I've watched you. I see the way you look at him."

"I think you need to get some rest," Angel said tightly.

"You wanna talk about self-destructive behavior," Faith said, laughing hysterically. "You only date gay or bisexual men because it keeps you from ever having to invest emotionally in them. How fucked up is that?"

"You don't know what the hell you're talking about," Angel said dismissively. "Now, it's late, so if you don't mind—"

"Have you ever been in love?" Faith asked. "Have you ever once allowed a man within striking distance of your heart?"

Angel stalked off, and Faith cringed when she heard the sound of the terrace door slam shut.

A few minutes later, she stepped out onto the terrace. To Angel's back she said, "I'm so sorry." Faith came forward and slapped the railing. "You can toss me over if you want."

Angel tilted her head up toward the heavens. "I guess it's safe to say that we both have some issues when it comes to choosing our men."

"We'll do better," Faith said softly.

In silence, the two women, the unlikeliest of friends, stood at each other's side watching the orange sun awaken from its respite, taking its place in the sky above them.

Faith turned to Angel, her eyes filled with the sadness of a truth she had finally come to accept. "I can't stay with him, can I?"

"You deserve better," Angel said sincerely.

Faith sighed. "We both do."

21

* * * * * * * *

Princes and Toads

"I'm still holding," Angel said, tapping her fingers.

"She's still on the other line," the assistant said in an acutely unapologetic tone. "I would be more than happy to take a message."

"Did I ask you to take a freakin' message?" Angel wanted to scream. "I'll wait," she said instead. "Do you have any idea how long? . . . ," she began, then stopped, realizing the assistant from hell had already placed her back on hold.

Angel looked up to the ceiling and sighed. "Lord, give me strength."

Down the hall, Faith slowed as she approached the dressing room door, mesmerized by a song that called to mind a sweet memory of her mother—one of the few she had. Whenever she felt especially suffocated by her bland existence as a makeup-counter girl, Loretta Molaney would sneak out to the large cherry tree behind their Tennessee home and sing tenderly to the sky above:

I love the Lord
He heard my cry
And pitied every groan
Long as I live
And troubles rise
I'll hasten to His throne . . .

As it had always done for her mother, the song helped to calm Faith's restless spirit. Just hearing the words somehow made her feel a little less afraid, a little less alone in the world.

Angel looked over at the door, slightly embarrassed to see Faith standing there. "Was I too loud?"

"Not at all," Faith said. "You have such a beautiful voice. That's one of my favorite songs."

"Yes, I'm still here," Angel spoke into the mouthpiece. "I'll continue waiting," she said, then looked back at Faith. "It's one of my favorites too," she said, pointing at the cord hanging from her ear. "I sing it whenever I need to remember that I'm blessed."

"I didn't know you were on a call," Faith said, turning for the door. "I'll come back."

"Stay—I could use the company," Angel said, motioning for her to approach. "I'm holding for *Helen*," she said deliberately.

"Ah, I see," Faith said as she took a seat in the chair. She was well aware of Angel's ongoing drama with her agent.

"Helen, it's Angel," she said finally. "Yeah, I'm fine," she snapped. "Listen, have you heard back from Weinstein's people yet?"

Angel's brow furrowed as the agent replied. "What do you mean 'not what they're looking for'?" She perked up. "What good news?" she asked. "*Ragtime* . . . the female lead," she said, excited. "A Broadway show could work," Angel said, grateful her agent had finally brought a role to the table that wasn't typically demeaning or blatantly stereotypical. "The touring company!" Angel's mouth fell to the floor. "Audition?" she shouted in total disbelief. "This is fucked on so many levels, Helen," she said, snatching for the cardboard box sitting atop the coffee table. "I'm an Emmy and Image Award–nominated actress," Angel pointed out. "I should be able to command better roles than the stuff you're bringing me."

Faith bit her lip as she listened.

"I know it's work, Helen . . . No, I'm not trying to be difficult, but I don't want to keep doing the same—" Angel exhaled. "Fine . . . bye." She disconnected the call, then resumed packing a box with the items she was taking home for the three weeks that production of *Brave* would be halted for the holidays. She turned to Faith. "Okay, let me just say that I have the very worst agent in the whole wide world."

"What has she done now?" Faith asked.

"Not even worth talking about. I'm feeling too good today to allow anybody to steal my joy," Angel said upbeat. "So what's happening with you, my dear?"

Faith placed a stack of scripts into the box. "I'm about to head over to *his* office."

Angel gave her a reassuring smile. "I'm proud of you."

"Like you said, if we're truly meant to be together, we will be," Faith said, hesitating as she raised her hand to her throat to catch the necklace that had come undone, "after the divorce is final."

"Exactly," Angel said, moving in to assist Faith. "Here, let me help."

"The clasp can be a little tricky," Faith said as Angel worked to refasten the necklace.

"Got it," Angel said. "And don't give this back either."

Faith sighed. "If he wants it back I'll—"

"The hell you will," Angel said, turning Faith around to face her. "Unless pretty boy can give you back all the coochie you've given him—"

Faith squealed, embarrassed. "Angel!"

"I'm serious." Angel said, laughing. "No coochie, no necklace."

Lucien walked into the dressing room. "I heard the most beautiful woman in the world was looking—" He stopped short when he saw Angel wasn't alone.

"I was just leaving," Faith said quickly.

"I can come back—"

"Absolutely not," Faith said, interrupting. "I'm late for a fitting."

Angel eyed her carefully. "You sure you don't want to talk some more first?"

"I'm sure," Faith said. "I know what I have to do."

"Okay," Angel said.

"I'll see you later, Lucien," Faith said, then turned back to Angel. "Thank you."

"Anytime, sweetie."

Faith returned Angel's smile, then walked out the door.

Lucien chuckled as he took a seat on the sofa. "You women have this whole subculture happening that we men don't have a clue about, don't you?"

"I'm not allowed to discuss that . . . one of the rules of the subculture," Angel said with mock seriousness. "You understand."

"I'll get it out of you one day," Lucien said. "So, you left a message that you wanted to see me. What's up?"

Angel reached over and picked up the folder from the chair. "I finished reading the screenplay last night."

Lucien immediately tensed up. "What's the verdict?"

"I laughed, cried . . . got angry, screamed in disgust one minute, then squealed with delight the next," Angel said. "When Giselle finally stood up to Jamal, I literally jumped up in my bed and applauded," she said eagerly. "This is amazing writing, Lucien."

He looked like he'd won a million dollars. "You think so?"

"Absolutely," Angel said. "The dialogue is fluid and unforced, the characters fully fleshed out," she said, flipping through the pages. "But the narrative . . . like this here," Angel said, pointing to a passage in the script. "This is poetry. And Giselle . . . she's an actor's dream. She's three-dimensional and complex, flawed and fallible."

Lucien's dimples danced as he smiled. "You really like it? Don't spare my feelings. I need your honest opinion."

"As surely as I am sitting here, a film studio is going to make this movie," Angel said with full confidence. "You might wanna go ahead and get your Oscar speech ready now."

"Get outta here," Lucien blushed. "You're just—"

"I'm telling you, man, *The Mad Season* is one of the best pieces of storytelling I've ever read," Angel said. "Every black actress in Hollywood will be lobbying to play Giselle." She pointed her finger at Lucien. "You mark my words."

He gave her a bashful smile. "Well, I kinda have an actress in mind for the role already."

"Let me guess. Halle Berry?" Angel nodded approvingly. "She's got the chops to handle this kinda role."

Lucien shook his head. "Not Halle."

"Vanessa?"

"Not Vanessa Williams either," Lucien said. "I wrote Giselle with only one lady in mind."

"Who?"

"You."

"No!" Angel stared at Lucien in total disbelief. "Are you serious? Oh, you can do so much better than me."

"I beg to differ," he said. "Besides the fact that you are one of the few black actresses in the business who doesn't play every character in broad strokes, you and Giselle have a lot in common." Lucien's eyes fixed on Angel. "Beauty, confidence . . ."

Angel looked down at the folder, trying to avoid his tender gaze. She wasn't sure if it was because he was being so complimentary or what, but at that moment she found herself terribly attracted to this man—the deliciously scary kind of attraction that made the hairs on the back of her neck rise to full attention.

"The two of you have enormous inner strength, vulnerability and an intense loyalty to the people you care about," Lucien said, his hand brushing against her arm in a way that was both tender and spine-tinglingly erotic.

Thoroughly unsettled by the feelings spiraling around inside her, Angel sprang up from the sofa and hurried over to the mini-fridge. "The movie studio's going to want a better-known actress to play Giselle . . . which is understandable."

Lucien stood to his feet. "But I want you."

Angel backed up as he approached. "And I appreciate that . . ."

Lucien drew her into his arms. "I want you," he said succinctly. "I want you."

Don't do it, a voice in Angel's head said as the desire to kiss Lucien's big, juicy lips—now only inches away from her own— became almost more than she could bear.

Then, as if reading her mind, he beat her to the punch.

Almost a minute later, Angel finally pulled away from the most sensual, toe-curling kiss any man had ever laid on her.

"Have dinner with me tonight?"

Angel covered her mouth like she was watching a scene in a horror movie unfolding.

"I'm not asking for your hand in marriage," Lucien said, noting the look of panic on her face. "Just dinner."

"I don't think that's such a good idea," Angel said, inching back.

Lucien took a step forward. "For just one day, let me believe that anything is possible . . . even if it isn't."

Angel studied his face as if seeing it for the first time. The silky smoothness of his deep brown skin, the tenderness in his eyes, the sound of his voice—she was fast becoming addicted to them all. And though everything in her gut implored her to run, Angel's heart demanded that she stand.

Lucien sighed in defeat. "Fair enough."

"Are you reading my mind again?" Angel asked with a raised brow. "We both know how bad you are at that."

"Then please don't make me try."

"Pick me up at nine."

Lucien looked at her skeptically. "You serious?"

"As a fat lady holding a candy bar," Angel said.

"Well . . . okay . . . uh, I'm gonna let you get back to your packing," Lucien stammered as he backed up toward the door. "I'll—I'll pick you up at nine."

"And, Lucien?"

"Yep?"

"No expectations," Angel said carefully. "Just dinner, okay?"

He gave her a respectful nod of the head. "I'll see you tonight."

And I'll see you naked, Angel thought as she watched Lucien's strong round backside make its departure. "I'll see you then."

22

* * * * * * *

The Things We Do for Love

Randall's lips curled into a self-satisfied grin. "President of Hiltop Films does have a nice ring to it, Paul," he said, careful to downplay his excitement. "But I'm pretty happy here at Wellington."

"Sure you are," Paul Hilary, Hiltop Entertainment's CEO, said. "But I'm offering you a chance to get out from under Jasper's shadow."

Randall listened with a raised brow as Paul continued making the sale. The offer was the second solid one he'd received since putting out feelers two weeks ago. And though he was playing it cool, he was quite eager to sever his ties—professional and personal—to the Wellington family.

"At Hiltop you'll be your own man, make your own mark."

"And I'd be in charge of the entire operations of the film division?"

"The whole kit and caboodle," Paul said.

Randall looked up from his desk when he heard the sound of raised voices outside his office. "Listen, Paul, let me get back to you," he said, sensing a problem.

"Ms. Molaney, you can't just go in there," Heather protested. "Please let me announce that you're waiting to—"

"We've only got a short window here, Randall, so I'm going to need—"

Faith stormed into the office, the executive assistant fast on her heels.

"Okay, Paul . . . sure . . . sure." Randall said, rising from his desk as Faith marched toward him. "I promise we'll talk this week. Bye." He removed his earpiece.

"Mr. Hunter, I tried to stop her, but she—"

Randall cut Heather off. "It's okay," he said. "Hold my calls please."

"Yes, Mr. Hunter," Heather said, then primly exited the office, closing the door behind her.

Randall didn't know what to make of the bold, fiery woman standing before him. "Is everything okay?"

"We can't do this anymore. I can't do this anymore."

"Tell me what's wrong."

"Everything is wrong," Faith said, the tears she'd promised herself she wouldn't shed filling her eyes. "You're a married man. My God, what have I done?"

Randall moved toward her, but Faith lurched to stay out of his grasp. "Don't . . . please don't," she said despondently. "This is hard enough."

"Can we talk about it?"

"There's nothing to talk about," Faith said with steely resolve. "You have a wife, and Erika is the mother of your child." She glared at him. "I should never have gotten involved with—"

"Please, let me explain," Randall said, reaching to touch her face.

"Don't touch me!" Faith snapped, her hand jerking up so quickly she inadvertently ripped the necklace from around her neck.

"I never expected to meet someone like you," Randall pleaded.

"It was all a lie," Faith said, shaking her head. "Everything was a—"

Randall grabbed her by the arms. "I never lied to you."

"You're hurting me!" Faith cried as she struggled to pull away. "Let go of me!"

"You mean the world to me," Randall said desperately, not releasing his grip on her.

"Let go of me, Randall!"

"Listen to me," he said, trying to keep his voice down. "I—*care* so deeply for you."

Faith snatched her arms from him at last. "You're married."

Randall moved closer. "In name only."

"But you *are* married."

"Is everything all right, Mr. Hunter?" Heather asked nervously from the other side of the closed door.

Randall cleared his throat. "Everything's fine," he said, taking a tentative step toward Faith. "Please just let me explain," he said in a low voice.

Faith shook her head. "I have made so many mistakes where men are concerned," she said, her extended arms, demanding that a safe distance remain between them. "But for once in my life I *choose* not to go down a path that I know will lead to unhappiness and shame."

"Let me fix this," Randall pleaded. "I can fix this."

Faith turned to leave. "Good-bye, Randall."

"I'm getting a divorce."

Faith stopped, but didn't turn around. "You filed for a divorce?"

Randall swallowed. "Not yet. But I plan to talk to Savanna over the holidays. . . ."

Faith continued toward the door.

"I love you!"

Faith kept walking.

"Please don't leave me!" Randall yelled at her back. "I'm begging you, don't leave."

Faith walked out the door.

Completely unnerved by what had just happened, Randall dropped back into his chair. He lowered his eyes to the floor, noticing the necklace. He picked it up, then fell back in his chair thoroughly dejected. It wasn't until the words came out of his mouth that he even realized that he was in love with Faith. But he did love her, and he knew that she loved him as well. He had to find a way to get her back. He simply couldn't let her get away.

"Mr. Hunter—"

"Not now!"

There was a moment of silence before Heather beeped again. "Mr. Hunter—"

Randall glared at the intercom. "I said—"

"Your wife is on her way—"

"Hello, darling," Savanna said smoothly as she came through the door. "Who was that who just left your office?" she asked, glancing behind her.

"One of the actresses from the show," Randall said, quickly slipping the necklace into his desk drawer.

"Pretty girl."

Randall pinched the bridge of his nose hard, though he knew it wouldn't ease the ache in his head. "What are you doing here?"

Savanna placed her wrap on the sofa. "Can't a wife come to visit her husband at work?" That's when she noticed the forlorn look in her husband's eyes. "Is something the matter, my love?"

Randall stiffened as the truth of his empty marriage hit him. "This has to end."

"What has to end, dear?"

"Us. This marriage—"

Savanna took a steadying breath. "Darling, you're under a severe amount of stress," she said carefully. "Why don't we take that vacation we've been talking about? I'll call our travel—"

"Listen to me, Savanna—"

"Where would you like to go?" she asked, ignoring her husband. "Negril? How about Belize? You always said how much—"

Randall slammed his fist on the desk. "I don't want a fucking vacation!" he shouted, standing up.

Savanna drew back, surprised by the uncharacteristic show of emotion from her husband.

Randall ran his hand over his dry lips. He took a deep breath and tried to compose himself. "I want a divorce, Savanna."

"Divorce is not an option," she said flatly. "We are married . . . till death do us part."

Savanna's words sent a chill up Randall's spine.

"My father has been *very* good to you—"

"And I appreciate all that Jasper has done to help my career," Randall said, cutting her off. "But this marriage is about you and me." He looked at Savanna intently. "Are you really satisfied—I mean, truly satisfied being married to a man who doesn't love you?"

Savanna's eye twitched, but she remained calm. "No marriage is without its imperfections."

"An imperfection is my leaving the toilet seat up," Randall said, dumbfounded by the woman's twisted perspective. "Savanna, we don't connect. I don't love you."

"I have put up with the affairs, and the rumors of affairs," she said, for the first time showing anger. "I say nothing about the apartment in Culver City."

Randall's mouth fell open.

"You didn't think I knew about your little love shack, my darling?" Savanna said tensely. "I know everything. But because I love you, you beautiful bastard, I allow you your *imperfections*."

She walked over to the desk, her eyes fixed on her husband. "We made a deal, Randall. My father and I have kept our end of the bargain. I expect you to do the same. We are husband and wife . . . period." Savanna kissed him on the cheek. "I'll see you at home tonight," she said, then walked out the door.

* * *

Savanna pulled her hair back into a tight bun. Dipping her fingers into the jar of cold cream, she applied a liberal amount to her forehead, beneath her eyes, and across her cheeks. She reached for a hypoallergenic tissue—specially flown in for her from France—carefully removing the cream and remaining traces of color from her face. After tossing the streaked tissue into the brass trash container beside the table, she scooped out a glob of the custom-made moisturizer and rubbed it precisely into her perfectly manicured hands.

There was a knock at the door.

"What is it?" Savanna asked, annoyed by the intrusion on her privacy.

The servant pushed the door open and stepped tentatively into the expansive master bedroom suite. "Did you enjoy your bath, miss?"

"It was acceptable."

"Will you be needing anything else tonight?"

"A glass of brandy," Savanna said, not bothering to look at the uniformed woman standing behind her. "And light the candles."

"Right away," Carlotta said, then rushed away. She returned a few minutes later with a snifter of brandy on a sterling silver serving tray. Making her way to Savanna, the servant carefully extended the drink toward her boss.

"Can you not see that my hands are full?" Savanna snapped. "Just put the damned drink down on the table."

Carlotta nodded, being sure not to make direct eye contact. Lowering the drink toward the table, her hand flinched ever so slightly, sending a splash of brandy onto the pink silken sleeve of her boss's nightgown jacket.

"Damn you!" Savanna bellowed. "Watch what you're doing," she admonished, dabbing at the barely-there stain.

"I'm so sorry, Mrs. Hunter," Carlotta said, wiping the sleeve.

"Get your dirty little paws off me!" Savanna snapped. "You've done enough damage."

"Sorry, miss."

"Light the candles, then get out," Savanna said with a dismissive wave of her hand. She took a sip of the brandy, then resumed applying the green-colored concoction to the skin around her eyes.

Carlotta gave a quick nod, then bolted from the room, closing the door behind her.

Moments later the door reopened.

Savanna sighed softly when her husband stepped inside. "Hello, darling."

Randall slipped off his suit jacket, resting it on the chair nearest the door to his walk-in closet. "We need to talk."

"I know we do, but it's been a terribly long day and I'm tired," Savanna said warily. "So, if you don't mind, I'd rather not *talk* until morning?"

"Savanna—"

"Please don't begrudge me one more night as your wife."

Randall sighed. "Fine."

Savanna smiled gratefully as she stood from the vanity table. She'd deal with her husband's restlessness tomorrow. Tonight she would allow herself to believe that he loved her as much as she loved him. "Let me help you with that," she said, going over to assist Randall extract himself from the French-cuffed shirt he was wearing.

"Thank you."

"Why don't I have Carlotta prepare a brandy while you take your shower?" she offered. "It'll take the edge off and help you sleep."

Randall unfastened his slacks. "That sounds nice." He gave her a quick peck on the cheek, then headed into his bathroom.

Savanna smiled as she listened to the sound of the running water. She walked over to the beige box perched on the wall beside the bedroom door. "Carlotta," she said, then waited for a response.

There was none.

Savanna pressed the button again. "Carlotta," she repeated, this time free of any of the tenderness Randall's appearance had inspired in her.

Still, no response.

"Carlotta, wake your daft ass up this instant and answer me!"

"Yes, Mrs. Wellington-Hunter—"

"I know my name," Savanna growled. "Prepare another brandy . . . Mr. Hunter is home," she instructed. "And try not to spill it this time."

"Right away."

Having instructed the household staff never to set foot into her bedroom when Randall was home, Savanna made her way over to the door when she heard Carlotta approaching. "I can hear your thumping a mile away," she said dryly.

"Sorry, miss," Carlotta said. She placed the snifter of brandy on the table, then made her way quickly to the door. "Will that be—"

"Mr. Hunter and I are not to be disturbed for the rest of the evening," Savanna advised, shutting the door in the servant's face. She returned to her vanity. Sparingly, she dabbed perfume behind her ears, between her breasts and inner thighs.

Rising to her feet, she removed her pink gown. Wearing only a revealing satin teddy, Savanna stood in front of the full-length mirror, carefully inspecting her reflection. Though she looked as good as any thirty-year-old from the neck down, the faint lines emerging around her eyes and mouth suggested another visit to the plastic surgeon was in order.

Satisfied that she looked as good as she was going to, Savanna headed over to the nightstand. Fighting the uneasiness building inside her, she removed a jar of hypoallergenic lubricant from the drawer.

Randall walked out of the bathroom, stopping short when he saw his wife lying in bed. "What are you doing?" he asked uncomfortably.

Savanna's eyes lowered discreetly toward her husband's marathon runner's thighs. Though the length and size of Randall's endowment made lovemaking her greatest fear, she found the sight of his manhood hanging majestically between his strong legs enormously appealing.

"I'm giving you what you've always wanted, darling," she said, slapping her firm backside with one hand, holding the lubricant in the other. If satisfying him sexually was what it would take to save their marriage, Savanna would make the sacrifice. "Come and get it," she said, her voice quavering.

"I thought you said you were tired," Randall asked, shrinking back.

Ignoring the look of disgust in his eyes, Savanna continued smiling seductively. "I'm never too tired to please my husband."

Randall swallowed. "Look, Vanna, I don't want to hurt you—"

"Then don't," Savanna said, cutting him off. Clinging to what little pride she had left, she said, "Darling, don't refuse me."

"I'm sorry," Randall said, avoiding her pleading eyes, "but I can't do this—"

"You are still my husband—"

"Savanna, listen to me."

"No, you listen to me." Savanna sat up in the bed. "I have put up with as much of your abuse as I plan to," she said, glaring at Randall. "I am your wife. Now get over here and fuck me . . . *please*."

Like a man walking to his execution, Randall made his way across the room and climbed into the bed he'd made.

23

* * * * * * *

Gotcha!

Angel sat at the vanity table applying the final touches to her face as Jade watched her from the bed. "You better be glad I like you," she said, smiling at the cat.

Despite her agent's attempt to rain on her parade earlier that day, she found herself in an especially good mood. She had sensed it the instant she'd gotten out of bed that morning; today was going to be one for the history books. Angel couldn't put her finger on it, but something about this day felt different, special. Life was interesting that way. You were never quite sure where each new day would take you. Of course, you had some idea of what to expect, but in the space between rising with the new morning and resting your head on the pillow each night, anything was possible.

Angel shook her freshly curled hair into place. "Dreamgirls will never leave you," she sang along with the CD player. She took another look at herself in the mirror, then stood from her dressing table. Walking into the closet, she retrieved the outfit she'd struggled for almost an hour choosing. The goal of the selected dress was to make Lucien's eyes pop out of his head when she opened her door tonight.

"And all you have to do is dream . . . we'll be there."

Angel slipped into the casually seductive black strappy number that said, "I look this good without trying too hard." Studying her reflection in the full-length mirror, she ran her hands down her hips to smooth out the line. "Mission accomplished." She turned toward the bed. "Do you like it, Miss Jade?"

The cat purred her approval.

Angel continued humming as she made her way over to the nightstand to answer the ringing telephone. It was most likely Lucien calling to make sure she hadn't chosen to back out at the last minute. "Talk to me."

"I did it."

"Oh, honey . . . you okay?"

"I guess so." Faith sighed. "It was the right thing to do."

"Yes, it was," Angel said as she walked over to the closet in search of her black Gucci pumps. "Where are you now?"

"In my car heading toward your house . . . if that's okay."

Angel stepped into her shoes. "It most certainly is," she said, scratching the cat's neck "This is your home . . . and Miss Jade's, for as long as you want it to be."

"Thank you," Faith said. "Keep me company while I drive?"

Angel took a quick peek at her watch. It was eight-forty-five. "Of course," she said easily as she rushed into the master bathroom. "So how did ole Randall take the news?" Angel asked as she riffled through the array of makeup on the countertop.

"I think he was genuinely unsettled," Faith said. "He said he's going to get a divorce."

"For your sake, I really hope he does," Angel said. "Are you just leaving his office?"

"No, I left a few hours ago," Faith said. "I've been sitting in the park . . . thinking. I believe Randall really does love me."

Angel didn't respond to that fantasy as she dropped the tube of lipstick and compact into the black rhinestone bag.

"I know, I know," Faith said, anticipating what Angel was about to say. "I deserve to be loved by someone who can love me exclusively. And Randall can't do that as long as he's married to Savanna."

"This calls for a celebration," Angel proclaimed as she headed toward the kitchen. "Hey, I know what. Why don't you come out to dinner with me and Lucien?"

"You have a date with Lucien!" Faith said, excited. "How militantly excellent!"

"It's not really a date . . . I don't think," Angel said, blushing. "It's just dinner."

"*Mm-hmmm,*" Faith cooed. "Well, thank you for the invitation to whatever it is you two are having, but I'm no longer doing the third-wheel thing."

"I could cancel and keep you company," Angel said, heading back down the hall. "We could have a girls night of movies, popcorn and Ben and Jerry's."

"You will do no such thing," Faith said, then shrieked. "Dagnabbit!" she shouted, swerving off the road to avoid an oncoming car.

"Faith?" Angel asked nervously. "What's going on?"

"It's a two-lane road, you moron!" Faith yelled out her window at the Mercedes whizzing by her. "All I want to do is come home, take a nice long bath, then hit the sack," she said, continuing around the curving road.

Angel walked into the guest bathroom. "Consider it done, sweetie."

"So you and Lucien are an item?"

"It's just a date—I mean, dinner." Angel blushed again. "Do you want strawberry or peach bath oil?" she asked, raising her voice to be heard over the rushing water.

"Angel!" Faith squealed. "Are you making me a bath?"

"Don't go getting all emotional, woman," Angel said. "Yes, I'm drawing you a bath."

"You are my best friend Ms. Angel," Faith said dramatically. "As God is my witness I shall never have a better friend than you."

"Bring it down a notch, Ms. Scarlett, it's just a bath," Angel said, pleased. She went back into the kitchen. "How close are you?"

"About a minute or so away," Faith said. "What time are you expecting Lucien?"

"Now," Angel said, reaching toward the wine rack. "You want red or white wine?"

"Belvedere on the rocks," Faith answered.

"Oh, you want the good stuff." Angel smiled as she removed the half-full bottle of vodka from the freezer.

"I'm pulling into the front gate now," Faith said. "And I think Lucien is behind me."

"Oh, shit!" Angel gasped, slamming the bottle onto the counter. She dashed down the hall toward her bedroom. "Stall him for a minute . . . need to check my face one more time."

"No, wait . . . false alarm," Faith said.

Angel clutched her pounding chest. "Girl, you gonna make me have a heart attack."

"Sorry," Faith said. "Hey, what are you wearing?"

"That black number I got when we were at Giorgio Armani a few weeks back," Angel said, checking herself again in the full-length mirror.

"Very nice," Faith said approvingly. "Great for a first date."

Angel blotted her lips with the napkin. "Shut up," she said playfully. "You're making me nervous."

"Lucien adores you—"

"Which is exactly why I don't want to lead him on," Angel said, walking into the guest bathroom. "Don't get me wrong, I like him and everything. I'm just not sure," she said, straining to be heard over the water filling the tub behind her. "Lucien isn't like the guys I'm used to dating. Well, of course he isn't, he's straight." Angel chuckled. "But you know what I mean, though," she said, sounding like a nervous teenager. "My God, I'm *sooo* acting like a giggly little schoolgirl, aren't I?" she asked, laughing. "Faith . . . Faith, you still there? Faith?"

There was no response.

Angel turned off the water. "Faith, are you still there?" she asked, listening for her voice on the other end of the line. "Faith, you there?" Angel asked again, the rising uneasiness inside her suggesting a problem bigger than a lost signal.

Worried, she charged down the hall as fast as her high heels would allow. Something was wrong; she could feel it in her gut.

When she opened the door, Angel's heart stopped. Everything seemed to move in slow motion.

"Get away from me!" Faith screamed at the man grabbing her. "Let me—"

"I just want to talk to you."

Lucien jumped out of his car and ran toward them.

"I don't want to hurt you," the man said as Faith tried to break free from him. Over her desperate screams, he yelled, "Please . . . stop trying to get away . . . I love you—"

Faith's eyes were filled with panic. "Let go of—!"

Lucien barreled into the man. "Get your fucking hands off her!" he shouted, taking the guy down to the ground.

Almost falling with them, Faith stepped back quickly. Standing there in stunned horror, she opened her mouth to say something, but no words came out.

"Oh, my God!" Angel said, racing toward the men as they rolled on the grass.

"I'll kill you!" Lucien said, landing another blow to the man's face. "I'll fucking kill you!"

"Stop it!" Angel demanded as she rushed up. The stranger had curled up into a protective ball. She tried to pull him off.

Pushing her away, Lucien continued landing punches to the man's turned head and torso with powerful, laser-like precision.

In a feeble voice the man cried out. "You're hurting me!"

Lucien refused to relent.

Angel had a horrible vision of another night, of another man striking a helpless victim. She grabbed him, struggling with all her might to pull him away. "He's not fighting. Stop hitting him!"

Faith cried out. "Lucien, please stop!"

Finally, Angel managed to pull him away, flipping him onto the grass. "What's wrong with you?" she asked, shoving him angrily when he tried to right himself.

"What the fuck is wrong with *you*?" Lucien said.

While the two argued, the man struggled to his feet. Holding his stomach, he scurried off into the darkness.

Lucien was about to give chase, but Angel grabbed his arm. "No!" she yelled.

"He's gonna get away."

Angel held onto his jacket sleeve with all her might. "Let him go."

Frustrated, Lucien stared at her. "What the—" he said, then caught himself when he noticed Faith had collapsed. He went over and helped her to her feet.

"Faith, are you okay?" Angel asked, pushing Lucien aside. "Let's get you inside, honey."

"He just came out of nowhere," Faith said, disoriented. "I didn't . . . I didn't know what to do."

"It's okay," Angel said, guiding her toward the house. "You're safe now."

"We need to call the police," Lucien said, following them.

Angel turned around, her eyes burning with anger. "I'll call them once I get Faith settled."

"I can do it now," Lucien said, reaching for his cell.

"You've done more than enough," Angel said sharply.

Lucien continued up the steps behind them, not realizing how furious she was.

Guiding Faith inside, Angel blocked him from entering. "You need to go."

Lucien took a step back. "Are you okay?"

"Go home, Lucien."

"Wait a minute," he said, reaching for her arm.

Angel shrank away, and a look of terror came onto her face.

"What's wrong with you?" Lucien asked, dumbfounded by her hostile behavior.

"Go home," Angel said harshly, then closed the door in his face.

24

* * * * * * *

All Eyes on Me

Faith awakened from another round of fitful sleep. Shifting her weight on the bed, she frowned as the warm air billowing through the open French doors of Angel's bedroom brushed against her cheek. At first she wasn't sure why she was in such a foul mood, but remembered instantly when she heard the voice coming from the television.

"Good morning, Los Angeles," the tanned anchor said with appropriate self-importance. "We have breaking news to bring you on this unseasonably warm Christmas Eve morning."

Sitting on the edge of the bed, Angel gasped when a photo of Faith appeared on the screen. "Son of a bitch."

"KCAL has learned that rising star Faith Molaney was attacked last night outside the home of her *Brave New World* costar, Angel Hart."

Faith sat up, focusing her sleep-deprived eyes on the screen.

"According to sources inside the Hollywood Police Department, the as yet unidentified assailant accosted the young starlet shortly before nine o'clock last night."

"This isn't happening," Faith said in a stunned whisper.

"Molaney had been staying with Hart since a break-in at her Westwood apartment a week ago. Besides riffling through the young starlet's lingerie, the intruder . . ."

Holding her breath Faith thought, *Please don't say it.*

". . . masturbated on Molaney's bed."

Faith winced. So much for hoping.

"What?" Angel asked snatching up the ringing phone. "How did you get this number?" she demanded. "No, we don't have a comment. . . . What did I just say?"

Faith looked over at her, then back at the television. Everything seemed so surreal. It was as if she had stepped out of her own body and was a spectator sitting on the sidelines, watching helplessly as her life played out like a movie of the week.

"Don't call here again!"

Groaning as the phone slammed against the receiver, Faith closed her eyes, praying that when she reopened them, she'd awaken from this horrible dream. No such luck.

"It was Luscious Alexander, a writer on *Brave New World*, who came to Molaney's aid . . ."

"It's Lucien," Angel barked at the screen. "You hounds can't even get minor details straight."

The telephone started ringing again.

"Neither Molaney, Hart nor their respective agents have returned our calls for comment . . ."

Glaring at the television Angel reached for the phone, stopping abruptly before her hand touched the receiver. She let the answering machine pick up the call instead.

"Stay tuned to KCAL for continuing coverage," the anchor said as a graphic popped up on the screen:

WHO ATTACKED FAITH?

"When something breaks . . . you'll hear it here . . . first," the anchor promised.

Pointing the remote at the screen, Angel replied, "I'm sure we will, you blood-sucking bastard."

Faith sat stone still as the walls began to close in around her. She wanted to crawl under the bed and stay there until the madness stopped.

"You okay?" Angel asked.

Faith nodded weakly as she made her way over to the window. Wrapping her arms around herself tightly, she gazed up at the morning sky. How had her new life gotten so far off course so quickly? she wondered. Was she so unworthy of being loved and respected? She really had tried to do things right this time. Okay, she'd been having an affair with a married man, but she'd ended that. That had to be worth something.

"Stop calling here, you vultures," Angel growled when the cell phone joined in the concert of noise. "Don't answer it," she said, heading into the bathroom.

Faith stared at the Hollywood sign in the distance, not hearing a word being spoken. A single tear trickled down her cheek. She felt utterly alone.

Distracted, she glanced over at the nightstand as the telephone rang again. Without thinking, she picked it up. "Hello?"

"Faith?" Jill asked quickly. "Is that you?"

"Mm-hmm."

"Let me in before I have to put my foot up in one of these barracudas' asses for pointing a camera in my face."

Faith glanced around the empty room. "Angel?" she called out. Hearing the sound of the shower, she looked at the phone, not sure what to do.

"Are you still there?" Jill asked, agitated.

"I'm here."

"Let me in."

Faith went to the door, taking care to stand out of view as she opened it.

"Don't you people have something better to do?" Jill shouted at the horde of reporters snapping her picture. "It's a fucking zoo out there," she said as she crossed the threshold. "I counted at least six news trucks as I pulled in."

Faith sat down on the sofa, lost in her own sadness.

"Are you all right?" Jill asked, concerned.

"Mm-hmm," Faith said unconvincingly.

"This is not your fault," Jill said, taking a seat beside her. "You are not responsible for this. You have to believe that."

"I know," Faith said, though she didn't believe it. As far as she was concerned, it was her fault. The bad karma she'd generated from her affair with a married man made her deserving of being violated by the stalker last night, and the media today.

Angel entered the living room. "When did you get here?"

"Just a few minutes ago," Jill said, eyeing the towel wrapped around her head.

"You want some coffee?" Angel asked.

"I'll get it," Jill said, standing. She turned to Faith. "You want some coffee?"

"No, thanks."

"What about something to eat? You hungry?"

Faith shook her head.

"Sweetie, you need to eat," Jill said. "I'll make you an omelet. Angel, you want anything?"

"No, thanks."

Jill was barely out of the room when the doorbell sounded again.

"Who is it?" Angel asked roughly.

"It's Ben."

Angel let him inside.

"Good morning," he said, then made his way over to Faith. "How you holding up?" he asked, giving her shoulder a gentle squeeze.

"I'm okay."

Ben took a seat in the chair. "I know you may not feel like dealing with much right now," he said, eyeing Faith. "But we really ought to give some thought to your safety."

Faith wasn't listening to a word he said. Her thoughts turned to Randall. How she wished he was here to hold her in his arms right now. Whenever he was near she always felt better. The time they'd shared in Malibu over the Thanksgiving holiday had given her such hope for the future. Why would God bring her so close to heaven, only to send her free-falling even deeper into the abyss of lonely despair?

"What do you think about that?" Ben asked. "Faith? You with us?"

"I'm sorry," she said, trying to pay attention. "What did you say?"

"I asked you what you thought about me hiring a bodyguard."

"For who?" Faith asked.

Ben gave her a strange look. "For you."

"I don't think that's going to be necessary," Faith said, squirming in her seat. "I should get ready for the Christmas party."

Angel's brow furrowed. "The producers will surely understand if you take a pass on it."

"I'm going," Faith said. "I promised those kids I'd be there, and no overzealous fan is going to stop me from keeping that promise."

"Okay," Angel said uneasily. "Will you at least consider Ben's offer to hire you a bodyguard?"

"I appreciate the offer, and the concern that prompted it," Faith said. "But I think you're both making a mountain out of a molehill."

Angel wasn't giving up. "Will you just humor us?"

"No," Faith snapped. "I have no intention of letting a man make me feel like a victim again," she said, shaking her head resolutely. "No bodyguards."

Ben and Angel exchanged concerned looks, but didn't fight her.

"I'm gonna go get ready." Faith said, then walked out of the room.

25

* * * * * * * *

Apples from Pear Trees

"Momma, it's a Christmas party for foster children," Erika said, tossing the fur-lined black dress on the bed. "I don't need a stylist to help dress me for it."

"This is so much more than handing out a few cheap gifts to some poor brats," Victoria said, motioning for Sasha to continue unpacking the outfits from which she wanted her daughter to choose. "The media is going to be camped out in droves now that Goldilocks has managed to attract a stalker. This is the perfect opportunity for you to reassert yourself as the *real* star of that show," she said. "Now come over here and pick out something fabulous."

Erika sighed tiredly as she walked over to the bed. Feeling like a bloated mad cow, trying on tons of expensive, too tight clothing was the last thing she was interested in doing.

"Yes. No. No. Maybe," Victoria said, pointing at each of the outfits Sasha held up for her review. She looked over at Erika, her eyes flickering with delight. "You need to steal the show today."

Erika scowled. "Momma, no one will ever accuse me of being a fan of Faith Molaney, but I wouldn't wish what happened to her on my worst enemy."

"She *is* your worst enemy," Victoria said. "If you ask me, that fake-friendly bitch got what she deserved."

"But I didn't ask you," Erika snarled under her breath.

"What was that?" Victoria asked, giving her daughter the evil eye.

"Nothing," Erika mumbled as she retrieved from her closet the simple black pantsuit she'd already chosen to wear.

"Oh, that's awful," Victoria cringed. "And about as flattering to your figure as that frumpy terry cloth bathrobe you're wearing now," she said, taking the suit from Erika and hurling it onto the bed. She turned to the stylist. "Don't you agree?"

Sasha offered his boss's boss a courteous smile, but kept his opinion to himself. It was Erika, after all, who signed his checks.

"Oooh . . . *yummy*," Victoria cooed, snatching a red rhinestone beaded suit from Sasha's hands. She walked over to the mirror with it. "This would look great on me," she said, taking off the sheer purple blouse and matching purple miniskirt she was wearing.

"Mother!" Erika shrieked as Victoria vamped in front of the mirror in her bra and panties.

Victoria slapped her firm behind. "Not too shabby for fifty, huh?" She smiled proudly, admiring her seminaked self in the mirror.

Erika tightened the belt of her terry cloth robe self-consciously. "You're fifty-five."

Sasha held Victoria's purse in the air. "Someone's ringing."

"Be a lamb," Victoria said, signaling for him to bring it to her.

"Here you go."

"*Hellooo*," Victoria sang into the cell phone.

"Listen, I'm sorry my mother wasted your time bringing you out here," Erika said to Sasha quietly. She was quite accustomed to apologizing to others for Victoria's actions.

"No need to apologize, darling," he said with a knowing wink. "I have a mother too."

Erika smiled gratefully.

Sasha removed another outfit from the garment bag. "How about this one?"

Erika studied the two-piece black pantsuit with mink trim. "This one's not too bad," she said, then lowered her voice. "What size is it?"

"Everything's a four," Sasha said, handing Erika the suit. "Your usual."

Victoria glanced back over her shoulder. "Of course I miss you too, love," she said absentmindedly into the phone.

Feeling her mother's eyes on her, Erika inched closer to Sasha, giving him a carefully raised brow. She mouthed, "Could you get it for me in an eight?"

"Certainly," he whispered back.

Victoria covered the phone with her hand. "Why the hell would you want an eight?" she asked rudely, then purred into the phone. "Oh, Charles, that sounds absolutely wonderful."

Erika ignored the question. "Could you have someone courier-service the eight in time for the party?"

"Of course," Sasha said, reaching for his cell.

"That was your horny-ass stepfather," Victoria said, scowling as she dropped the phone back into her purse. "I rue the day they ever created Viagra."

"It'll be here in an hour," Sasha said to Erika.

"What'll be here in an hour?" Victoria asked.

"I found something to wear," Erika said.

"Let's see," Victoria said, ready to give her opinion on the selected item.

Erika held up the suit and prayed her mother wouldn't insist she try it on.

"Well, aren't you going to try it on?" Victoria asked with a raised brow.

"It's got a snag," Erika lied. "Sasha's having another one sent over."

Victoria turned to the stylist. "A snag," she said disapprovingly.

"It was my fault," Erika said, hoping to spare Sasha from her mother's wrath. "I'll make it to the studio with time to spare."

Victoria glanced down at her watch. "Well, I don't have time to wait. I've got to be at the airport to retrieve my oversexed husband in exactly forty-five minutes," she said, redressing in her own clothes.

"Traffic is going to be a mess," Erika said, brightening. "You better get going."

Victoria turned from the mirror, considering the too-happy look on her daughter's face. "Not so fast," she said, returning to the bed. Victoria picked up the supposedly snagged suit. "Try it on anyway," she said smoothly. "We can at least get some idea of what it looks like on you."

"It's fine. Mother . . . really," Erika said, backing up as Victoria approached her with the suit. "What are you doing?"

Snatching open the robe, Victoria growled, "Tell me you've done what we agreed you would do?"

Sasha gasped when he saw Erika's stomach.

"Well, I'll be damned," Victoria said with contempt. "How is it possible for you to be so stupid . . . with me for a mother, no less?"

Erika stood humiliated and thoroughly afraid. "Please, Momma, try to understand."

"Understand, my ass!" Victoria shouted. "Do you have any idea how tacky this is going to look to the public?"

Sasha backed away from the dueling mother and daughter.

"I really don't care how it looks," Erika said, retying her robe.

"Well, I do," Victoria said. "You stupid, stupid girl!" she screamed at Erika. "It's one thing to marry a white man. It's a totally different story to have a married white man's baby!"

Sasha bustled over to the opposite side of the room, busying himself with the clothes.

Turning from her mother, Erika went over to the window. "I've decided to keep the baby, Momma."

"The hell you are!" Victoria's head snapped toward Sasha. "You're not hearing any of this."

"Of course not," he said, well aware that the confidentiality agreement Victoria forced everyone working for her daughter to sign precluded him from sharing this tasty little morsel with anyone.

"I will not allow you to have this baby."

Erika continued looking out at the estate that her income had made possible. "If I want to have *my* baby, there's nothing you can do to stop me."

Victoria slithered up behind her. "I'll push you down a flight of stairs myself if that's what it'll take to keep you from making the biggest mistake of your life."

Erika blinked.

Sasha gasped.

Victoria spun around. "Get out!"

Dropping the pile of suits to the floor, Sasha raced from the room.

Victoria turned back to Erika. "There's nothing I wouldn't do for you . . . *nothing*," she said with haunting sincerity. "Now, I need you to do this one thing for me. Can you do this for me?"

Erika nodded, giving in.

Victoria kissed her gently on the cheek. "It's for the best, you'll see," she said. She picked up her purse from the chair. "I'll make the appointment with Dr. Sheridan," Victoria said, then walked out of the bedroom.

Erika sighed. "Yes, Mother."

26
* * * * * * * *

I'm O-Freakin'-K

ngel frowned as she pulled up to the gates of Wellington Broadcasting's Manhattan Beach production studios. "Fucking vultures," she said, maneuvering through the obstacle course of television crews and photographers blocking the main entrance. She glanced over at the passenger seat. "You ready?"

Faith swallowed as she eyed the media crowds. "As ready as I'll ever be."

"It's them!" a KNBC reporter screamed, directing her crew toward the approaching Jaguar. "Get 'em on camera!"

Instantly, the car was surrounded.

"Faith, how you are holding up?" the reporter asked, shoving a microphone into her stunned face.

How the fuck do you think she's holding up, you skinny skank? Angel thought as she glared at the offending voyeur through her red-tinted sunglasses.

Shielding her face from the blinding camera flashes exploding like gunfire outside her open window, Faith said nothing.

"Ms. Hart, can you give us a comment?" a writer from the *L.A. Times* yelled, almost pushing a competitor to the ground.

"Please move so we can pass," Angel said with a snarl.

The man turned his attention back to Faith. "Is it true that your attacker declared that if he couldn't have you, no one would?"

Angel glowered at him. Apparently, the truth wasn't titillating enough for these people. They were now making up "facts" as they went along to help spice up the spectacle they'd made out of Faith's personal pain.

"Are you afraid he'll try again?"

Faith shuddered, but had the presence of mind not to respond.

The questions continued to come in rapid succession.

"Do you think this will have any impact on your career?"

"Is it true that you and Lucien Alexander are dating?"

"That's it!" Angel snapped. "She said 'no comment.' Now get away from my car!"

"Come on, Ms. Hart," one of the reporters said, frustrated. "You have to give us something . . . this is a big story."

Angel could feel her blood rising to the boiling point as the pack of greedy wolves prodded her and Faith to give them something they somehow believed it was their right to have. The nerve of these people was beyond her. Yes, she and Faith were actresses, which by definition meant they were in the business of courting the media's attention. But this was different. This wasn't about some movie, or season premiere. Faith had just been through a horrendous experience, and none of these bastards gave a damn about her pain.

"Here's a comment for you," Angel said, revving up the engine. "Move the fuck away or I'll run you over!" She slammed her foot into the gas pedal, sending the reporters scattering like bugs as she sped past them into the lot.

Faith was clearly impressed as they got out of the car and made their way toward the back entrance.

Ernesto rushed toward them as they entered the building. "Mommie, are you okay?" he asked, hugging Faith.

"I'm fine," she said.

Ernesto took Faith by the hand, leading her toward the makeup suite.

Angel sighed as she followed. It was only two o'clock, but the day had already proven to be a long one. And there was still the dinner at Jill's to get through later. She had an urge to call her and cancel.

"When Jackson called me from the police station to tell me what had happened, my mouth just fell to the floor," Ernesto said, talking a mile a minute. "Here you go, sweetie."

"Thanks," Angel said as he handed her a red Santa hat.

Ernesto turned back to Faith. "You must have been so scared."

"I think I may have overreacted." she said sheepishly. "The guy was probably just trying to get my autograph and I freaked."

"Well, I would freak too," Ernesto said, placing the hat on Faith's head. "If some crazed lunatic jumped out of a tree in the dead of night, I would pee my pants." He shivered at the thought. "If Angel and Lucien hadn't come to your rescue, who knows what that freak might—"

Angel shot Ernesto a look that stopped him cold.

Embarrassed, he glanced down at his watch. "Where is Erika?" he asked, quickly changing the subject.

"I'm right here," she said, rushing through the door.

"Here," Ernesto said, handing her a third hat. "Hurry up."

When Angel saw Erika easing her way over toward Faith, her first thought was to intervene. But something told her to let this one play out on its own.

"Hello."

"Erika," Faith said, continuing to adjust the hat in the mirror.

Erika shifted her weight from one leg to the other as she stood behind her. It was as if she wanted to say something but couldn't bring her lips to form the words.

Finally, Faith turned to face her. "Did you want something?" she asked coolly.

Angel and Ernesto both swallowed.

"I just wanted to . . . umm," Erika said, struggling. She took a nervous breath. "Are you okay?"

Faith was taken aback. "I'm okay."

"Good, well . . ." Erika said, hesitating. "Okay, then," she said, turning to walk away.

"Erika?"

"Yes?"

Faith smiled. "Thank you."

Erika's lips curled into something resembling a smile as well. "You're welcome."

Angel exhaled a sigh of relief as the production assistant popped her head into the room. "Ladies, are you ready?"

Erika and Faith now standing on either side of her, Angel smiled at her costars. "We're ready."

The picture of charmed-life perfection, the three women strolled onto the set to the enthusiastic cheers of the foster children gathered to meet them. For the next hour, Angel, Erika and Faith were able to put their own problems behind them, enjoying their roles as Santa's helpers.

"Merry Christmas," Faith said, presenting an oddly shaped gift to one of the children.

The little boy looked at her with the kind of awe that made adults feel like superheroes. "Thank you, miss."

Faith smiled into his wide eyes. "You are very welcome."

"Let me do that for you," Angel said, refilling the cup of cider.

"Thank you," the little girl said before dashing away.

"No running," Angel said, chuckling to herself. She sounded like Jill overprotecting Jasmine or Junior.

Her expression hardened when she noticed Randall standing in the far corner, his eyes glued on Faith as she made her way around the set handing out gifts. He looked like a lovelorn teenager. Angel almost felt sorry for the man. If she didn't know better, she'd have sworn he really did love Faith.

"Look alive, Kenyatta," Erika said as she strutted past, the young girl fast on her heels.

Angel couldn't help but smile. From the moment the girl had laid eyes on Erika, she'd been clinging to her like a child to its mother. Surprisingly, Erika didn't seem to mind the attention one bit.

Angel studied the happy faces of the children running around the studio. Despite lives filled with more pain than any child should know, they found reason to smile. She was reminded how, if you looked hard enough, joy could be gleaned even in the worst of times.

"Hey, you," said Lucien.

"I didn't see you standing there," Angel said, flinching. The warm holiday cheer she was feeling not a moment ago was instantly replaced by the coldness of harsh reality.

"Didn't mean to scare you."

Angel looked down at Lucien's bandaged hand.

"It looks worse than it really is," he said with a sly grin.

Staring into his eyes, Angel searched for any residue of the monster she'd seen the night before.

Lucien gave her a curious look. "Is something the matter?"

Angel took a breath, bracing herself before responding. "What happened to you last night?"

"What do you mean?" Lucien asked, confused.

"You almost killed a man," Angel said, recoiling at the memory. "That doesn't bother you at all?"

"Is that what your behavior was about last night?"

Angel drew back. "*My* behavior."

"The way you dismissed me like the hired help," Lucien said acerbically.

"That's not what I did," Angel said. "Are you not at all bothered by your actions last night?"

"You're mad at me for defending Faith?"

"Of course not," Angel said. "But I do think the level of punishment you were dealing out was totally uncalled for."

Lucien lurched back. "What?"

"You tried to kill that man—"

"What would you rather I'd done, Angel?" Lucien asked, interrupting. "Tap the guy on the shoulder and say, 'Ah, excuse me mister stalker, but would you mind terribly taking your hands off the young lady . . . *please*?' "

Angel didn't appreciate the sarcasm one bit. "You could have simply restrained him until the police arrived," she said snappishly.

Lucien looked at her as if she was speaking in a foreign tongue.

"Do you have any idea how many times you hit that man?"

"I don't care how many times I hit him," Lucien said, becoming angry. He tried to compose himself. "Look, I'm not sure why you're having such a problem with what I did last night, but I don't."

Ernesto rushed over, inserting himself between them. "Could you two decaffeinate it please?" he asked, nodding toward the group of kids playing nearby. "You're going to scare the babies."

Lucien stared at Angel disbelievingly. "I'm outta here."

Ernesto eyed him as he stormed off. "What was that all about?"

Angel's attention had already shifted to Randall and Faith, who appeared to be having a heated discussion in the back corner of the studio. "About last night," she said distracted.

"What about last—?" Ernesto asked, but Angel was already marching across the studio. "Ai . . . this can't be good."

"I don't want to talk," Faith said, pulling away from Randall.

"Please just hear me out," he said.

Angel approached them. "Let go of her."

"This isn't your business," Randall said, maintaining his hold on Faith. "I'm not trying to upset—"

"I said, let her go!" Angel said, pushing his hand away roughly.

Surprised, Randall turned to Angel. "I'm going to act like you didn't . . ." He hesitated when Faith ran away in tears. He was about to go after her, but Angel stopped him.

"Don't you think you've caused her enough pain?" she asked.

Randall gave her a dismissive wave of the hand, moving to get around her. "This doesn't concern you."

"Like hell it doesn't," Angel said, refusing to get out of his way.

Standing a few steps behind them, Jasper observed the unfolding drama with keen interest.

"Move, Ms. Hart," Randall said, glaring at Angel.

She stood her ground. "I'm not going to let you hurt her."

Jasper moved in quickly, grabbing Angel by the arm. "Get control of yourself this instant, young lady," he whispered in her ear. "You are making a scene."

Angel glared down at his hand. She was about to show the old man what a real scene looked like, until she noticed the nervous stares of the kids starting to gather around them. Forcing her lips into a tight smile, she looked Jasper straight in the eye, "Take your hands off of me . . . *now.*"

"Careful, dear," he advised, smiling back. "You don't want to go to battle with me.

"Is that a fact?" Angel laughed for the kids' benefit. "You've got two seconds to get your paws off me," she said. "One . . ."

Jasper removed his hand.

"Thank you," Angel said, then turned to Randall. "If there is an ounce of decency in you," she said, still smiling, "you'll leave that girl alone."

"I just want to talk to her—"

Angel cut him off. "Go talk to your wife instead."

Stunned, Randall didn't say a word. Jasper was about to interject, but Angel's eyes dared him to open his mouth.

"Now, if you gentlemen will kindly step to one side," she said, turning to leave, "my friend needs me."

27

* * * * * * *

Clean Break

Glen Jr. glanced back over his shoulder. "You wanna play the winner, Auntie Angel?" he asked as he and Jasmine sat perched in front of the plasma-screen TV.

"No, thanks," Angel said. "I've never played that one."

"I can teach you," Junior offered.

Jasmine elbowed him playfully. "After I finish schooling you."

"Yeah, right," Junior countered.

"Ha!" Jasmine said, frantically manipulating the joystick. "Die, pirate, die!"

Jill shook her head in feigned annoyance as she handed Angel the cup of eggnog. "I put a little kick in it for you."

"Thanks," Angel said, taking a sip. "Ah, yes . . . just how I like it."

Jill sat down on the sofa beside her.

"No fair!" Junior yelled out as his sister decimated another of his pirates. "Your hands are bigger than mine."

"In your face!" Jasmine said, slamming the joystick down on the floor like a football in the end zone. She rose to her feet, doing a victory dance. "*Loooooserrrr*," she sang out, taunting her little brother.

Junior bolted up from the floor. "Shut up," he said, pushing her. "You only won 'cause you cheated."

Jasmine shoved him back. "And you're just mad 'cause you're a *loooo—*"

Jill's head snapped toward her bickering offspring. "If you two can't play without World War III breaking out over there, I will put that Xbox away . . . for good." She gave them the dreaded eye. "Am I making myself clear?"

Jasmine and Junior nodded in unison. "Yes, ma'am."

A melancholy smile spread across Angel's face as she watched. She loved spending the holidays with Jill and her family, but it was always a bittersweet time for her. Growing up, Christmas had been her favorite time of the year—until her mother's death, anyway. During the holiday, even her father managed to be on his best behavior. If only for a couple of weeks, Steven and Marcella worked together to ensure that their daughter's Christmas would be a happy one. Angel loved helping her mother prepare the big dinner. They'd laugh, sing and talk the entire time. The smell of ham and turkey, candied yams and sweet potato pies, made from scratch, filled the air with mouth-watering aromas.

"Ben said he and Phallon might be a little late." Jill glanced down at her wristwatch. "But Glen's family should be here by now." She looked over at her daughter, playing another round with Junior. "Jaz, honey, will you go ask your father to call his mom and make sure everything's okay?"

She continued playing. "As soon as we—"

"Now," Jill ordered.

"Yes, ma'am," Jasmine said, bounding to her feet.

Angel sighed longingly as she raised the cup to her lips. She would give anything for one more chance to hug her mother, smell her sweet perfume, wrap herself snugly in the love that radiated from those kindly brown eyes.

"Hello?" Jill said, snapping her fingers. "Earth to Angel."

"I'm sorry," Angel said, lost in thought. "What did you say?"

"I said I understand why Faith decided not to come, bless her heart," Jill said with empathy. "But where's Lucien?"

Angel's face darkened. "He's not coming."

"That much I get," Jill said sardonically. "Why not?" she asked, noting Angel's tense expression. "Did something happen?"

"Let's just say he proved not to be the man I thought he was," Angel said, hoping that would be the end of it. With everything going on, she hadn't had an opportunity to go into detail with Jill about what had transpired. As far as she was concerned she never needed to speak of the ugliness again.

"Why isn't Lucien the man you thought he was?" Jill asked, not willing to drop the subject.

Angel cut her eyes. "He just isn't."

"Will you tell me what happened please?" Jill pressed.

"Lucien almost killed that man," Angel blurted out.

Jill drew back.

"No, let me restate that," Angel said. "Lucien *tried* to kill that man."

"Angel, he was protecting Faith from a man who, for all he knew, was a deranged killer," Jill said, defending Lucien. "Of course he was going to use some force."

"Appropriate force is one thing," Angel said. "Lucien went over the line. Way over."

Jill listened intently as her best friend recounted the violent events that had soured her on Lucien.

"Even after he had the guy down—who wasn't fighting back, by the way—" Angel said darkly, "Lucien kept beating him, and beating him. By the time I finally pulled him off, the guy was covered in a pool of his own blood."

Jill cringed. "Well, it wasn't as if Lucien didn't have just cause—"

"There was no excuse for what he did to that man," Angel snapped. "As far as I'm concerned, anything Lucien and I *might* have had is over."

"Angel, I appreciate your discomfort over what happened," Jill said, eyeing her friend incredulously. "But don't you think you're being a bit extreme?"

"No, I don't," Angel said. "You know how I feel about men who are too fucking weak—" she said, catching herself when she caught Glen Jr.'s curious eye.

"Uh . . . baby, will you go check on your daddy for me," Jill said, giving her son an appreciative smile.

Junior was already halfway out of the room before she'd finished. "Yes, ma'am."

"Thank you," Jill said, turning back to Angel. "What is this really about?"

"What do you mean?" Angel asked guardedly.

"Are you really so outraged by Lucien's behavior?" Jill asked, studying her closely. "Or are you just looking for any excuse—"

To Angel's relief, her cell phone started ringing. Glancing down at the caller ID, she frowned. "What the hell does that woman want?"

"Who?" Jill asked.

"My agent," Angel said. "Do you mind?"

"Take your call," Jill said, rising from the chair. "I need to go make sure the two Glens aren't burning down my kitchen."

"Raise those men to your hand, girl," Angel said, laughing as she flipped open the phone. "Yes, Hel—"

"What have you done?"

Angel stared at the phone. "Excuse me?"

"I just got off the phone with a livid Jasper Wellington!" Helen said frostily. "He's threatening to blackball me and this entire agency if I don't get you in check."

"Get me in check?"

"Are you trying to torpedo your career?" Helen asked. "How could you to do something so bloody stupid?"

Angel leapt from the sofa. "Hold up!" she yelled into the phone. "Who the fuck do you think you're talking to like—?"

"I don't think you fully understand the severity of this situation."

"And I don't think you fully understand that you work for me, Helen," Angel roared back. "Not the other way around."

"Your outburst at the studio today caused Mr. Wellington a great amount of discomfort."

"Don't blame me for the discomfort of the almighty Jasper Wellington."

"I'm not blaming you, Angel."

"You just did."

"Then you misheard—"

"I didn't mishear shit!"

Helen took an exacerbated breath. "Mr. Wellington expects an apology," she said.

Angel laughed. "Oh, *that's* gonna happen."

"I *strongly* suggest you swallow your pride and apologize to Mr. Wellington the first chance—"

"I'm not apologizing to that man for a damned thing," Angel said flatly.

"Need I remind you that you work for Mr. Wellington's network?"

"And, need I remind you *again* that you work for me, Helen, *not* Jasper Wellington?"

"Do you have any idea what your little outburst could mean to my company's reputation?"

Angel's brow rose as a very appealing idea popped into her head. "Hold, please," she said, interrupting Helen. She hit the SEND button, speed-dialing Ben. "Hey, it's me. . . . Everything's fine," she said hastily. "Listen, does your offer to represent me still stand?" Angel smiled, pleased at his answer. "Great. I'll call you back in a few." She hit the SEND button again. "I'm back."

"We need to correct this situation immediately," Helen said, not missing a beat.

"I totally agree."

Helen exhaled a relieved breath. "I'm glad you've come to your senses—"

"You're fired."

"Wha . . . what did you just say?" Helen asked, staggered.

"You heard me," Angel said. "I should have gotten rid of you and that fake British accent a long time ago."

"Dear, I realize these past days have taken a toll on you," Helen said in that condescending tone that always made Angel want to bitch-slap her. "But I implore you to take a breath, then give some real consideration to what your next steps could mean to your career."

"Buh-bye, Helen," Angel said, then closed the phone.

"Is everything okay, Auntie Angel?" Junior asked, standing in the doorway.

"It is now," she said, giving him a huge wink. "Hey, you still interested in teaching me how to play that video game?"

The pensive look on his face morphed into a wide smile. "Sure."

Angel followed him over to the Xbox. "Then let's do this."

28

* * * * * * * *

To Thine Own Self . . .

"Grandma, did she call yet?"

"Dammit, little girl!" Ethel yelled at Faith as she wiped the vodka from her shirt. "How many times have I told you about running into this house screaming like a lunatic?" she admonished. "You made me spill my damned drink."

The smile that had been plastered across Faith's young face that entire day disappeared. "Sorry, Grandma," she said. "Did she call?"

"Did who call?"

"Momma," Faith said. "She said she'd call me on my birthday."

Ethel took another swig of her drink. "Well, she not gonna call you, so go on outside and play or something."

"Can I just stay inside and wait for Momma's call?" Faith asked pleadingly. "I hardly get to talk to her since she moved to Nashville."

"Don't you defy me, little girl," Ethel said, turning away so Faith wouldn't see the tears forming in her eyes. "You go on and do like I said."

Faith didn't budge. "I want to talk to my momma," she said defiantly.

Ethel snatched her by the arms. "You can't talk to somebody who's dead!" she shouted.

Faith let out a horrified gasp. "Don't say that!" She started swinging wildly at her grandmother. "How could you be so cruel to say something like that?"

Relenting, Ethel pulled a sobbing Faith into her arms, offering her two things she'd never offered before or would again—compassion and understanding.

"I didn't want to tell you like this," Ethel said sympathetically.

Faith looked up at her grandmother with strangely vacant eyes.

"I'm sorry, baby," Ethel said, hugging her. "I'm so sorry."

*   *   *

Shaking off the intense memory, Faith picked up the phone. Not certain if she was doing the right thing, she dialed the number she still knew by heart. Tonight she needed to belong to someone.

"Yeah," the gruff voice answered.

"Merry Christmas!" Faith said brightly.

There was no response on the other end of the line.

Faith's heart sank, but she pressed forward. "Grammy, are you there?" she asked, still holding out.

"Who is this?" Ethel asked stiffly.

"It's me . . . Faith."

After a few more seconds of silence, Ethel responded, "What do you want?"

"I just wanted . . ." Faith, hesitated, her words sticking in her dry throat. Gripping the phone tighter, she exhaled. "Have you had a chance to see the show?"

"Hang on," Ethel said, covering the phone. "Give me a minute," her muffled voice instructed someone.

Faith closed her eyes as a feeling of emptiness chilled her entire body. What she wouldn't give to know what it felt like to be a part of a big, loving family like the ones she saw in the movies. Just once she wished Ethel could find it in her heart to say something kind or supportive. Tell her that she was proud of her. Wish her well. Was that really so much to ask for?

"You still there?"

Her bottom lip trembling, Faith replied. "I'm still here, Gram."

"I asked you, what show."

"*Brave New World* on WBN," Faith said, trying to remain upbeat.

"Never heard of it," Ethel said, bored.

Faith steadied her breathing as she leaned back in the sofa. "I thought I mentioned it in the last letter I sent you," she said, knowing full well she'd expended at least two pages worth of ink on the subject. "But maybe I forgot to mention—"

"Hold your horses, big fella," Ethel instructed her guest. "You know what I think about you being in that business," she said into the phone. "My feelings haven't changed."

"I know, Gram." Faith's voice was paper thin. "But this is a national show. They're paying me thirty thousand dollars a week," she said, hoping the figure might serve as some sort of validation.

"You must be showing your tits or something," Ethel said derisively. "Why you're so hellbent on following in your mother's sad footsteps I'll never understand."

The comment caught Faith off guard. "I'm nothing like her," she said, feeling the need to defend herself. "This is legitimate. The producers say I'm very good at it too."

Holding the phone to her ear, Faith gazed around Angel's elegantly appointed living room. She had done it. She'd made her dream come true. She was a costar on a hit television show. The whole world knew her name. All of the hard work, the speech lessons and acting workshops, the late nights and early rises had paid off, just as she knew they would.

"Why did you call me?"

Faith lowered her head. Even though she knew that no answer she gave would be an acceptable one, she tried anyway. "I know how you feel about me being an actress, Gram, but I've made my choice," Faith said, calling up her own inner strength. "You're all the family I have—"

"Don't!" Ethel barked.

"Grammy, please, for once can you just be happy for me?" Faith implored. "This is what I've always wanted—"

"How can you expect me to be happy for you?" Ethel asked. "You are so selfish and starved for attention. Just like your mother. . . ."

As she sat there being made to feel worthless, Faith had an epiphany. Ethel was never going to give her the love and validation she so desperately craved. The sooner she accepted that fact, the sooner she would find acceptance from a more important source . . . herself.

"I love you, Grammy. I won't bother you again."

Faith hung up the phone.

29

*　*　*　*　*　*　*

Mother, May I?

The Oak Grove Women's Center administered its highly sought-after services with strictly enforced secrecy. Just behind a six-foot cement wall surrounding the fifty-acre campus, a sprawl of buildings housed clinics, spas, residential bungalows and surgical suites. The famous, infamous or otherwise image-protective women who used the facility affectionately referred to it as the "other" Magic Kingdom. From breast reduction to liposuction, drug rehabilitation to drug distribution, Oak Grove was the ultimate in one-stop shopping for those rich enough to afford its services.

"Ms. Dee Vah is here for her appointment," the driver spoke into the black box.

"Suite 10," the box answered back.

The steel gates separated, allowing the limousine to enter the grounds. Oak Grove didn't do walk-ins.

Victoria glanced over at Erika through her Jackie O. sunglasses. "By this time tomorrow it'll all be over."

Erika continued staring out the tinted window.

The driver opened the door.

Stepping out of the limo, Erika turned back to her mother. "I want to do this alone."

Victoria gave her a "you must be out of your mind" stare as she scooted toward the door.

Erika blocked her from getting out. "I said *alone*."

Victoria snatched off her sunglasses, raising her brow at her insolent offspring. "I'm going in with you," she said firmly. "And that's final, young lady."

"Then I'm not doing it," Erika said, her hands fastened on her hips.

"Oh, yes you are," Victoria insisted. "And I'm coming in with you to make sure that you do."

Erika glared into the limousine. It was bad enough her mother had strong-armed her into doing this in the first place. Now the power-greedy oppressor wanted the added satisfaction of watching it happen. "Don't push me, Mother . . . not today," she said in a stern tone that sent Victoria drawing back into the leather seat.

Power was a strange commodity. It wasn't something that was taken from you but something you gave away. And once gone, it was terribly difficult to get back.

Victoria studied her daughter's face for any trace of weakness. "Fine," she said, putting her sunglasses back on. "Whatever you think is best."

Erika turned to the driver. "Please take my mother to *her* home," she said, then began walking toward the suite. "I'll call when I'm ready to be picked up."

*   *   *

After changing into the gown the nurse had given her, Erika hopped up onto the examining table, careful not to tear the paper covering. She lowered her hands into her lap, feeling dejected. Soon it would be over. Things would be back to normal. Her life would return to the empty void it had been before.

Swinging her legs restlessly, Erika glanced around the room, searching for something to concentrate on besides the incessant pounding in her head. The place was a cold, sterile bore. She looked over at the door, annoyed. Where the hell was that damned doctor?

The flutter inside her abdomen gave Erika a start. She fought against the instinct to put her hand on her stomach, instead shutting her eyes tightly, praying the movement inside her would cease.

Erika raised her hand to her face, tracing the outline of her full nose with her index finger. How would she react if her baby was born with a similar nose? Would she make the child feel as imperfect as Victoria had made her feel, or would she see the nose as the big beautiful perfection that God had intended it to be? Erika couldn't be sure. A tear rolled down her cheek.

Damn you, Momma.

"Hello, Ms. Bishop," the doctor said as she stepped inside the room.

"Dr. Sheridan."

"How are you—"

"Can we just get this done, please?"

"All right." Dr. Sheridan motioned for Erika to lie back on the table. "As I explained to Mrs. Steinberg, the dilation and extraction procedure is a two-part process," she said as she prodded between Erika's legs. "Today I'm going to insert a dilator into your cervix in order to soften and widen it. Then tomorrow you'll come back in and we'll perform the extraction. Now the extraction is—"

"I don't want to know the details," Erika said. "Just do it."

The doctor nodded understandingly. "Slide down a bit farther for me," she instructed. "You might feel a little—"

Flutter.

"Wait!" Erika cried, slamming her legs together so quickly the force sent the doctor tumbling from her stool.

"Are you okay?" Dr. Sheridan asked, pulling herself up off the floor.

Erika sat upright, burying her face in her hands. "I'm sorry," she said. "Just give me a minute to think."

"Are you having second thoughts?"

"I don't know."

"You don't have to go through with the procedure if you don't want to," Dr. Sheridan advised. "It's absolutely your choice."

Freedom of choice was a concept foreign to Erika. Over the span of her thirty-two years, she couldn't recall one instance of making a decision on her own, certainly not one as important as this. Choosing what to do with her life had always been Victoria's job. From career to the color and length of her hair, from where she lived to the clothing she wore, her mother had decided everything, just as she had decided Erika wasn't having this baby.

Flutter.

"You do have to make a choice soon, though," Dr. Sheridan cautioned.

Flutter.

"Why don't you take a day or two?" Dr. Sheridan suggested. "We can reschedule when you're ready."

Flutter.

Erika shook her head no. There was no need to reschedule. She had made her choice.

*   *   *

Randall took another sip of the vodka, then sighed. It was no use. As much as he wanted to drown his sorrows, the reality that his life was a complete mess was as clear to him now as it had been four drinks ago. So much wasted time amassing power and influence, unwilling to feel anything besides the incessant need to succeed. Then Faith stepped into his life and changed everything. She had awakened in his heart emotions he never thought he was capable of feeling. Things that were acceptable and tolerable before—a loveless marriage, sex for sport—now felt repugnant. Faith had inspired in Randall a desire to be a better man. Now she was gone and he felt lost without her.

Though he knew he could never go back to his old ways, he wasn't sure he could go forward either.

The sound of the cell phone snapped Randall out of his funk. He looked at the caller ID before answering. "What is it, Savanna?" he asked tiredly.

"Heather said you'd left the office for the day," she said. "When are you coming home?"

Randall took a long sip of his drink, closing his eyes as the vodka burned its way down his chest. "Soon," he said. "We need to talk."

"I forgive you, Randall," Savanna said stoically.

"It's not that simple."

"Darling, I love you," Savanna said. "We'll get through—"

Randall cut her off. "I need you to hear me out."

"I've spoken to our travel agent," Savanna continued, ignoring her husband. "She has put together the most delicious—"

"I don't want a fucking vacation, Savanna!" Randall shouted. "I want a divorce."

There was no response.

"Savanna, did you hear what I said?"

She took a labored breath. "I let you have your fun, Randall, but play time is over. Now you *need* to come home and be the husband we agreed you'd be when we got married."

"I can't do this anymore," Randall said. "I love Faith."

"She's gone," Savanna said. "She realized she was just another of your little flings. But I'm still here, Randall, ready and, despite everything, willing to continue loving you."

Randall shuddered at the thought. "But I'm not in love with you."

"But, I love you."

"I don't want to stay married—"

"Shut up!" Savanna roared. "Please . . . *please* don't do this to me."

"You need to listen—"

"No, *you* listen, Randall," she hissed. "That bitch is gone. And I'll be damned if I let that home-wrecking tramp ruin my life."

Randall stared at the phone in stunned disbelief. Though his wife was certainly justified in her dislike for Faith, the severity of her contempt floored him.

Sensing that she'd crossed the line, Savanna softened her tone. "This is just a bump in the road, *darling*," she said. "All marriages have them. But we'll get through this . . . *together*."

Randall heard the sound of the doorbell. "Ah, someone's at the door," he said dully.

"Ignore—"

"I'll be home in an hour," Randall said, not letting Savanna finish. "We'll finish this then."

Closing the cell phone, he rose from the sofa moving across the room like a shell-shocked zombie. Though he had no idea who would be at his door at two o'clock in the afternoon, he was too discombobulated to consider asking who was on the other side.

"We need to talk."

Randall glanced down at Erika's protruding stomach as she stepped inside the apartment. "Just perfect," he said, making a bee-line for the bar.

"Great to see you too," Erika said, closing the door behind her. "You look like hell, by the way."

Randall poured another glass of Grey Goose. The liquor wasn't affording him the escape he wanted, but on an empty stomach it was giving him one helluva headache. "I thought you were taking care of that."

Erika walked over to the bar. "By 'that,' I assume you mean the *life* growing inside of me," she said, pouring herself a glass of orange juice. "I've decided to keep the . . . my baby."

Randall sat down on the sofa, lowering his head into his hands.

"Don't get nervous," Erika said, taking a sip of the juice. "I don't expect anything from you. I am totally prepared to raise this child on my own. . . . It's probably better that I do, anyway."

"Better than having to tell the world that the father is an asshole," Randall said solemnly.

"Enough with the pity party, already." Erika lowered the glass onto the counter and walked over to the sofa. "You are not an asshole," she said matter of factly. "You're a triflin', selfish, spineless son of a bitch."

"Geez . . . thanks," Randall said tonelessly.

"*Loook*," Erika said, "I'm trying to be sensitive here, but as we both know, it goes against my nature." She took a seat beside Randall. "What I meant to say was that I'm not having this baby in the hopes that you'll divorce the old crow and marry me."

"Then why?" Randall asked. "You're not the most maternal person around."

Surprisingly, Erika didn't reach over and slap him across the face. Instead, she leaned back on the sofa and pondered his question. "I guess I'm doing it for the same reason you're such a funky mess right now . . . Love."

"Love," Randall sighed.

"I've never felt this way about anyone or anything in my life," Erika said, caressing her stomach. She chuckled nervously. "It's all a little scary if you really want to know the truth."

Randall listened intently as Erika continued. It wasn't lost on him that this was quite possibly the first conversation the two had ever shared that didn't involve screaming or sex . . . or both.

"I'm no saint," Erika said with a sardonic grin. "So there's a pretty good chance I'll screw my child up the way my mother fucked me up. But I don't think I could live with myself if I didn't try. My baby is counting on me to do better . . . be better."

Randall reached over and touched Erika's hand as it rested on her abdomen. Sitting beside him was a woman quite different than the hard-ass he'd met three and a half years ago. Impending mother-hood had softened her.

"I'm sorry about Faith," Erika said.

Randall started to turn away from her, but she placed her hand on his chin to stop him.

"Look at me," Erika insisted. "I know you're all messed up right now, but you are not the type to just sit around and feel sorry for yourself. You're stronger than that."

Randall wasn't so sure about that. Glumly he said, "No matter what you might think of me, I really do love her."

"I know you do," Erika said softly.

"I was planning to leave my marriage for her . . . stop messing around," Randall said. "What am I supposed to do now?"

"First off," Erika said, patting his arm, "stop *planning* to file for divorce. File for divorce already. Today is not too soon."

"Uh-huh," Randall said. "Then what?"

"Then go find Faith and pledge your undying love to her . . . and only her," Erika said pointedly.

"What if she won't take me back?"

Erika looked him square in the eye. "Do you love that girl as much as you say you do?"

"Yes," he insisted.

"Then failure isn't an option, is it?" Erika asked with a shrewd grin.

Randall's face brightened. "No, I guess it isn't."

30
* * * * * * * *
Can't Let Go

"Mmm, this is *sooo* good," Angel said, savoring the chocolate mousse. She smiled at Jill, who was eyeing her plate enviously. "You sure you don't want at least a bite?"

Jill shook her head. "I've eaten my quota of fun food through spring," she said with a chuckle.

"Y'all worry too much about weight," Ben said, stuffing more of his fudgy pecan brownie into his mouth.

Both women rolled their eyes simultaneously. "What do you know about weight issues?" Angel asked. "You ain't got an ounce of body fat."

Jill popped him playfully upside the head. "Yeah."

Ernesto and Jackson gave Ben sympathetic looks, but were smart enough not to get involved.

"More coffee, Miss?"

"Yes, please," Jill said, nodding to the server.

"And for you, sir?"

"No," Ben said, raising his hand to stop her from pouring, "I'm good."

Service at the Ivy was what one would expect of a restaurant that catered to Hollywood's celebrity elite. On any given day, the overpriced two-room cottage was overflowing with the likes of Jennifer and Brad, Will and Jada and the Toms—Hanks and Cruise. While the food was decent enough, it was the desserts, made by pastry chef Richard Irving, that made the place a standout.

"So, Benjamin," Ernesto said, playfully pressing his finger into Ben's shoulder. "Were you able to get passes to the *Catwoman* premiere for me and Jackson?"

"Sure did," Ben said, giving Angel a guilty shrug.

"Don't feel bad," Angel said. "Cassandra Douglass is your client. I'm happy she's costarring with Halle and Sharon," she said, feigning an eye twitch. "*Really*, I am . . . dammit."

Everyone laughed.

"Your day is coming, Mommie," Ernesto said, giving her a wink.

"Maybe you can be the first female action star," Jackson said. "You got the body for it."

Angel waved her hand at him. "Stop it," she said, blushing.

"*The Terminatrix*," Jill said with a chuckle.

"That could work," Angel said, nodding her approval.

"Ooh, ooh, ooh," Ernesto said eagerly. "How 'bout, *Rambolina: Breast of Fury?*"

The table erupted with laughter.

"Y'all crazy," Angel said.

"I wasn't going to mention this until the situation was a bit more concrete," Ben said, eyeing her. "But . . ."

Angel perked up. "But what?"

Ben smiled. "Your wonderful, talented, handsome, incredibly good in the sack—"

"Get to the point, already," Jill said anxiously.

"Patience, pussycat," Ben said, then turned back to Angel. "I think I've found the perfect star-making vehicle for you."

"A movie role?" she asked skeptically.

Ben nodded. "Yep."

Angel squealed. "Boy, you better not be playing with me."

"Scout's honor," Ben said, raising his hand. "Hiltop Films has expressed strong interest in securing the rights to a screenplay written by one of my clients."

"And you're going to get me an audition?" Angel asked hopefully. Finally things were going her way. After the past few months she was starting to lose hope that she'd ever get over the great divide separating television and film.

"Oh, better than that, Grasshopper," Ben said, brimming with pride. "The lead is already yours."

Angel hit him. "No freakin' way."

"Yes, way," Ben said, rubbing his arm. "And ouch!"

"Sorry," Angel replied, though she really wasn't. "So?"

"Well, said client will only sign the contract if Hiltop guarantees you right of first refusal to the role."

Everyone sitting around the table gasped.

"You are the *man!*" Angel said, kissing him on the cheek.

Jill smiled. "Yes, you are."

"I don't even care if the script sucks," Angel said, excited.

"It's rather good, actually," Ben said. "In fact, you've already read it."

"This is so—" Angel said, then stopped cold. "Wait a minute. I haven't read any scripts." Then the truth dawned on her. *"The Mad Season."*

"Mm-hmm."

The smile on Angel's face disintegrated. "I'll pass."

"What do you mean, you'll pass?" Ben did a double take. "Whatchoo talkin' 'bout, Willis?"

"I'm not interested in doing that movie," Angel said tersely.

A wrinkle formed on Jill's brow, but she remained silent.

"I don't understand," Ben said, flabbergasted. "Lucien said you loved the script."

"The script is great," Angel said, returning to her mousse. "I just don't think I'm right for it."

"For Giselle?" Ben asked, his voice inching higher. "What are you talking about, lady? You're perfect." He stared at Angel, baffled by her cool response. "Do you know how many A-list actresses would give their first-born—?"

"Then give the role to one of them," she snapped. "And when did you start representing *him?*"

With a clenched jaw Ben reached for his ringing cell phone, immediately softening when he saw his wife's name on the caller ID.

"I need to talk to my woman," he said, rising from the chair. He turned to Jill. "Will you try to talk some sense into your friend, please?"

Jackson gave Ernesto a nudge. "Men's room?"

Ernesto nodded as they hastily stood up. "Men's room."

Jill waited until they were gone, then opened fire. "And why exactly are you passing on a role you told me you would give your eyeteeth to have?"

"I think you know why," Angel said.

"Uh . . . no, I don't. And you should know, Glen feels the same way," Jill said, placing her napkin on the table. "He said that if he were in Lucien's shoes, he would have made sure that man was no longer a threat."

Angel frowned. "That's sick."

"No, that's human nature," Jill said.

"Are you telling me that you support Lucien's actions?" Angel asked, stunned.

"As a general rule, I don't condone violence," Jill said. "But in this specific instance, yes, I think Lucien was totally justified." Angel was about to interrupt, but Jill's finger flew up. "Before you even go there, don't," she said sharply. "What happened to your mother was horrific, but this is not the—"

"How the hell isn't it?" Angel said angrily. "Violence is violence."

"That psycho set the ball in motion," Jill said. "Lucien was only reacting to—"

Angel became furious. "Are you implying that had my mother—"

"Don't!" Jill shouted at her. "That's not what I mean and you damned well know it."

Angel drew back, but her fingers kept drumming the table. Other diners were staring at the two, but neither woman saw anyone else in the room.

"There is absolutely no acceptable justification for the violence inflicted upon your mother," Jill said, trying to calm down. "But Lucien is not your father, and every act of violence is not unprovoked or unreasonable . . . it just isn't."

Angel bit down on her trembling bottom lip.

Jill reached across the table, taking her hand. "Baby, you gotta stop trying to outrun the memory of what happened that night," she said sincerely.

"I don't know if I can," Angel said, her eyes tearing.

"If you don't, you will continue to live in fear with a heart unable to give, or receive, love."

Angel lowered her head in despair. "God help me."

31

Crazy Love

From her car, Faith stared at the apartment complex. The prospect of returning home was proving more difficult than she had anticipated. She took a deep breath. "You can do this," she told herself as she removed the keys from the ignition. "Now get out of this car and walk into that building."

Collecting Jade's cage from the back seat, Faith closed the car door. As she made her way through the tree-lined courtyard, she had an eerie feeling that someone was watching her. She glanced nervously over her shoulder. Seeing no one, she quickened her pace toward the building.

Stale, musty air assaulted her as she stepped inside the darkened apartment. After freeing the cat, Faith made her way over to the window, opening it to allow in fresh air. She continued down the hall to the bedroom.

Faith dropped the garment bag on the bed, then surveyed her bedroom. "Home, sweet home," she said with a bittersweet sigh.

She picked up the photo of her and Angel from the nightstand and studied it closely. It was hard to believe she was so happy only a few weeks ago. How quickly life could turn sour, she thought.

Lowering the gold frame, Faith went over to the dresser. Melancholy swept over her as she fingered the diamond tennis bracelet Randall had given her. She really thought he would be the man to save her. She realized now that that was her responsibility and hers alone.

Faith gasped when she felt the pressure against the small of her back.

"Don't scream," the raspy voice warned. "I don't want to hurt you, but I will if you scream."

Bone-chilling fear coursing through her, Faith closed her eyes. This was it. She was about to die.

Waiting for her killer to pull the trigger, she focused on the array of images whizzing by in her head. It really was true what people said. When your life was about to end, it actually did pass before your eyes.

"I'm sorry about the other night."

Faith reopened her eyes. Taking a careful breath, she tilted her weight forward ever so slowly in order to confirm the weight against her back was no longer there. Carefully, she turned around.

A young blond man was now standing on the opposite side of the bed fidgeting with the gun in his hand. His bloodshot eyes darted nervously about the room.

Faith swallowed. It was the same guy who had tried to attack her outside Angel's house. He was a little less menacing in the light of day, but just as unwelcome.

Reverentially, the man-child picked up the brown teddy bear from the bed, rubbing it tenderly across his pimpled cheek.

Her heart racing like a mad horse, Faith considered her options. She could try to make a run for it, but considering the fact that the psycho was closer to the door than she was, he'd probably shoot her before she got halfway down the hall. Her eyes eased over to the window. Jumping wouldn't work either. Assuming she survived the two-story fall, the crashing glass would most surely cause career-ending scarring, not to mention hurt like hell. Her eyes returned to the lunatic, still fondling the poor bear. Soaking wet, he couldn't weigh more than one hundred forty pounds. Maybe if she caught him off guard—which, considering his perverse fixation on the stuffed animal, shouldn't be too difficult—she could overpower him and take the gun.

Jimmy kissed the teddy bear, then placed it back on the bed. "I'm not sure what to do next."

Faith was speechless. How exactly did this AC/DC T-shirt–wearing freak expect her to respond? Was he hoping for some instruction on how to properly execute the murder, robbery or whatever it was he had come here to do to her? And why in the hell was he crying? He was the one holding the gun.

Nothing about this entire exchange was making a bit of sense to her. One minute the man's sticking a gun in her back, threatening to kill her, the next he's roaming aimlessly about the room like a lost puppy, touching and caressing her belongings. Faith wasn't sure what kind of sick mind game he was playing on her, but it was starting to make her more angry than scared. "Who are you, and what do you want?"

The man looked over at Faith, studying her with the unnerving attention one might give a famous painting they'd happened upon in a gallery. "My name is Jimmy."

Faith took a step back as he moved toward her. "Why don't you just take what you want and leave . . . *Jimmy?*"

"You are so pretty." Coming close, he brushed the back of his dirty hand across her cheek. "Your skin is so soft and smooth." His eyes eased down to her chest heaving up and down beneath her sweater.

Faith snatched for air as the most likely reason why she was still breathing dawned on her. This bastard was going to rape her. Why else hadn't he killed her already? The thought of him inside her, grinding away, made her sick with disgust.

"I never meant to hurt you," Jimmy said. "All I was trying to do was tell you how much I love you."

Faith realized that Jimmy was most likely the same man responsible for breaking into her home, violating her space and personal things. And now he was going to violate her again. *How dare he*, she thought. He had no right to do this to her.

"But that black guy started beating me . . ."

Faith could feel her throat constricting as she fought against the overwhelming urge to strike him. Her eyes went to the gun.

"I wasn't trying to hurt you . . . I promise," he said, tugging at the mop of stringy blond hair atop his head. His voice deepened. "Bad. Jimmy. Bad, bad Jimmy."

Though her impulse was to panic, Faith knew that if she had any chance of getting out of this alive, she had to keep it together. "I know you weren't trying to hurt me," she said.

Jimmy pulled back, surprised. "You believe me?"

"Of course I do," Faith said with a practiced smile. This was certainly one of those times when being an actress paid off. "You would never *purposely* hurt someone you loved, would you?"

"I wouldn't."

"I know you wouldn't," Faith said, lifting her hand from her side.

Jimmy lurched back. "What are you doing?" he asked, the gun rising to his waist.

"I just want to touch you," Faith said softly. "Can I touch you, Jimmy?"

He nodded a weak yes.

"Doesn't that feel nice, Jimmy?" she asked, stroking his pimpled cheek.

"Uh-huh," Jimmy croaked.

With her free hand Faith removed the band from her hair.

Jimmy licked his cracked lips as he watched the blond locks fall to her shoulder.

"Do you like me, Jimmy?"

"Oh, yes."

Faith smiled seductively. "Would you like to touch me?"

Jimmy stammered, "I don't—I don't think I should—should . . ."

"Don't be afraid," Faith said, easing his trembling hand onto her breast. "Mmm, that feels so good."

His eyes fluttering madly, the tip of Jimmy's awakened manhood poked through a hole in his blue jeans.

"Squeeze them harder," Faith instructed. "Use both hands."

Jimmy was only too happy to oblige.

As he groped her, Faith's eyes moved toward the gun, now resting on the dresser. "Oh, that's it, baby . . ."

Jimmy let out a high-pitched shriek as her knee connected with his aroused groin. He keeled over, writhing in agony.

Faith snatched up the gun, pointing it at him.

"What did you do that for?"

"Lie down on the floor!"

"What did I—"

"I said, lie down on the floor!" Faith shouted. "And keep your nasty hands where I can see them."

Jimmy lay down on the carpet, bringing his knees to his chest.

Not taking her eyes off him, Faith backed toward the phone on the nightstand.

"Nine-one-one emergency."

"Uh, yes, I need the police," Faith said, fighting to keep her breathing steady.

"What is the nature of your emergency, ma'am?"

"A man tried to attack—"

"Look what you've done now!" Jimmy said in a deep, angry voice. "You always make things worse!"

Faith's brow rose as she watched Jimmy.

"I just wanted to make her like me."

"Ma'am, are you still there?"

"Uh, yeah . . . I'm here," Faith said.

"Where is the man now?"

"He's right here," Faith said. "I got his gun from him."

"Bad Jimmy. Bad, bad Jimmy."

"Will you shut the fuck up?"

"Who are you talking to, ma'am?"

"Uh-oh . . . you've gone and made her mad, Jimmy."

"Not another peep from you or any of the voices in your head—" Faith said, stopping short when she saw Randall in the doorway.

"Are you okay?" he asked, rushing toward her. "What's going on?

Faith felt her knees beginning to buckle. "He's the guy who attacked me."

"I got it," Randall said, taking the gun out of her unsteady hand.

"Oh, you've really done it now," Jimmy scolded himself. "Bad Jimmy."

Randall's eyes widened.

"Stop it!" Jimmy said, rising from the floor. "I didn't mean to—"

"Move another muscle and I'll bust a cap in your ass," Randall growled, his finger wrapping around the trigger.

Jimmy sat back down. "Bad Jimmy. Bad, bad—"

"*Shut up!*" Faith shouted.

"Ma'am? Ma'am, is everything okay?"

"Yes," Faith said hastily into the phone.

"Is someone else there?"

"Yes, my—Randall . . ." Faith said. "Could you just send the police, please?"

"I've already dispatched a car to your address."

"Thank you," Faith said, then hung up the phone.

The gun fixed on Jimmy, Randall glanced over his shoulder. "You okay, baby?"

Faith nodded. "I am now."

32

* * * * * * *

Power Play

"How does Friday at noon work for you, Ms. Bishop?"

"That's fine," Erika said.

"Wonderful," the receptionist said. "I'll let Dr. Mariman know."

Erika closed the cell phone and stepped out of the limo. "Hello, sunshine," she said, gazing up at the sun, no longer an enemy to be avoided for fear it would darken her rich mahogany skin.

As she made her way into the house, her head raced with ideas for how to turn the sterile mansion into a warm and inviting home for her unborn son or daughter. Erika had been transformed. Tomorrow, she'd begin transforming the room closest to her own—currently a mini-mall of shoes and purses—into a wonderland of bright colors and plush toys guaranteed to delight even the most finicky baby. And, considering his or her lineage, the chances were high that Erika's offspring would be überselective.

"Maria, you in there?" Erika called out.

Getting no response, she continued floating down the long hall, humming to herself. Today had represented an important turning point for her. Erika had made a choice for herself, and in doing so moved a major step toward taking full ownership of her life. She knew her mother's reaction would be anything but positive, but it didn't matter. The decision to continue the pregnancy, as well as the repercussions of that choice, belonged to her.

Hearing the sound of the television playing, Erika headed toward the great room. "Maria, you—?" She hesitated when she saw Victoria. "I thought I told the driver to take you home." The soft glow on her face dimmed. "You do realize this isn't your home, right?"

"I thought you might need some help getting around after the *procedure*."

"Well, I don't," Erika said, motioning toward the door. "Now, if you don't mind—"

"You still look fat," Victoria said, eyeing her daughter like a slab of meat.

Erika rolled her eyes. "Don't start with me, Mother," she said, not bothering to mask her annoyance. "Maria, get your ass in here!"

Victoria smirked. "Someone's in a mood."

"A great mood, actually," Erika said smugly. "I just don't appreciate unannounced and *uninvited* guests."

"Yes, Ms. Bishop," Maria said, racing in from the kitchen.

Erika eyed her housekeeper. "I'm going to say this to you only one time, so listen to me carefully," she said, buoyed by her new-found confidence. "No one is to come into *my* home without me saying it's okay for them to do so."

Maria's eyes eased over to Victoria.

"Don't look at her," Erika barked. "Contrary to popular belief, this is not my mother's house, it's mine."

Victoria watched the exchange with bemusement.

"Am I making myself clear?"

"Yes, ma'am," Maria said, nodding.

"Good," Erika said.

"Will there be anything else, Ms. Bishop?"

"Yes, actually," Erika said, remembering what she wanted Maria for in the first place. "I'm going to need your help clearing everything out of the bedroom closest to mine."

Victoria leaned forward on the sofa, her curiosity piqued.

"What we can't fit in the storage closet we can give to charity," Erika said before she caught herself. "We'll talk about it later."

"Yes, Ms. Bishop," Maria said, then got the hell out of Dodge.

Erika turned back to Victoria. "We need to talk."

"About?"

Erika sat down on the sofa beside her mother. She took a deep breath. "I'm about to tell you something, and I really need for you not to go off the deep—"

"So long as you're not about to tell me you didn't take care of the problem," Victoria said, her eyes lingering on Erika's full stomach.

"Mom, please try to understand—"

"Tell me you've taken care of it." Victoria demanded.

"I've decided . . . I'm having my baby."

"Oh, no you're not," Victoria said with unmistakable certainty. "I've worked too damned hard to get you where you are to *allow* you to fuck it all up now."

"Look, Mother, I appreciate everything you've done for me," Erika said, getting to her feet. "But you have absolutely no say in this. I'm having my baby, and that's final."

Victoria shot up from the sofa. "Who in the hell do you think you're talking to?"

"I'm talking to you, Mother," Erika said. "And I don't care what you say, I'm having my—"

"Girl, I will knock the—"

Erika grabbed her mother's hand in midair.

Victoria's mouth fell open. "Let go of—"

"If you ever raise your hand to me again . . ." Erika said, then faltered and dropped the hand like a useless rag. She stepped back, for the first time seeing her mother for the imperfect woman that she was. "It would be nice if my child could have a *healthy* relationship with his or her grandmother . . . but I can go either way on that," Erika said with indifference. "It's really up to you."

Victoria's hand rose to her throat. "Are you having a breakdown?" she asked, certain her daughter was going crazy.

"I'm more together than I've ever been," Erika said, softening when she noticed the look of genuine concern on her mother's face. Though she would never win any prizes for mother of the year, she knew that in her own special, borderline sadistic, way, Victoria did in fact love her.

"I want you in my life, Momma, but the days of you controlling every aspect of my existence are over," Erika said, ushering Victoria toward the door. "I'll call you tomorrow. Maybe we can do lunch or something."

"Maybe you should lie down."

"I'm fine . . . really." Erika kissed her mother on the cheek, then tapped her gently on the rear. "Now, off you go."

Victoria walked toward the door with the unsteady gait of a drunk who'd just been in a bar brawl and lost.

Erika called after her. "And, Mom?"

"Huh?"

"You are always welcome in my home," Erika said. "But from now on you'll call first . . . right?"

Victoria gave her a weak nod, then left.

33
* * * * * * *
Unbreak My Hart

Angel retrieved the video cassette from the back of the top shelf of the closet and returned with it to the bedroom. She slipped the tape into the VCR, picked up her glass of wine from the dresser, then sat on the chaise longue. Pointing the remote at the screen, she braced herself.

"Steven, will you stop following me around with that video camera?" Marcella protested, covering her face with her hands. "I swear, you're like a child with a new toy," she said, laughing.

"Come on, baby, wave for the camera," Steven prodded. "My beautiful wife is shy this Christmas morning," he said, grinning into the camera.

"You're silly, Daddy!"

Steven pointed the lens toward the little girl sitting on the floor beside the Christmas tree. "Now, there's a face that could melt a million hearts," he said brightly. "What's your name, pretty lady?"

"You know my name, Daddy!"

"Princess?"

"Nooo."

"How about Aphrodite?"

"My name is Angel Madison Foster."

"And who loves you more than the whole wide world two times over?"

"You do, Daddy!"

Steven turned the camera back on himself. Smiling, he said, "She's right."

Angel hit the PAUSE button when the doorbell sounded. She was about to get up but thought better of it. Company was the last thing she wanted right now. She needed to be alone. The tense exchange with Jill yesterday had her up most of the night unable to sleep. The painful memories she'd managed to keep dormant for years had been reawakened. Like a prison she couldn't escape, her childhood was playing out over and over in her head,

Staring at the frozen image of her father on the screen, Angel took another sip of the merlot. She expelled an unsteady sigh. Jill was right, and Angel knew it. If she was to have any shot at happiness in the future, she was going to have to finally come to terms with her past.

Angel scowled when the bell rang again. Irritated, she rose from the chaise, marching down the hall. God help the poor soul waiting on the other side of her front door.

"Who is it?" she barked.

"Uh, it's Lucien."

Angel stopped short. Despite trying her damnedest not to, she missed Lucien terribly. No man had ever moved her enough to consider the possibility of falling in love.

"Will you open the door, please?"

Angel continued to vacillate. Though part of her wanted to see Lucien, another part wanted nothing more to do with him.

Finally she opened the door. "Yes?"

"Can I come in?"

Without responding, Angel turned on her heel, walking back into the living room.

Stepping inside, Lucien closed the door behind him.

Angel exuded cool detachment. "What do you want?"

Lucien's eyes locked on hers. "I don't want to lose you over this."

"You never had me," she said tightly.

Standing firm in the face of Angel's arctic chill, Lucien said, "I've been searching my mind trying to come up with some reason for why you're acting this way."

"Why I'm acting this way?" Angel asked. "I'm not the one with the problem here," she said bitingly. "You are."

Lucien shook his head in disappointment. "I see trying to have an adult conversation—"

"It boggles my mind how you can stand there acting so fucking pious," Angel said, cutting him off. "You really do think it's okay to attack people, don't you?"

Lucien took a step back as she stalked toward him. "I think you need to calm down."

"Or what?" Angel asked, getting up in his face. "You're gonna give me a nice hard slap across the face?"

Lucien gave her a strange look but didn't respond.

"Answer me!" Angel shouted. "Would that make you feel like a man?"

"I think I should go—"

"Don't walk away from me!" Angel grabbed Lucien by the shoulder, spinning him back around to face her. "How would you feel if I knocked the hell out of you every time you said or did something I didn't like?"

Lucien was slack-jawed. "You are a fucking head—" Before the words were out of his mouth, Angel slapped him. Stunned, he raised his hand slowly to his reddening cheek.

Angel's eyes widened. "I'm sorry," she said, horrified by her own behavior.

Glaring at her, Lucien said, "I'm not going to let you make me into the monster you need me to be." He lowered his tightly fisted hands to his sides. "I'm not the bad guy here."

Angel stood there stunned by her outburst. "I know that," she said, extending her hand toward his reddened cheek.

"Do *not* touch me." Lucien said, jerking back.

"Please let me try to explain."

Lucien studied her face as if committing it to memory before turning to leave. "Goodbye, Angel."

"Please wait!" she called out after him. "Let me explain."

Lucien kept walking.

Fearing she was about to lose him forever, Angel panicked. She blurted out, "My father killed my mother."

Lucien stopped in his tracks.

"And for eight years before that he beat her," Angel said, sitting down on the sofa. "Violence was his way of controlling her."

Slowly, Lucien turned around.

"Every time he slapped her face, busted her lip, blackened her eye or simply told her she was worthless, a little piece of my mother would die," Angel said, reliving a flurry of memories she'd spent most of her adult life trying to forget. "But no matter how many times he abused her, she stayed with him because she loved him."

Lucien's tight jaw unhinged as he listened.

"Even after he started using drugs . . . and lost his job . . . Momma stayed with him, certain that the sheer magnitude of her love would get him through the madness." Angel glanced at the television. "It didn't."

Lucien sat down beside her on the sofa.

"When she wouldn't give him the funds from a money-market account, he beat the hell out of her," Angel said, fighting back her tears. "But Momma stood her ground, for once refusing to give in to him." She closed her eyes. "I hid behind my bedroom door watching as my father ransacked our house searching for enough money to satisfy his jones," she said, reliving the horrible memory. "When he didn't find anything, he stormed into the kitchen and got a steak knife."

Lucien winced.

"I will never for as long as I live forget the look in his eyes when he raised the knife to Momma's throat." Tears cascaded down Angel's cheeks. "It was the same look I saw in yours that night."

Lucien pulled her quaking body into his arms. "I'm sorry," he said rocking her gently.

"That's why I was so scared," Angel said, struggling to catch her breath. "You reminded me so much of him."

"Look at me," Lucien said, lifting her head from his chest. "I am not your father."

"I know that, but—"

"But nothing," Lucien said. "Girl, I love you. Don't you get it?"

Angel gasped for air.

"You are my queen, baby. I could never hurt you," Lucien said, wiping the tears from her cheek. "I would kill myself before I harmed—"

"Make love to me."

Lucien drew back. "Baby, maybe we should just talk—"

"I need you to make love to me." Angel kissed his lips greedily as if they were the nourishment her starving soul craved. "Please," she said, her tone beseeching. "Make love to me now."

Lucien scooped her up into his arms and carried her toward the bedroom. "I love you."

Angel exhaled. "I love you too."

Epilogue

* * * * * * *

Prisoners of Hope

Hope is not pretending that troubles don't exist. It is the trust that they will not last forever, that hurts will be healed and difficulties overcome. It is the faith that a source of strength and renewal lies within to lead us through the dark into the sunshine.

—Elizabeth A. Chase

"What a beautiful day the Lord has made."

"Let us rejoice and be glad in it."

Angel spied the faces of the people sitting around her in the church. These past eight months, her family of friends had helped her through myriad troubled days and sleepless nights. At times the pain she felt had been so intense it sent her to her knees, begging God for mercy. She'd faced her anger and guilt over her mother's death head-on and then released the bitter emotions from her heart once and for all. Like the brightly shining August sun, she had emerged from the darkness that had surrounded her. Today was a beautiful day indeed.

"God is truly a miracle worker . . ."

As Pastor Woodson continued speaking, Angel's mind wandered back to the day that Wellington Broadcasting announced that after three successful seasons it was canceling *Brave New World*. Certain that Jasper, still bitter over Randall's leaving his daughter, would make things messy, Angel was floored when he tore up her contract, thanked her for her work on the show, then handed her a check for $264,000, representing her salary for the forty-four shows she would never tape. Erika had received a similar parting gift. Faith got Randall.

"The miracle of life is a gift that must never be taken for granted. . . ."

Angel looked back at Ben, beaming like a peacock as he held his wife's hand. In five months he and Phallon would be experiencing that miracle firsthand. She glanced over at Lucien sitting at her side. It had only been three weeks since she'd accepted his marriage proposal, and already he was picking out names for each of the five children he wanted them to have together. Sharing Lucien's enthusiasm, Jill had arrived on the set of *The Mad Season*—a movie being executive-produced by one Randall Hunter—the other day armed with a stack of bridal magazines. She pronounced herself Angel's official wedding planner.

"Who are the grandparents of this blessed child?" Pastor Woodson asked, cradling the sleeping infant in her arms.

Victoria stood with her husband. "We are," she said proudly.

"Please come forward."

Angel smiled as she made eye contact with Faith. Any reservations she might have had about her picking up with Randall had been quelled. Determined to rebuild their relationship on a more solid footing—and punish him a little—Faith withheld sex for almost five months, insisting he court her slow and proper. To his credit, Randall went along with the program without complaint. By the time he finally got some, the poor guy was pretty much a born-again virgin.

"Grandparents are the history teachers," Pastor Woodson said, handing the baby to Victoria. "You represent Hope's living link to her past. The lessons you teach her will serve as the foundation on which she builds her future. Teach her well."

Angel glanced over at Erika. She and her mother had certainly come a long way these past months. Victoria remained a handful, to be sure, but she was making a sincere effort to treat her only child like the adult she'd become. Erika had shared with Angel how in one of her therapy sessions, Victoria had broken down in tears, apologizing for not being a better parent, and promising to do better by her grandchild. It was only the second time in Erika's life that she'd seen her mother cry—the day she won the role on *Momma Knows* was the first.

"Will the godparents please stand."

Lucien and Angel stood.

Pastor Woodson extended her arms. "Come forward, spirits."

"Careful with her head," Victoria said to Lucien as she handed the baby to him.

"Godparents are the spiritual guides," the pastor said. "Encourage and foster Hope's relationship with the Father. Take care with your words and actions, for they help set the coordinates of the moral compass she will utilize to direct her journey through life."

Lucien and Angel nodded. "We will."

Pastor Woodson smiled out into the first row of pews. "Mom and Dad, would you come forward, please?"

Erika and Angel exchanged knowing glances as Lucien placed the baby in Randall's waiting arms. Of the slew of positive changes Hope's birth had provoked in the lives of the people closest to her, the most notable was the transformation her arrival had effected in her father. Not hours after she was born, Randall showed up at Erika's hospital room. Angel and Jill watched in stunned silence as he asked Erika if—despite everything—she might consider allowing him to be a part of his daughter's life. Surprisingly, Erika didn't bust his chops. She looked him dead in the eye and said, "Don't let her down." So far Randall hadn't.

"There is no purer love than that of parents for their children," Pastor Woodson said. "With diligent, loving hands tend the soil from which Hope's sense of well-being and self-worth grows. Sow the seeds of respect and trust early and you will reap delicious bounty the likes of which you have never known."

Lucien took Angel's hand as they stood there.

Pastor Woodson turned to Erika. "The relationship between a mother and daughter is a special one. In you, Hope will see her future self," she said. "The example you set will inform the type of woman she becomes." She looked at Randall. "And your relationship with Hope will serve as the litmus test by which she judges her dealings with other men throughout her life. When you tell her that she is a princess worthy of nothing less than love and respect, she'll believe you."

Jill waved her hand in the air. "Amen," she sang out.

Erika looked back at her and smiled. The two of them had grown quite close in the past months. The only mother Erika knew besides her own, she turned to Jill for advice on everything from colic to diaper rash. When she'd made the decision to get rid of her weave, it was Jill who Erika asked to accompany her to the salon for moral support. Later that day when Angel commented on how fabulous she thought the new short do looked, Erika thanked her, saying, "Once the little diva arrived, the rented hair had to go."

Angel gazed at Hope as she cooed in Pastor Woodson's arms. She was pure, unconditional love, uncomplicated by agenda, untainted by experience, heartache or past mistakes. Her life was just beginning. It wasn't going to be a perfect one, but it would always be a life worth living.

"Let the church say amen."

Angel smiled. "Amen."